GH01085923

Reckless Obsession

Reckless Obsession

DAVID WILDE

authorHOUSE®

"LIFE IS LIKE A ROAD, YOU DRIVE ALONG WITHOUT A CARE THEN SUDDENLY YOU TAKE A WRONG TURN. AFTERWARDS NOTHING IS EVER THE SAME AGAIN."

AuthorHouse™
1663 Liberty Drive
Bloomington, IN 47403
www.authorhouse.com
Phone: 1-800-839-8640

Published by AuthorHouse   06/18/2012

ISBN: 978-1-4685-8631-2 (sc)
ISBN: 978-1-4685-8632-9 (e)

To my wife Katherine, I love you very much and thank you for all the support and faith you have given, throughout our marriage and the writing of this book.

CHAPTER ONE

Oh No . . . . Tilley Watson mumbled to herself as she left her apartment building. Raining again and my umbrellas broken, still at least its Friday. Tilley was on her way to work as she had done for the last five years since she started working at Coopers Insurance Services in Bromworth High Street. She had a quarter of a mile walk to her local train station in Parkview—a small Hamlet fifteen miles west of the town of Bromworth. Her train normally left at ten minutes past nine then after a ten minute journey to Bromworth she had a five minute walk to her office.

Today however—Friday the ninth of October nineteen eighty three—was going to be very different indeed because, as she was walking down a narrow overgrown lane she often used as a short cut to the station she heard a noise like a thump, it came from behind some bracken and gorse bushes which lined the left hand side of lane. Tilley being Tilley she just could not resist investigating because to say the least Tilley had a tendency to be curious which had landed her in a few scrapes in the past.

Worming her way through the wet grass and bushes Tilley caught a glimpse of a man but, he had his back to her and was walking away from the other side of the bushes.

She could only see the top half of him but noted that he was wearing a light blue coat and had short hair. However she couldn't get any further into the dense bushes so reluctantly she made her way back to the path. She was wearing light grey trousers and the bottoms were soaked as was her shoes and hair, of course she missed her train making her late for work which was the first time ever.

When she finally arrived at work her colleagues—Rob and Lucy, were anxious to know why she was late and in such a state. Tilley told them but they just looked at each other with that "here we go again look" because they were well aware of her inquisitive nature.

After a relatively uneventful day at work she left work and went to the station to catch the five fifty pm train to Parkview, where she lived. Being a moonless damp October night she avoided taken the short cut and arrived home at six twenty.

On entering her apartment she kicked off her muddy shoes and chuckled to herself, remembering her escapade earlier that day. "A nice hot bath" she thought as she placed a ready meal in the microwave.

While her meagre supper was heating up she went to the bathroom to run her bath. Once there was enough water in the bath she went back into the kitchen and her meal was ready, however as she opened the microwave door her phone rang, she lifted the receiver and it was her mother, she said: 'Hello Tilley how's things?'

'Everything's fine thanks, I was just going to eat my supper actually, then have a bath.'

'Ok, I won't keep you but your dad and I were wondering what you had planned for your birthday next Wednesday.'

'Oh don't worry about that mum I wasn't planning anything, you know me.'

'Yes we do but it is your thirtieth and you should do something special so dad and I have booked a table at Christos restaurant in Bromworth.'

'Oh mum I wish you wouldn't do this I hate dressing up and all that stuff, I'd much rather curl up on the sofa with a TV dinner.'

'Yes we know that but this time we are not taking no for an answer.'

'Fine if that's what you want but I've got nothing to wear.'

'Well that is the second part of your birthday present, you are coming shopping with me tomorrow and your dad's paying.'

Tilley knew it was a waste of time arguing with her mum so she just said: 'Alright then what time are you picking me up?'

'About ten thirty we can have some lunch then hit the shops.'

'Ok then mum, I will have to go now though or my supper will be cold.'

'Alright Tilley see you tomorrow.'

Tilley hung up and took her meal from the microwave but it was only lukewarm and she didn't fancy it anymore so she threw it in the bin.

She took a bottle of spring water from the fridge and headed for the bathroom, she tested water with her toe and it was still just about hot enough so she climbed in.

After a long refreshing soak Tilley climbed out and towelled herself off and slipped her dressing gown on. By now she was hungry so she made a cheese and tomato sandwich and a cup of hot chocolate.

Sitting at her small table she ate her sandwich afterwards she washed her plate and made her way to her bedroom taking the hot chocolate with her.

She sat up in bed and finished her hot chocolate, noticing that the time was nearly ten forty she switched her bedside lamp off and settled down to go to sleep.

However Tilley found it difficult to drop off, she just tossed and turned, her mind drifting back to the mysterious man in the bushes. She mulled it over for a little longer then eventually she dropped off to sleep.

She awoke with a start as her radio alarm came on and the newsreader was in the process of reporting a newsflash saying: "The woman's body was discovered around seven thirty last evening on the edge of Parkview common by a woman walking her dog. A spokesman for the Police stated that the death is being treated as suspicious.

Her identity is being withheld until her family has been notified . . . . And now for the weather".

Tilley stirred not really taking in what the newsreader had said. She slowly got out of bed and slipping on her dressing gown and slippers began the morning routine of preparing her breakfast. She had just put two slices of bread in the toaster when it suddenly come to her that it was Saturday and wondered what made her set her alarm so early.

She was just about to turn the toaster off and go back to bed when it dawned on her that she was going shopping with her mother and was relieved to know she wasn't losing the plot.

It was ten thirty five when her mum pressed the intercom buzzer and Tilley called down that she was on her way, she locked her door and went down and met her mother.

Her mother remarked: 'Hello darling you look tired.' Tilley replied: 'I'm fine thanks mum I didn't sleep very well actually though I am looking forward to today.'

'My word you must be ill girl.' Her mum quipped and with a mutual giggle they set off.

The traffic was quite heavy with people starting their Christmas shopping early and it took over forty minutes to reach the shopping centre. Finding a parking place was very difficult but eventually they managed to park the car and headed for the shops.

By this time they were ready for a cup of tea so they decided to have lunch. They found a cafe and ordered their meals and a pot of tea. Tilley's then mum said: 'Did you hear about that body they found near you?'

'Body what body? I haven't heard anything about that.' Suddenly Tilley froze and her mother said to her: 'Whatever's wrong Tilley? You've gone as white as a sheet.'

I remember now! 'It was on the radio this morning, I saw him.'

'Saw who? What are you talking about?'

'The murderer, I saw the murderer.'

Tilley related to her mother what she saw on the way to work the previous morning, her mother listened intensely with horror on her face, when Tilley had finished her story her mum said: 'You are going to get yourself into a serious of trouble talking like that my girl, what you saw couldn't have anything to do with that body and there has been no mention of murder yet, so if I were you I would forget all about it.'

They ate their lunch in relative silence, when they had finished and paid the bill they headed for the shops. Tilley's mind was not on shopping however and her mum said: 'Look Tilley you said you were looking forward to today.'

'I know and I am sorry but I'm so sure I saw the murderer.' Her mum was annoyed and said with a moan: 'Tilley for Pete's sake let it go will you? And concentrate on finding something to wear for your birthday meal.'

'Ok mum I will, I have ruined your day haven't I?'

'No you haven't ruined my day but you will if you carry on with that ridiculous business, now come on.'

After trooping around the shops for over two hours Tilley finally found an outfit she was happy with. They made their way back to the car neither saying very much because despite her mother's efforts to distract her daughter from the news of the dead body, Tilley just couldn't get it out of her mind.

The atmosphere on the journey home was very subdued with Tilley feeling guilty for ruining her mum's day and her mum was worried that Tilley was going to do something stupid. She knew that once her daughter got her heart set on something there was no reasoning with her.

When Tilley's mum arrived home her husband greeted her with a hug but he could see she was not herself and asked: 'What's the matter Joyce?'

'Oh Bob I'm worried about Tilley, she thinks she saw a murderer yesterday.'

Murderer! 'Hang on, back up a minute, look take your coat off and I will make us some tea, I swear that girl will be the death of us one day.'

Bob made the tea, brought it into the lounge and said: 'Now for god's sake tell me what is going on?'

'Well do you remember that news on the radio this morning about the body they found last night?'

'Yes but what has that got to do with Tilley?' Joyce explained what Tilley had told her and Bob sat back in his chair and looked up at the ceiling saying: 'When will that girl ever learn?'

Tilley spent that evening relaxing reading magazines with the TV on low. The national news was on and she just heard the news reader say: "Police have stated that the woman who was found dead in Parkview yesterday was in fact murdered. The name of the dead woman is Mrs Angela Johnson she was identified by a staff ID badge found with the body. She was aged thirty three.

Mrs Johnson had been dead for approximately twelve hours and had been missing since Friday morning when she failed to turn up for work at "Your Type Secretarial Agency" in Parkview. Police are also anxious to know the whereabouts of the woman's husband—Andrew

Johnson—last seen leaving his place of work "Halls Estate Agents" also in Parkview at four thirty Friday afternoon.

Mr Johnson was wearing a black knee length coat, blue suit, white shirt and black shoes. He has curly red hair. If anyone has any information regarding either of these two people please contact your local Police station ASAP".

Tilley's mind was racing not knowing whether to call the Police or follow her mother's advice and leave well alone. After a long think she decided to wait until the morning and went to bed although she knew it was going to be a long sleepless night.

Sunday morning was a long time coming, Tilley couldn't stop thinking about the news item from the previous evening. She looked at the clock and saw that it had only just turned seven am. She laid there for a while longer but eventually she had to get up. She couldn't stomach the thought of breakfast so she got dressed. By this time she had made her mind up to call the Police to tell them about the events of the Friday morning. She looked up the number for the local Police station and dialled it. A female voice answered: 'Hello this is Parkview Police, WPC Wright speaking, how can I help you?' Tilley said: 'Hello I am Tilley Watson, I think I have some information regarding the woman's body found on Friday.'

'Right hold the line please.' After a pause a man's voice came on the line: 'Hello my name is Detective Inspector Harper, who am I talking to please?'

'Hello I'm Tilley Watson.'

'Is that Mrs or Miss?'

'It's Miss actually.'

'Ok Miss, I understand you may have some information regarding the body found last Friday, is that correct?'

'Yes it is.'

'Would it be convenient to come into the station and talk to a member of the investigating team? It would be an informal chat.'

'Yes of course, will later this morning be ok?'

'Yes that's fine just come to the front desk and ask for me.' Tilley said goodbye and hung up.

She now had to decide whether to tell her parents of her decision or wait and tell them after she had spoken to the Police. After pondering over it for a while she decided to bite the bullet and tell them, her dad answered the phone: 'Hello Bob Watson.'

'Hello dad, did mum tell you about the man I saw on my way to work on Friday?'

'Yes she did what about it?'

'Well please don't get mad but I have decided to tell the Police and I am going to see them today.'

'Why on earth do you want to do that Tilley?'

'Well it is a murder enquiry now and I couldn't live with myself if I kept quiet and what I saw turned out to be vital evidence.'

'Well in that case you are not going alone, I'm coming with you.'

'No dad there's isn't any need for that.'

'Yes there is and no argument, when are you going?'

'About eleven o'clock.'

'Ok I'll pick you up.'

'Ok dad thanks, I'll see you then.'

Bob Picked Tilley up and drove her to the Police station but there wasn't very much conversation, Tilley knew her father was not best pleased but she knew he would always support her even though she had gotten herself in many awkward situations due to her curious nature, and she was glad of that.

At the front desk the duty Sergeant said: 'Good morning can I help?'

'Yes my name is Miss Watson I am here to see Detective Inspector Harper, he is expecting me.'

'Ok Miss please take a seat, I will let him know you are here.' After about three minutes DI Harper appeared—a tallish man about thirty five years old Tilley surmised. He greeted her saying: 'Hello Miss Watson, I'm DI Harper.' The DI held out his hand and shook Tilley's she gestured to her dad, and said: 'Hello this is my father, he insisted on coming with me.'

'That's fine it's always a good idea to have some support.' The DI shook Bob's hand and then continued: 'If you would follow me I'll take you to the investigative officer who is leading the enquiry.'

DI Harper guided them to an office on the second floor, there sitting at a desk was a man with thinning brown hair, he greeted them saying: 'Hello, Detective Chief Inspector George Carter, and you are?'

'I am Tilley Watson and this is my father.' After inviting them to sit down DI Harper left the room, DCI Carter then asked: 'Ok Miss tell me what you know?'

'If you don't mind I prefer Tilley.'

Tilley! 'That's a nice name.'

'In actual fact my real name is Natalie which I will explain if you wish.'

'Well maybe later, now what have you got for us?' Tilley took the DCI through the events of the previous Friday morning, when she had finished DCI Carter asked: 'Could you see his face?'

'No as I said he was walking away so I could only see his back and only the top half because the bushes were quite high.'

'That is very interesting Tilley, tell me would you be able to show us exactly where this was?'

'Yes no problem.' The DCI then showed Tilley and her father a picture of Mrs Johnson and asked if they knew her. After carefully looking they both said they didn't. The DCI then asked Tilley if she could show them where she saw the man, he said they would take her and her father in a Police car. Tilley got excited saying: Oh yes! 'I have always wanted to ride in a Police car.'

'Actually it would be an unmarked car.'

'Oh how disappointing.' Her father told her not to be so daft but DCI Carter said: 'No if Tilley wants to go in a patrol car that's fine.' Tilley though said that she was only joking so the DCI left with a smile to arrange a car.

While they were waiting Bob asked Tilley: 'Are you alright with all this? You could be letting yourself in for a whole lot of trouble, particularly if what you have told the Police leads to an arrest, you will have to go to court and give evidence and God knows what that could lead to.'

David Wilde

'I'm fine dad honestly and I am aware of what I am doing, I just want to do the right thing.'

'I don't know Tilley you have been in some right scrapes in the past but this takes the biscuit, however your mother and I will stand by you no matter what.'

'I know dad and I really do appreciate it and I do love you both very much.'

A few moments later a Police Constable arrived and said: 'Hello I am PC Walker, if you would like to follow me I will escort you both to the car.'

When they reached the car—a blue Volvo—DCI Carter helped them both in. While they were on their way DCI Carter turned to Tilley and asked: 'Now do tell me Tilley how did your name come about?' She explained a little tentatively: 'Well it all started in junior school, there was an older girl also called Natalie in my class, we all called each other by nicknames, so it was decided that she would be called Nat and I would be called Tilley—they reckoned the last part of my name sounded like Tilley so it has been my name ever since.' The DCI appeared a little bemused and said: 'Ok I think I get it.' Looking at Mr Watson with a wry grin.

As the car approached the Common Tilley guided the driver to the beginning of the path. They all left the car and the DCI said: 'Ok Tilley maybe you would like to take us to the spot and go through the events as you recall them.'

'Yes sure.' Tilley replied and started walking along the path. When she stopped at the spot where she saw the man she pointed and said: 'There, he was behind those bushes.'

'Right Tilley I must point out that is not where the body was found.'

'Really I don't understand, I definitely heard something being dropped and then there's the man.'

'I'm sorry I am not disbelieving you, I am sure you did see and hear something but it was most definitely not the body being dumped, that occurred further along the common. However I will get a couple of uniforms to search this area in case there is something interesting here.'

Tilley's father had a noticeable expression of relief on his face which Tilley saw and remarked: 'Ok dad, tell me you told me so.'

'I'm sorry love but I am relieved, now apologise for wasting the detective's time and let's go home.' DCI Carter chipped in: 'There is absolutely no need to apologise, we would rather you report something and it come to nothing than ignore it and a villain gets away. You go home and I will let you know if uniform find anything of use here.' DCS Carter shook Tilley's and her father's hands and thanked them both for their time.

CHAPTER TWO

It was one fifteen when Mr Watson dropped Tilley off, she said sheepishly: 'Thanks dad I am really sorry for wasting your time today but I thought I saw something important.'

'You didn't waste my time sweetheart but hopefully it is all over now, so go and put your feet up, I'll shoot off your or mother will be worried.'

'Ok give her my love and I will call if there's any more news,'

'Ok love, bye for now.'

Later that afternoon the ringing of the phone startled Tilley for a second as she had dozed off while reading a magazine on her sofa. She lifted the receiver and it was DCI Carter, he said: 'Hello Tilley I just thought I'd let you know that the officer's we sent to check the scene of your sighting found nothing of interest, so you can rest easy. If you remember anything else though please don't hesitate to call. Thank you for your interest Miss, goodbye.'

After thanking him for calling Tilley said goodbye to the DI and hung up. She rung her parents to let them know the news then sat back letting out a sigh but, whether it was with relief or disappointment she wasn't sure.

DCI Carter had only just hung up the phone when DI Harper knocked his door and came in, he said: 'George; I have the Pathologists report on Mrs Johnson, it seems that death was due to asphyxiation, believed to be caused by a red silk cushion or something similar held over her nose and mouth as there was strands of red silk in her mouth. There are no signs of a struggle though so she either knew her killer or killers or was taken by surprise. However she was killed somewhere else and most probably taken in a vehicle to the edge of the common and carried to where she was found.'

'Thanks for that Mike, is that all we have?'

'At the moment apart from a sweet wrapper found at the scene—a glacier mint actually. It was bagged and is being tested, SOCCO are still going over the area but that's it for now.'

'Ok, is there any news on the husband?'

'No, DC Price spoke to his employers and they are completely baffled. He was a good worker apparently, good with customers but, there was no sign he was worried about anything. He only started there just over six months ago and had excellent references.

SOCCO and Forensics checked their house but there was nothing much there, it doesn't look like she was murdered there as they found no red cushions or anything like the material found in her mouth, they did find credit card bills in both their names, all paid up but no cards, they bagged up a comb belonging to Mr Johnson to test for DNA and we have requested their phone records.

Uniform did speak to the neighbours, they were shocked but said the couple kept themselves to themselves and didn't go out very much. There doesn't appear to be a trace of any relatives of Mrs Johnson but Mr Johnson's employers say that he has elderly parents living in the area problem is they are both in a nursing home. I have sent a Constable and a WPC along to talk to them.

The victim's boss said she had only worked there for five months and as with the husband she had outstanding references and was a good worker with no signs of problems. She told them she had been living in London prior to starting there the husband had said the same thing to his employers.

She got on well with her colleagues but said nothing about her past, she was a loner and didn't mix well at work but there is one woman she talked to on occasions, a Beth Goodwin. She told her she had been married for over four years but that's all we have.'

'Ok Mike thanks, tell Pathology to let us know if they discover anything else.'

The DI walked out of George's office and met a PC heading towards him, he said: 'Oh hello Gov I was just on my way to the DCI's office, a woman's bag has been found, it's a shoulder bag.'

'Oh so you are an expert on women's bags are you Constable?' DI Harper asked smiling.

No! The Constable replied his face reddening. 'WPC Evens described it.'

'Ok Constable, where was it found?'

'I don't know Gov it was handed in at the front desk, the lab has it.'

'Alright I'll go down there.'

In the lab the Chief Forensic Technician Dan Phillips was testing the bag. The Di asked if he had found anything useful. Phillips replied: 'No just some lipstick, make up, small hair brush and a few tissues.'

'No credit cards?'

'I'm afraid not, there are a few clear print's on the bag though, which are mainly the woman's but the rest are from the guy who handed it in.'

'What's his name?'

'Paul Archer, I've run his prints but he has no record.'

'Thanks Dan, is he still here?'

'Yes DC Briers is talking to him.'

'Cheers Dan, I'll nip along and listen.'

In the interview room DC Briers had just finished talking to the man, he came out and met Mike, he shook his head and said: 'I don't think he knows anything and he has an alibi for the time of the murder. He was in London and has at least five people that can substantiate it.'

'Ok we'll release him but tell him not to leave the area.'

When Tilley's alarm went off on Monday morning she was not in the mood to get up and go through the tedious routine of getting ready for work. The trials of the weekend had taken their toll especially as it was all a waste of time. However she forced herself out of bed and had a shower, not fancying any breakfast she had a cup of coffee and set off for work.

She reached the area of the path which triggered the weekend's events but walked past as quickly as she could, not wanting to linger any longer than necessary. She arrived at work at the usual time and she was the first one in so after taking her coat off she put the coffee machine on.

Shortly afterwards Lucy arrived closely followed by Rob. Lucy raced straight over to Tilley and took hold of her arm asking: 'Was that body they found anything to do with what you saw last Friday morning?' It was obvious Tilley was uncomfortable with the question so Lucy asked: 'Whatever is the matter Tilley have I hit a nerve?'

No! 'Well in a way.' She then gave them a brief account of the weekend's events. Lucy and Rob listened intently then Lucy said: 'Well you certainly don't have a boring life, do you Tilley?'

'I wouldn't put it like that exactly but I do have my moments. Anyway enough of the chatter we ought to get on with some work.' They took their coffees to the desks and began the day's work.

When lunchtime arrived Tilley intended spending the hour in the local park, her usual routine. She often bought a sandwich and a drink from a mobile snack bar and sat watching the ducks and birds at a small pond. Her colleagues however had other ideas, Lucy grabbed Tilley's arm and said: 'You are spending lunchtime with Rob and me today we want to hear everything about your weekend.' Before Tilley could protest Rob and Lucy linked their arms through hers and marched her off to the Spread Eagle pub just down the road from their office.

They reached the pub and walked in, they found some seats and Rob said he would get the drinks, he asked Tilley what she wanted, Tilley answered: 'To be back by my pond.'

'Well you can't so there.' Lucy told her. Tilley replied: 'You are so cruel.' She grinned and said to Rob: 'I'll have a tomato juice and no ice please.' Rob asked Lucy what she wanted and she asked for an orange juice and lemonade with lots of ice.

Rob brought the drinks over on a tray with three menus and they browsed through the food on offer, they chose their meals and Rob went and ordered them. When he returned Lucy said to Tilley: 'Right come on Tilley tell us all.'

'Well there isn't much to tell, my mum called me on Friday evening to discuss taking me out on Wednesday evening for my birthday . . . . Rob and Lucy looked at each other and then at Tilley and almost in harmony said: 'Your birthday? You kept that quiet.'

'You say that every year but all along you have some devious plan up your sleeves, anyway I'm thinking of taking Wednesday off.' Lucy retorted: 'Don't you dare, anyway let's get back to your weekend.'

'Well as I said my mum phoned and said that her and my dad had booked a table at Christos in Bromworth High street and that she was taking me shopping Saturday to find something for me to wear.

I set my radio alarm and when it went off in the morning the news of the body find was on.

Because I was only half awake it didn't sink in but, then when my mum mentioned it at lunch it suddenly hit me and much to my mum's dismay I couldn't concentrate on anything else after that.'

'What happened when you went to the Police, did you have to make a statement?' Lucy asked. Rob cut in saying: 'Let Tilley tell her story Lucy, we only get an hour and you know Tilley's tales are never short.' Lucy poked her tongue out at Rob grinning and said: 'Ok carry on.' Tilley continued: 'Well my dad came with me bless him, I could tell though he was worried sick about it all but he said he would support me, and no I didn't have to make a statement, I just told the detective—who was quite cute actually—what I'd seen and they took me to where I saw the man and heard the noise, they said though that it wasn't where the body was found so they thanked me for reporting it and took us back to the Police station. They did a search there later but found nothing. I know my mum and dad are relieved but I feel awful, I was convinced I had seen something suspicious.'

'And you said you don't have an exciting life, all my weekend consisted of was washing and ironing and buying groceries.' Lucy said.

At that moment there meals arrived and Rob went to get another round of drinks. When he returned Tilley asked him: 'What did you get up to the weekend then Rob?'

'Not a lot, I took Jill and the kids to town to buy some shoes for Amy and of course Daniel wanted something so we bought him some jeans. We then went to a cafe and the kids stuffed themselves with burgers and milkshakes.' Oh memories! Lucy said: 'When I was younger every Saturday I would go for burgers and milkshakes with my friends eying up the boys. I bet you did the same didn't you Tilley?'

No! 'I used to go the pictures on Saturday afternoons or sometimes I would go to town wondering around looking at the fancy gowns and dresses, wishing I could look nice in one instead of looking like a sack of potatoes.'

'Why? You have a nice figure, doesn't she Rob?' Lucy remarked

'I'm not complaining.' Rob said looking Tilley up and down with a cheeky grin on his face.

'Stop it you two I can feel my face glowing.'

'Oh I wouldn't say that but when you turned and looked out of the window all the cars came to a halt.'

'I hate you both, come on let me pay the bill then we must get back to work our hour is nearly up.'

On their way back to the office Tilley suddenly stopped dead and pointing to the other side of the road she stuttered: 'That . . . That's him.'

'That's who?' Lucy asked.

Him!!! 'The man I saw in the bushes.'

'How can you tell? You only saw the back of him.'

'Yes but that is the same coat and he has short brown hair.'

'Yeah and so does half the men in Bromworth.' Lucy remarked.

'You sound just like my mother.'

'Good then perhaps you will listen and not be too quick to jump to the wrong conclusions.'

'Alright then but I am going to follow him for a while and see where he goes.'

'That won't do any good, besides you will be late back to work.'

'I know but I need to do this, cover for me will you please Lucy?'

'Well I suppose, what shall I tell the boss though?'

'Oh tell him I have a migraine or something and I've gone home to bed.'

'You are pushing your luck my girl but if you must you must, be careful though ok?'

'I will, thanks Lucy and you Rob you're both the greatest.'

Tilley said goodbye and crossed the road, she hurried off in the direction that the man went and was soon walking behind him keeping a safe distance so he wouldn't know she was following him.

Tilley continued to follow him and he headed into the train station. He went into the station shop and Tilley waited outside, after a few minutes he came out carrying a newspaper and a bag of sweets. He then went to the ticket window. Tilley took a chance and stood behind him so she could hear where he was going. She heard him ask for a single to Parkview and waited until he had walked onto the platform.

Tilley didn't need a ticket as she had a season ticket so she walked onto the platform and looked to see where he had gone. She spotted him sitting on a bench reading the newspaper, she moved as close as she could and noticed that he was reading a story about the murder, there was a picture of the woman and the headline read "Murdered woman's husband still missing". As soon as he had read the story he threw the paper in the waste bin.

A few minutes later their train arrived, Tilley held back to see what carriage he chose and followed him on board. To avoid being spotted she sat at the end of the carriage but in a position where she could keep an eye on him.

At Parkview the man left the train but several other passengers also left by the same door meaning Tilley could not get close enough to follow him out of the station. She pushed past people but she had lost him. She was furious as she really did think he was the man she had seen in the bushes and knew she may never know now.

Dejected Tilley went into a pub situated just outside of the station called "The Junction". After ordering a bloody Mary she looked around the bar noticing it was very quiet but then it was a Monday afternoon so she decided that it was not so strange after all.

The barman brought her drink and after paying him she sat on a stool. 'No work today?' The barman asked her. Not realising he was talking to her she didn't respond straight away, then remembering she was the only one at the bar she said: 'I'm sorry, were you talking to me?'

'Yes I hope I wasn't being nosey?'

'No of course not, I was miles away.' She said smiling.

'Somewhere nice I hope?'

'No not really, just something playing on my mind.'

'Well I am a good listener, by the way I'm Simon the landlord.'

'Ok, well I'm Tilley, I'm sure you don't want to hear about my silly antics though.'

'Hello Tilley.' Simon reached over the bar and shook Tilley's hand and replied: 'You never know, try me.'

Tilley thought about it for a while then said: 'Ok but if you laugh at me you will wear this drink.'

'Well there's a challenge, go on fire away.'

Tilley told him about the murdered woman and the events leading up to her ending up in the pub. Hmm! Simon muttered: 'I think you need another drink, allow me and I think I will join you.'

'Thank you that's very kind.'

'Think nothing of it it's an amazing story, after all It's not every day I get a real Miss Marple in my pub.'

'I thought I warned you not to laugh at me.' She lifted her drink as if to throw it at him, he put his hands up in front of his face and laughing he said: 'Ok, Ok I submit.'

They both laughed then Simon said: 'Seriously though I think you are right, if you feel sure about something then you should pursue it until you have proved it one way or the other.'

'Thank you Simon you are the only person that doesn't think I'm bonkers accept for my mum and dad although they don't think I saw anything suspicious, they just support me because they are my parents.'

'Well that's natural but you follow your heart and if I can be of any help then don't hesitate to ask.'

'Thanks again Simon I appreciate it, oh my look at the time I must go home.'

'Ok then Tilley, it was nice to meet you, would you like me to call a taxi?'

'No I think I would like to walk but thank you anyway, goodbye.'

Leaving the pub and walking into the fresh air and Tilley not being a drinker, she felt a little woozy, she also felt a little hungry so she stopped off to get some fish and chips and ate them while walking home.

She arrived home and felt tired, she slipped off her shoes and coat and taking a bottle of spring water from her fridge she went and sat in the lounge. She switched on the TV and sat back on the sofa, in no time at all she nodded off.

The ringing of the phone woke her, she answered and was glad to hear her dad's voice, he asked: 'How are you darling?'

'Oh I'm alright thanks dad, how's you and mum?'

'We're great love we were just wondering whether you have gotten over the weekend.'

'Yes thanks dad.' "Not daring to tell them about her exploits of that afternoon". Her dad continued: 'Good have you heard anymore about that terrible business?'

No! 'I've got the TV on but I was tired and fell asleep almost as soon as I sat down.'

'I'm sorry love, did I disturb you?'

'Yes but I'm glad you did because I have a kink in my back now from this old sofa.'

'Why you don't get rid of that old thing, I don't know? It was old when you begged us to give it to you when we bought our new suite.'

'Yes I know but I could not afford to buy a new one then and I'm not that well off now either.'

'Well in that case we will buy you a new one.'

'No you won't dad you both do more now than you should I'll be alright, stop worrying about me.'

'Well we will discuss that on Wednesday evening. By the way your mother wants to know if you are happy with your outfit.'

'Yes it's lovely dad, thank you.'

'Ok then love, I've booked a taxi for seven thirty for you.'

'Ok thanks dad, look I'm going to say goodnight now if you don't mind, give my love to mum for me.'

'I will goodnight Tilley.'

The next morning DCI Carter was having breakfast when his phone rang, it was Mike Harper, he said: 'George; a man's body has been pulled from the river near the marina, I'm heading there now. Are you coming?'

'Yes Mike, I'll see you there.' Mike gave George the directions and left his office.

George arrived at the scene a few minute after Mike. The body was naked and laying on the river bank and being examined by the pathologist, George asked him: 'Any ID Roy?'

'No not at the moment George, I can't give a time or cause of death yet either but, he has been in the water for quite a few hours I would say, I won't know anymore until I get him on the slab.' DCI Carter thanked Roy then asked one of the uniformed officers: 'Who called it in constable?'

'It was discovered by a yachtsman earlier this morning sir, the body was wrapped in blue plastic sheeting which became caught in the yachts propeller. The guy dropped anchor and put his waders on, the water was shallow enough to allow him to clear the plastic away from the prop then he saw the body so he climbed back aboard and radioed it in.'

'Where is he now?'

'We have put him in a car sir, he was quite shaken it wasn't a pretty sight.'

'No of course not, what's his name?'

'Peter Crabtree.'

'Ok Thanks Constable.'

George Carter went over and opened the car door and climbed in beside the man. He said: 'Good morning Mr Crabtree how are you feeling?'

'A little better thanks.'

'Do you feel like taking me through this morning?'

'Yes I will try.'

'Ok then tell me in your own time what occurred.'

'Well I was taking my boat down to the marina to take it out of the water for the winter and just as I approached a narrow bend I felt a bump on the portside then the engine stalled. I looked over the stern and saw some blue plastic just below the water. That part of the river isn't very deep so I put on my waders and slipped over the side and saw the plastic was entangled around the prop. I started to pull it off and that's when I saw the body, the prop had sliced through the plastic and into the body, it was horrible.'

'I imagine it was sir, did you see anything else out of the ordinary such as a boat or anyone hanging around?'

No! 'I don't think so but as I said I was a little shook up.'

'Ok thank you, we would like a statement at your convenience Mr Crabtree but, in the meantime if you should remember anything else please contact the station.'

'Ok Inspector I will, when will I get my boat back?'

'When forensics are finished, there are still several tests they need to complete, someone will contact you when they are finished. Now I will arrange for a car to take you home.'

'That's ok I have my own car at the marina.'

'I would rather we took you home you are still a little shocked, we will pick you up tomorrow and take you to your car, your boat should be released by then as well.'

'Ok thank you, my boat will not be left unattended will it?'

'Not at all, we will have it towed into the marina onto your berth. Actually I do have one more question Mr Crabtree, if your car is at the marina, how did you get to where the yacht was moored?'

'I used a dinghy which I tow on a trailer with my car.'

'Ok sir thanks again, I'll go and arrange your lift.'

After leaving Mr Crabtree George arranged for a patrol car to take him home, George then called DI Harper over and asked if anything had been found that may identify the dead man, the DI told him: 'No nothing, the Pathologist has finished here though, he is on his way back to the lab and as soon as the body gets there he will commence a full post mortem.'

'Is there anywhere a vehicle could have got close enough to the water and dump the body?' Mike pointed out that there was a spot about a mile upstream and told him: 'There is a narrow track leading down to the water, it is an ideal spot as it is at the end of a tree lined lane with no houses close to it.'

'Has it been checked for tyre marks etcetera?'

'Yes George and there are fresh tracks in the mud at the water's edge, SOCCO have taken a plaster cast of them.'

'How can they tell the tyre marks are fresh?'

'Well it rained just after two o'clock this Morning so they would have had to have been made after that.' Looking at his watch Mike said: 'Its eleven twenty now and Roy hoped to have some answers in three or four hours.'

'Well in that case Mike let's get back to the office, will you get the team together in the incident room for about two thirty for an update on the Angela Johnson case.'

George Carter entered the incident room at two thirty five and the team were all present. He went to the front and stood at the side of the incident board on which was pinned Mr and Mrs Johnsons photos and all the information that was currently available.

He read out what written evidence they had then said: 'Well people we haven't got very far have we? There is still no info on the husband . . . . Excuse me sir . . . A WPC said: 'PC Clerk and I questioned his parents in the nursing home but they both have serious dementia. The Matron said they have only been there for just over five months, the son visited once and he paid a whole year's fees up front.'

'How much was that?'

'Just over seven thousand pound's sir.'

'That's a lot of money let's find out how and when they came into that sort of cash. One thing that is clear is these two people only seem to have appeared on the scene in the last six or seven months, do some digging and find out more about them.

Mike; we know they came from London so contact the Met and see if they can shed some light on them. Any luck with finger prints or DNA?'

No! 'They are not in the data base Gov. I have asked both of their employers for their CV's, I'll go through them when they arrive.'

'Ok team thank you, please let me or DI Harper know if any of you discover anything, however small.'

As George was dismissing the team Mike gave him a brown envelope a Constable had came in with. George opened it and read it aloud: "It's the preliminary Post Mortem report on the man's body. It confirms it had been in the water for some time which is hampering the PM, the Pathologist says he won't know much more before tomorrow.'

CHAPTER THREE

Wednesday morning Tilley arrived at work to find her desk covered in birthday cards, banners and balloons with thirty all over them were hanging from above.

There were no cards from Rob or Lucy which was unusual as they were normally the first to give theirs however they were also known for their pranks, so she put the coffee pot on then cleared a space on her desk and commenced opening her cards.

She was just wondering why no one else was in yet when the office door opened and a young man entered and asked: 'Are you Tilley Watson?' She said yes then he said: 'Well I am your birthday card from Rob and Lucy.' With that he started singing happy birthday while pulling off his long overcoat revealing just a pair of tight red trunks. Still singing he commenced writhing around close to her, he then pulled her head towards his pelvis area.

Tilley was stunned and speechless not knowing where to look, her face was redder than a tomato and she wished the floor would open up and swallow her.

Suddenly the rear door to the office opened and in walked the boss James and all the staff clapping and singing happy birthday. Lucy shouted to Tilley: 'Well we really caught you this year didn't we girl?' Tilley shook her fists at Lucy saying: 'I'll get you for this.' The stripper gram put his arm around Tilley and kissed her on the cheek and Lucy took a photograph. He picked up his coat and after wishing Tilley happy birthday again he said goodbye and left.

After the door closed James produced a bottle of champagne style drink and poured everyone a glass, he gave a toast to Tilley and they all took a sip of their drinks. After a few minutes James suggested they all start work, Tilley having to clear all the cards from her desk first.

When she arrived home that evening Tilley was ready to just put her feet up and have a nice cup of tea but, she had to get ready to go out for her birthday meal with her parents. After showering and putting on her makeup, she slipped on her new outfit then sat on her sofa waiting for her taxi to arrive.

The taxi picked her up on time but the driver asked her whether she minded if he made a little detour, he said he had left his wallet at home and it would only take a few minutes.

She said she didn't mind and they set off. When they finally arrived at Christos her mum and dad were waiting outside, they both kissed her and wished her happy birthday, her mum remarked: 'Oh you look lovely darling, doesn't she Bob?'

'She certainly does, quite stunning.'

'Oh don't you two start, I have been embarrassed enough today.'

'How was that then?' Her dad asked. Tilley replied: 'Don't make me tell you please?' Her dad continued: 'Ok let's go in and sit down and maybe we can persuade you to tell us.'

'I don't think so.'

Meanwhile DCI Carter was leaving his office to go home when his phone rang. It was Roy the pathologist, George said: 'Hi Roy, I hope you have some news for me.'

'I have, although a lot later than I expected and I don't think you are going to like it.'

'Ok I'll come on down.' On entering the lab George put on a gown and mask, he joined Roy who was looking at some tissue samples under a microscope, George asked: 'Ok Roy what have you got for me? Put me out of my misery.'

'As I said George you won't like it.'

'Let me guess, its Angela Johnson's husband, am I right?'

'Dead right, if you forgive my pun.'

'How long has he been dead?'

'It's hard to determine at the moment but I would estimate about two days, he was dead before he went into the water though.'

'What about cause of death, any ideas?'

'Not yet, two days is a long time to be in the water and its hindering me but, I will let you know as soon as I have completed the Post Mortem.'

'How did you identify him.'

'I matched his DNA with the sample from the brush.'

'Have you found anything else of importance?'

'No accept for an old scar on his right shoulder, It's small and round but I'm not sure what could have caused it, I would have thought it was about a year or so old.'

'I was just thinking Roy, if he has been in the water about two days, wouldn't he have had to been put in the water much further than a mile away, surely he would have travelled further along the river wouldn't he?'

'Not necessarily, there are several bends and it could easily have been caught up several times on overhanging bushes etcetera, anyway it is only an estimated time.'

'Right then thanks Roy, I'm going home now but please call me as soon as you have more.'

Back at the restaurant Tilley and her parents were looking at the menus while waiting for the waiter to bring some wine, her dad asked her: 'Come on then what happened to embarrass you today?'

'Oh it was nothing.'

'Never mind nothing, it's our turn to be curious now, so out with it.'

'Oh lord, alright but if either of you laugh I swear I will walk out.' Looking at his wife her dad said: 'We promise we won't, don't we love?' Joyce nodded her agreement, so Tilley set about telling them: 'Ok, well when I got to work this morning there was no one else in but there was thirty birthday banners hanging above my desk and that was covered in birthday cards and streamers.

While I was opening my cards the office door opened and a guy came in wearing a long overcoat and asked if I was Tilley Watson. I told him I was and he said he was Rob and Lucy's birthday card, with that he began dancing and singing happy birthday while taking his coat off, oh I can't I can feel my face glowing.' Her mum said: 'Don't stop now darling, we won't embarrass you we promised.'

'You better not, anyway all he was wearing under his coat was a pair of tight red trunks, he danced over to me and started writhing around and pushing his pelvic area up to my face. Oh I can't carry on, I'm sure you get the picture.'

'Yes I think we do.' Her dad said trying hard not to burst into laughter. Tilley saw this and pointed her finger at him screwing her eyes up saying: 'I warned you.' Still struggling not to laugh he asked: 'Who organised that then?'

'Who do you think? Rob and Lucy.'

'They get you every year don't they?'

'They sure do, I am going to get my own back one day.' At that moment the waiter arrived with the wine rescuing Tilley, he asked if they were ready to order. Glaring at her parents Tilley said. 'Yes we are, aren't we?' They got the message and gave their orders to the waiter.

Later after they had eaten their deserts they were quietly enjoying their coffee's when Tilley's mum said: 'Well Tilley I think it's time for the rest of your birthday treat, she looked at her husband and said: 'Call the stripper gram on darling.' That did it her parents just split their sides laughing. Tilley pulled her wrap around her face hiding until her mum and dad calmed down. When they did and after wiping their weeping eyes Tilley's mum said: 'Sorry darling but I just couldn't resist it.'

'I don't believe you two, you promised.' Her mum said: 'I know you must admit though it was funny.' Tilley turned away from her parents as if to snub them and said: 'I'm never talking to either of you again.' Her dad chipped in: 'Does that mean you don't want the last part of your birthday present.' She turned back around and asked him: 'What last part? I don't know whether I can trust you two anymore, it would have to be something very special to get you both out of this mess.'

'Ok then let's go and find out shall we? The taxi will be here in five minutes.' Her dad paid the bill and they went outside and sure enough the taxi was waiting.

The taxi dropped them off and Tilley let them into the building, they approached the apartment door and as Tilley unlocked it her father said: 'Now close your eyes.'

'Why there's nothing in there I don't know about.'

'Just humour us.' Her dad said. Tilley gave him that "I'm warning you look" and closed her eyes. Her dad placed his hands on her shoulders and guided her into her apartment. He stopped her and then said: 'Ok you can open your eyes now.' She slowly opened her eyes not knowing what to expect, standing in the place of her old tatty sofa was a brand new white leather one. She was speechless for several moments then blurted out: 'Oh mum, dad it's lovely, how—when did you get it in?' Her dad explained: 'I was waiting outside in the van from the furniture store when your taxi picked you up and I had tipped the driver to delay your arrival at the restaurant. I used the spare key you gave us to hold and the van driver and I brought it up. Have we redeemed ourselves?'

'I should coco, thank you both so much it's fantastic, I've had a wonderful time tonight.

Her mum asked: 'Even though we wound you up?'

'Yes mum but I forgive you both this time.' Her mum added: 'I must say though I do wish we could have been there this morning.'

'I don't—Her daughter replied grinning all over her face—now sit down on my "new sofa" and I will make us all a hot chocolate.'

'Ooh that sounds lovely.' Her mum remarked.

While drinking their chocolate they mulled over the evening, then kissing her goodnight her mum and dad went home and Tilley went to bed exhausted.

When her alarm went off next morning, to say she was not happy would be an understatement. Slowly getting out of bed and tenderly placing her feet into her fluffy slippers she began the morning routine, although with her head spinning and her tummy a little unsettled breakfast was definitely not going to be part of it, so she had a quick coffee and left for work.

Leaving her apartment the memories of the previous evening slowly began to come back, she smiled to herself remembering her mum pretending to have a stripper gram lined up.

At the station she walked past the station shop, a bulletin board outside read "Local Police investigating double murder". Intrigued she went in and bought the local newspaper. On the train she read the story—"The man' body that was pulled from the river on Tuesday morning was Mr Andrew Johnson, husband of the dead woman found on Parkview common last Friday. Police have not yet confirmed whether Mr Johnson was also murdered. Detective Chief Inspector Carter who is leading the investigation stated: "We are putting all of our recourses into the investigation but at this time we have little to go on. If anyone has any information however small please notify the Police".

Tilley thought to herself: "I bet that man I saw has got something to do with this". Consequently the rest of the journey was spent with her wondering what will happen next.

Later that afternoon DI Harper received a phone call from the front desk, it was the duty Sergeant, he said: 'We have a young man here who says he saw someone in a boat around the time, and close to where it is thought the man's body went into the river.'

'Ok put him an interview room, I will try to contact DCI Carter.' Harper hung up and called DCI Carter and gave him the news and arranged to meet him downstairs.

When they reached the interview area DCI Carter asked the PC on duty: 'Where have they put this guy?'

'He's in interview room four Sir.'

'What is his name?'

'Mr Simpson.' George thanked the PC and said to Mike: 'You interview him I'll observe from next door.'

The two rooms were separated by a two way mirror and a microphone relayed the sound into the room".

DCI Carter positioned himself so he could see the man clearly.

The man was looking relaxed, he had short fair hair and was wearing a grey hooded top, blue jeans and white trainers.

Milk Harper entered the room and introduced himself he then asked: 'Can I have your full name please?'

'Yes it's Gareth James Simpson.'

'Ok Mr Simpson.'

'You can call me Gary.'

'Ok how old are you Gary?'

'I'm twenty two.'

'I understand you have some information regarding the body found in the river, before you answer though I must inform you that this is an informal interview and is not being recorded. If your information does result in and arrest however, we will ask you for a written statement, is that ok?'

'Yeah, that's fine.'

'Right then tell me, what have you got to tell us?'

'I had been night fishing on the night before the body was found. I was on my way home and as I made my way up the bank something caught my eye to the right where the river bends. I got closer and shone my torch and I saw a figure in a rowing boat moving away in the direction of the marina.'

'Could you see if it was a man or a woman?'

'It was definitely a man and he was wearing a light coloured coat, blue I think and dark trousers.'

'Did you get a look at his face?'

No! 'As soon as I shone my torch on him he put his head down and started rowing away fast.'

'Is there a road or track leading down to the river near that area?'

'Yes it is about twenty or thirty yards from where I was.'

'At about time was this?'

'Around four to four thirty I would say.'

'Could you see if there was anything in the boat?'

'Not that I could see but, I didn't get much chance to see as he rowed away too quickly.'

'So what made you contact us today Gary?'

'I heard the report on the radio and thought there may be a connection.'

'Ok Gary is there anything else you can tell us?'

No! I'm afraid not.'

'Ok well thank you for coming in, if you remember anything else please call us, if we need to talk to you again we will be in touch. Goodbye Gary.'

Mike Harper met George outside of the interview room and asked: 'What do you think George?'

'Interesting the timing is about right, actually Mike that girl, what's her name? Tilley something wasn't it? Anyway didn't she say the man she saw wore a blue coat and had dark hair?'

'Watson George and yes she did, it's a bit of a long shot though.'

'Maybe but it's the only shot we have at the moment, by the way while you were interviewing Roy called, Mr Johnson was also suffocated and as with his wife there are no defensive marks. On a more sour note, the deputy Chief Constable called, it appears that the top brass feel we could do with some help so they are sending down a couple of people from the MET—a

Superintendant David Shaw and a female Profiler, her name is Francis Temple.'

'A profile that's all we need.'

'I thought you might say that Mike but it's out of our hands I'm afraid, they will be here first thing tomorrow.'

'Does the team know?'

'Not yet I will tell them in the morning, it will be a nice surprise for them.'

'You have a mean streak don't you George?'

'Whatever gave you that idea? Anyway I have to go, it's my daughter's birthday today and she is coming to dinner with us tonight so I'm in charge of buying the wine.'

'Ok George, have fun and say happy Birthday to Jodie for me.'

'Why don't you come along Mike? Marie won't mind she only said the other night that you haven't been around for a long time and you know she always cooks enough to feed an army.'

'Thank you George but I couldn't intrude on Jodie's night.'

'Don't be daft Mike Jodie thinks the world of you and after all you're as close to being her uncle as anyone.'

'Ok if you're sure I'd love to, it will be nice to see them both again but, I'm buying the wine.'

'You won't hear any complaints from me on that score, especially on a poor DCI's salary. See you at seven thirty then Mike.'

'I look forward to it I'll stop off and find a present for Jodie and some flowers for Marie.'

'Ok Mike I'll call Marie she will be thrilled.'

CHAPTER FOUR

Nine o'clock Friday morning the two officers from the MET arrived. Chief Superintendant Shaw—a smart, portly, middle aged man—and Consulting Profiler Francis Temple—a slim blond haired woman in her mid thirty's—were in DCI Carter's office discussing the files on the two murders with George and Mike Harper.

The Superintendant remarked to George: 'What is most obvious is that no one seems to know much about these two people. What about National insurance records?'

'Nothing from before they appeared on the scene about six months ago, we have posted their names and images around all the forces in the country but we've drawn a blank, it's as if the sky opened up one day and they fell to earth. There has been no finger prints or other any other evidence found on either body, so whoever is responsible are desperate to make sure there is nothing to incriminate them.'

Mike joined in and turning to the Superintendant he said: 'They are supposed to have come from your patch sir.'

'Yes that's right but we have drawn a blank in our investigations there as well. What about this Tilley Watson and Gary Simpson?' George answered: 'Miss Watson thought she saw something on her way to work on the morning after the wife's murder but it was nowhere near where the body was found. We did search the area but we didn't find anything. Her description of the man she saw does have a resemblance to the one Gary Simpson gave of the guy rowing the boat but that's about it really.' David Shaw turned to the Profiler and asked: 'Have you been able to come up with anything?'

'No not yet, it's a bit early and there are too many holes in what little information there is but, I would like to talk to this Tilley and Gary, could you set that up for me?' George responded: 'Of course, Mike will see to that won't you Mike?' Mike looked sideways at George and nodded his agreement.

Mike Harper called Tilley at home on Saturday morning, and asked whether she would be willing to go to the station and tell the profiler exactly what she saw on her way to work on the morning of the woman murder. Tilley could not speak for a second or so but when she regained her composure she said: 'Does this mean I did see something suspicious?'

'Nothing is clear at the moment Miss.' Feeling the excitement seeping back into her she asked: 'What time would you like me to come in?'

'Two o'clock this afternoon please, if that is ok?'

'I'll be there.'

Tilley couldn't believe what had just happened, she decided though that she was not going to tell her parents, she did not want them worrying needlessly.

After Mike hung up he called Gary Simpson, he also agreed to go in.

It was five minutes to two o'clock when Tilley arrived at the front desk. She was escorted to Mike Harper's office, he was with Francis Temple. Harper shook Tilley's hand and introduced her to Francis, he then said: 'I hope it isn't too inconvenient for you to come in today?' Tilley replied: No! 'In fact it's a little bit exciting actually.'

'Well I hope we haven't given the wrong impression, this is just an informal chat with our profiler here.' He pointed to Francis.

'I understand but it's just that I am a little intrigued.' Francis said to Tilley: 'Is it ok if I call you Tilley?'

'Yes of course, that's fine.'

'Good, well I am Francis. So Tilley, can you describe the person you saw last Friday Morning?'

'Well he had his back to me but I noticed he had short dark hair and was wearing a light blue coat.'

'Was there anything in his manner that caught your attention at all?'

'I don't think so, no.'

'I mean, was he was he hurrying away or just casually walking?'

'Casually walking I would say.'

'Lastly Tilley, was he heading towards the common or the road?'

'He definitely headed for the road.'

'Right thank you Tilley you have been very helpful.'

Oh! 'Is that it?'

'Yes I don't think there's anything else.'

'What about the thumping noise I heard?'

'Well we did get some officers to check the area but nothing was found but we have it on record in case it becomes relevant.' Tilley thought for a minute then said: 'Look I don't know if this any help at all but on the following Monday I was on my way back to work from lunch and I'm sure I saw the same guy.'

'Where was this Tilley?'

'Bromworth, my workmates and me had lunch in a pub, when we came out I saw him on the other side of the road. He was wearing the same coat with black Joggers. He also had short, dark, curly hair.'

'Did you get a good look at him?'

'Not straight away but I followed him. He went to the train station and bought a newspaper, he then went to the ticket window and bought a single ticket to Parkview so I decided to follow him further. I didn't need a ticket because I have a travel pass.'

'How did you know what ticket he bought then?'

'I stood behind him so I could hear.'

'Well you are quite the little detective.' Francis saw straight away though that Tilley was not amused and said: 'sorry Tilley, do carry on.'

'Well as i was saying, he went out onto the platform and I walked a little way behind him, he sat down and opened the newspaper. By this time I had managed to stand behind the seat and I noticed that he only read the story on the murdered woman then threw the paper in the rubbish bin. I did notice though he had a scar just below his left ear. Anyway a few minutes passed and the train arrived and I followed him aboard.'

Tilley continued on with the rest of her afternoons antics. Francis considered what she had heard then said: 'Ok that's very interesting, do you think you could work with our sketch artist and maybe get a description of this man?'

'Yes I will try, it sounds like fun.'

'Ok if you will follow me I will I will take you to him.'

Francis took Tilley downstairs to the artist's room and introduced her to him, she asked Tilley if she would like a cup of tea and Tilley accepted. Francis fetched some tea then left Tilley with the artist and went to speak to DCS Shaw. She said: 'David I think we may have a lead.'

'Tell me more Francis.' She repeated Tilley's story then said: 'I think it is significant that he only read the story on the murder then disposed of the paper.'

'I agree, is the girl still here?'

'Yes I have put her with the sketch artist to try and get a description.'

'Well done Francis, good work, by the way Mr Simpson has just arrived, he is having a cup of coffee so you take a break then have a word with him, it would be good if the sketch is ready to show it to him, hopefully something may twig with him.'

A little later DCS Shaw went to see George Carter and asked him to call Mike in. When Mike arrived Shaw told them that they may have a lead and went on to relate Tilley's account of following the man. He told them: 'She is currently working with the artist so hopefully we may have a face to work with.' Fantastic!

George exclaimed. Mike agreed enthusiastically saying: 'Good old Tilley.' David Shaw warned: 'It may not pay to get too excited just yet gents.' George replied: 'It's hard not too though after all this time Sir.'

'I can understand that, this is a very testing case so yes, I do get your excitement at the first sign of a breakthrough, I can also understand your resentment at Francis and myself barging in and seemingly taking over the case. Well we are here to help and not take over.' DCI Carter replied: 'I wouldn't say we resent you it is more that we are so frustrated that we couldn't get anywhere ourselves.'

'Of course and we understand that but, we are just another part of your team so why don't we all go down and see if we have a face to Tilley's mystery man?'

On their way downstairs Mike told his colleagues about a thought that had been niggling at him, he said: 'I have been wondering if we may have a witness protection program gone wrong.'

'That is a very feasible possibility Mike. David Shaw said. That would explain why there are no records of them before they appeared out of the woodwork. Has their CV's turned up yet Mike?'

'I don't know I'll check on them when we have finished here, we have got there phone records but they hardly made any calls, there were a few incoming calls a couple of which were blocked, we have to investigate those a little deeper.'

'Good thanks Mike.'

When they arrived at the artist's room David Shaw stood back and allowed George to take the lead, he asked the artist whether the sketch was ready. He said that it was and showed George the result. The sketch showed a thin faced man with dark short hair and brown eyes and a scar bellow his left ear. He was wearing a light blue coat with white tee shirt, black joggers and white trainer shoes. George asked Tilley: 'How good a description of the man would you say that was Tilley?'

'Very close, I got a good look at him that Monday.' David Shaw added: 'Great you have done magnificently, would you mind staying a little longer and I will have a word with you before you go.'

Meanwhile after Francis had finished talking to Gary Simpson she asked him to stay on for a while, he agreed and she went outside and met up with Superintendant Shaw, he asked her: 'Did you get anything useful?'

'No he virtually repeated word for word what he said in his interview.'

'Ok let's see what he makes of the sketch?' Francis and the Superintendant entered the room and Francis introduced Gary to David then asked: 'Would you mind looking at this sketch and tell me if you recognise the person?'

'No I don't know him.'

'Are you sure Gary? Take another look and take your time.' Gary looked again and said: 'I suppose it could be the bloke I saw in the boat but, I can't be sure.'

'So you wouldn't be prepared to swear to it?'

'No sorry.'

'That's fine Gary thank, you if we want to talk to you we will call you.'

David and Francis met up with George and Mike, the Superintendant said to Mike: 'Take some copies of the sketch and put it through the data base, also post it around all the forces Nationwide. Put it out to the media and the press as well, someone must know him.'

David Shaw then went back and spoke to Tilley, he said: 'I see from my notes that you thought you heard a noise that sounded like something being dropped.'

'Yes I am sure of it.'

'You didn't actually see anything though did you?'

NO! 'I'm positive I did hear something though.'

'Don't worry Miss Watson you have been very helpful but, we have taken up enough of your time. Go home and we will be in touch if we should need to talk to you again. I will arrange for a car to take you home. By the way we are putting your sketch in the papers and on TV.'

'My name won't be mentioned, will it?'

No! 'I can assure you, your name will be left out of it.'

'Thank goodness my parents would have kittens.'

'I'm sure they would. Now if you go down to the front desk you will be taken to a car.'

When the Superintendent had finished with Tilley he met up with the other three officers. He said to them: 'I have been thinking, Tilley said she heard something being dropped in the bushes that Friday morning. What if that guy was testing with a large rock or something similar to see if it would be dense enough to hide a body? Don't forget the woman's body was reasonably well hidden.' George responded: 'Very possible, if it hadn't been for that dog sniffing it out it could still be there. Mike; when they searched there was there anything like a rock there?'

'I don't know actually but then they wouldn't have been looking for anything like a rock of suchlike.'

'No I suppose not, ok send some more officer's back there tomorrow to have another look, it's too dark to start now.'

'Ok I will see to it.'

Tilley was dropped off outside of her apartment building at just past five twenty. She was of course very much on a high as the Police seemed to believe she had given them something to help the enquiry. She still wasn't sure if she should tell her parents though as she didn't want to worry them, she was bursting to tell someone though so she bit the bullet and rang them. Her mother answered and Tilley said: 'Hi mum.'

'Hello darling, how are you?'

'I'm alright, how are you and dad?'

'Very well, dad's just nipped down the shop to get some milk actually.'

'Well you both may not feel so good when I tell you my news.'

'Oh Lord what now, should I sit down?'

'Well maybe it's just that the Police asked me to go and see them today because something has turned up, and they wanted me to run through my story of that Friday morning.'

'What's happened then?'

'Someone saw a man in a boat rowing away from the area where they think the man's body was put into the river.'

'What has that got to do with you for heaven's sake?'

'Well his description of the man was similar to the person I saw.'

'How come, you only caught a glimpse of him and that was just his back wasn't it?'

'Yes but there is something I haven't told you.'

'Right now I am going to sit down, ok now what haven't you told us?'

Tilley gave her mother a detailed account of following the man, she then said 'So you see mum I was able to give the police a description of him.'

No! 'I don't see really because there is still no proof that he is the same man.'

'That's true but don't you think it's rather suspicious that he was only interested in the story of the murder then threw the paper away?'

'He probably only had time to read that story before the train came.'

No! 'It was at least five minutes before the train arrived, anyway they asked me to help create a sketch and it will be in the papers and on TV.'

'They aren't giving out your name are they?'

'No they assured me of that.'

'Ok but I'm still not convinced I hope you're not keeping any more secrets from us, we worry enough about you as it is.'

'I know mum and that is why I kept it from you, and no there are no more secrets.'

'Thank Heavens for that, now please keep us informed in future darling. I'm dreading what your father is going to say when I tell him.'

'You tell him not to worry. I would only have to give a written statement if my information should help catch the man anyway.'

'I'm not so sure Tilley, you may have to give evidence in court and that will put you in danger once your name has been announced as a witness.'

'Oh mum stop being so dramatic, I thought I was the one with the imagination. Anyway how would they find where I Live? The Police wouldn't release it.'

'These People have their ways of finding out these things love.'

'I think you have been watching too much television mother, now stop getting yourself in a stew and go make a cup of tea, I will give you a ring if I hear anything.'

'Alright darling but don't be surprised if your father calls you after I have told him.'

'Ok mum cheerio.'

Tilley's dad didn't call her but she could guess what he said to her Mother'.

CHAPTER FIVE

At eight thirty Monday morning four Police Constables plus a Sergeant began the second search of the area Tilley first saw the man. It was not long before one officer shouted that he had found something. The sergeant went to see and the officer pointed to a black plastic milk crate semi hidden by long grass and shrubs about nine feet away from the bushes Tilley said the man was. The Sergeant photographed the find then he examined the crate. He remarked to the Constable: 'That could easily have made the thumping noise the girl heard, he carefully picked up the crate with his Forensic gloves and after a further search, nothing else large enough to have made the thumping noise was found.

One officer did find a wrapper to a Glacier mint and it was bagged. The Sergeant announced that there was nothing else of any use there and ended the search.

On his arrival back at the station the Sergeant reported to George Carter, after which George went to Mike Harper's office and told him that the search team was back. Mike asked: 'Did they find anything useful George?'

'Possibly, they found a plastic milk crate that could be heavy enough to make a thumping noise. I've sent it to Forensics but, that's it accept for a sweet wrapper, I sent that to the lab too.' Mike then said: 'The CV's have come in they both had glowing written references, so far though it appears that their previous employers are either bogus or gone out of business because the phone numbers on the CV's are none existent.'

'Your theory of witness protection could be spot on then Mike, I think we should have a team talk and put this new information to them, we can also introduce our guests from the MET.'

George arranged a team meeting for eleven fifteen and he introduced David Shaw and Francis Temple, he then began to run through everything they had so far, he stated: "Ok people, we have Angela Johnson murdered early on the morning of the ninth. Her body was found that evening on the edge of Parkview Common. She was suffocated with a red cushion or pillow. Forensics can confirm this.

Mr Johnson was found in the river on the morning of Tuesday the thirteenth. His naked body was wrapped in a blue plastic sheet which caught in the prop of a yacht that was on its way to the marina. He was also suffocated in the same manner. There was no ID on or near the body he was identified by DNA from hair in his hair brush. Mrs Johnson was identified by a staff badge around her neck but there have been no other items of interest discovered.

We do have a young woman who saw a man—although a fair distance away from the site where woman's body was discovered—on the morning of her murder. She also thought she heard something being thrown or dropped in the area.

The young woman—Miss Watson—was able to create the sketch you see on the board with the aid of our sketch artist. She was able to give us the image because she thought she spotted the same man while on her lunch break in Bromworth on the Monday of the twelfth and followed him. While she was following him he bought a newspaper and only read the story of the woman's murder after which he threw the paper away. This leads us to believe him to be a person of interest. We have released his picture to the press and media as well as all other forces.

Mike Harper took over saying: 'There is also a young man—Gary Simpson—who had been fishing over night in the river and spotted a man that fits the description, rowing a boat in the direction of the marina at or about the area we think Mr Johnson's body was placed in the water, the timing is also about right. With the ID from Miss Watson and Simpson it is more than an assumption they both saw the same man.

One theory is that we may be looking at a witness protection gone wrong as both victims only seem to have appeared about six months ago. We want everybody to check all the companies who allegedly gave them references on their CV's. They seem to have disappeared.

We have had no luck with their phone records but there are two blocked numbers of which we are waiting for details.'

George clapped his hands and said: 'We are on unlimited overtime now people so all of you can spend the necessary time on the investigation. The DI and myself as well as our friends here from the MET are available twenty four seven so if you come up with something or need help with anything don't hesitate to call us.'

Later that lunchtime Mr and Mrs Watson were shopping in town and were having some lunch in a cafe. Mr Watson was reading the newspaper, the headline read: "Police have released details of a man they wish to question in connection with the murders of Angela and Andrew Johnson". There was a picture of the sketch Tilley had helped produce and Mr Watson gasped when he saw it, his wife asked: 'Whatever is the matter?'

I know that man!

'What man?' Pointing to the picture he said: Him! 'He comes into the shop, he's only been coming in for about three weeks but, he has been in at least three times in the last week. He only buys packets of sweets, Glacier mints actually.'

'Are you sure Bob? I'm worried enough with Tilley being involved in this dreadful business, she could end up testifying. I don't think I could cope with you having to go to court as well.'

'Yes I am sure love and I do understand your feelings but my information could help capture this man, so I'm duty bound to tell the Police.'

'They haven't printed her name have they?'

'No thank goodness.'

'That's something at least. I just knew one day Tilley's inquisitiveness would come back and bite her, I never for the life of me though imagined you or I would be involved. These people are obviously dangerous and you both could be in grave danger if you appear in court.'

'Don't fret Joyce, we are a long way from a court appearance and if there was a threat to Tilley or me we would probably be able to give our evidence from behind a screen.'

'I hope so Bob but as you say thankfully it is a long way off yet.'

When they got home Bob decided that he would tell the Police right away but he couldn't remember the name of the DCI he met when he and Tilley went to the station. He decided to wait until she got home from work and phoned her and asked for the DCI's name. Tilley asked: 'Why do you want that dad?'

'Well darling I saw your sketch in the paper today.'

'Yes so did I but why do you want that Detectives number?' Her dad went on to explain the situation and Tilley was speechless which amazed him, so he asked her: 'Are you alright Tilley?' She hesitated then said: 'Yes dad, I just can't believe I may actually have seen the murderer.'

'No one has said he is the murderer yet but he does seem involved somehow.'

'No one believed me though did they dad? I knew he was dodgy. Anyway you need to speak to DCI Carter.' She gave Bob the DCI's direct number from the card he gave her. He said: 'Thanks love I'll call him right away.'

'Ok dad let me know how you get on.'

'I will, I'll speak to you later.'

Bob hung up and called the number, a female voice answered: 'Hello, Parkview Police, WPC Haines speaking, can I help you?'

'Hello my name is Robert Watson, I have some information about the double murder and I would like to speak to DCI carter please.'

'Ok sir I'll see if he is still here.' A few moments later the WPC came back on the line and told Bob: 'I'm sorry DCI Carter is not in his office but he will be in about eight o'clock. DI Harper is in though and he is working alongside the DCI in the investigation, would you like to speak to him?'

'Yes that's fine I have met him, thank you.' The WPC said she would put him through. There was a short pause before DI Harper answered: 'Hello DI Harper here, what can I do for you?'

'Hello Detective, I am Robert Watson, we met the day my daughter Tilley showed DCI carter where she thought she saw the man in the bushes.'

'Ah yes I remember I understand you have some information for us.'

'Yes that's right, I recognised the man in Tilley's sketch from the paper today.'

'Where do you know him from sir?'

'Well I work in a convenience store in Parkview and he has been in the shop at least three times in the last two weeks. It was the scar just below his ear that convinced me. The odd thing is he only buys bags of Glacier Mints.' When Harper heard about the Glacier mints he said to Bob: 'Ok that's very interesting Mr

Watson, would you be able to come in and repeat what you have just told me to the DCI?'

'Of course, yes.'

'Good because you may have some vital information, although I can't say anymore at this stage but you may well give us a turning point.'

'That's good to know, when would you like me to come in?'

'Would you be able to come in tonight?'

'Yes no problem, what time?'

'About eight o'clock if that's alright?'

'Yes of course.'

Bob arrived at the station at ten minutes to eight, the front desk was unoccupied so he pressed the bell on the wall, after a few seconds a woman Police officer came to the window, she said: 'Good evening sir, how can I help?'

'Good evening, I'm here to see DCI Carter.'

'Is he expecting you?'

'Yes he is my name is Robert Watson.'

'Very well sir, please take a seat and I will notify him you are here.' He had only just sat down when the DCI came out.

'Hello Mr Watson nice to see you again.'

'Hello Inspector.'

'Will you follow me please?'

DCI carter led Bob to an interview room and invited him to sit down. He asked if Bob minded the interview being recorded.'

'No not at all, I just hope I can help.'

'Well I am sure you can Mr Watson, let's get started shall we?' Switching on the tape machine the DCI said:

'Ok Mr Watson in your own time, why have you come here this evening?'

'I was reading a newspaper today and I saw the sketch of the man you are seeking in connection with the murders of that couple.'

'What was it about the sketch that drew your attention?'

'Well the scar under his left ear really, he has come into the shop where I work at least three times in the last two weeks.'

'What shop is that sir?'

'Leslie's convenience store in Parkview Avenue, he just bought Glazier Mints each time.'

'Are you sure it is the same man.'

'Yes positive, although he was wearing different coloured trousers, he did wear a light blue coat and the hair and scar are the same.'

'When was the last time to your knowledge did he come into the store?'

'Lunch time last Friday about twelve thirty, I am sure of the time because I finish work at twelve thirty and he was the last customer I served. He was unshaven and looked exhausted.'

'Has your shop have CCTV?'

'Yes it does.'

'Do you know if anyone else in the store has seen him?'

'No but they would have had no need to mention it up to know.'

'Of course not, ok would it be possible to look at the security tapes for last Friday?'

'I would think so, would you like me to call the manager and ask him?'

'Yes please, will he still be there?'

'Yes the shop doesn't close until ten o'clock.'

'Fantastic, you can use the phone in my office, would there be any other tapes with him on?'

'It's possible they are marked Monday to Sunday and recorded over each week'

'That's good news, were you at work today Mr Watson?'

'No Monday is my day off.'

'Ok, obviously I will have to interview all the other staff members, will that be a problem?'

'I wouldn't think so but there is only the Les manager, his surname is Taylor and Helen Miller who works the opposite shift to me, I will mention it when I call Les about the tapes.'

'Thank you Mr Watson you have been most helpful.'

'That's ok, now if I can use your phone I will call about the tapes.' The DCS took Bob to his office and pointed to his desk and said: 'There you are, be my guest.'

Bob called his manager who agreed to take the tapes in that evening, he also remembered the man going in the store. He said he would talk to Helen when she came back from her break. Bob relayed les's response to DCI Carter. He asked Bob if he objected to his interview being used in evidence if needed and if he would attend an identity parade if required. Bob agreed and the two men said their goodbyes.

At the store Les asked Helen if she minded being questioned by the Police, she said she didn't but she didn't remember him going in the store when she was working. Les said he would tell the Police and asked her to lock up at ten o'clock if he wasn't back.

Les t retrieved the tapes and took them to the station, he agreed to his conversation being recorded then said: 'I remember the man coming into the shop about a day or so ago. As usual he only bought a packet of Glacier Mints.' The DCI showed him the sketch and he agreed it was the same man, he also confirmed Bob's account that he wore different trousers then the ones in the sketch.

He signed agreeing to his statement being used in evidence as well as attending an identity parade, George Carter then said: 'You can tell Helen that we will not need to talk to her at this stage however give me her details in case we need to talk to her at a later date? . . . . In the meantime if the man should come in the shop again please let us know as soon as possible.' Les agreed then asked when he could have his tapes back. Carter said he would get them copied that night and returned to him the next morning. Les thanked the DCI and said goodnight.

George called Mike Harper to bring him up to speed, he told him: 'It looks like we may have a break at last, we will get the tapes checked soon . . . . Before he could finish talking Roy Sharpe the Pathologist knocked Georges door and went in, he said: 'I'm sorry to barge in George but you need to hear this.' George told Mike he would call him back and hung up, he said to Roy: 'This had better be good Roy I was going home when I had finished talking with Mike.'

'Well, I have found something on both bodies.'

'Ok hit me with it, you have my attention.'

'Something has been troubling me about the cause of death, I thought it strange there were no defensive wounds so I had another look and found puncture wounds on the right buttock on both bodies. They probably injected the drug into them from behind. The amount of sedative in the woman's bloodstream indicates she would have been rendered unconscious almost immediately, making it easy to suffocate her. Mr Johnson however had less in his body which means he could have been conscious for a lot longer.' George thanked him then said: 'Well this is really a night for surprises.' Roy asked: 'Why what else has happened?'

'We have had a breakthrough on the man in the sketch he's been seen in a convenience store in town buying glacier mints.'

'Well I was just coming to that, if you remember glacier mint wrappers were found by uniform when they searched the area that girl took you to on that Sunday, and near the woman's body.'

'That's right they did yes.'

'Well you will be pleased to know I found a partial print on one, it was just enough to put through the data base and I got a hit.'

'Fantastic Roy who is it?'

'He's a known felon by the name of Shane Rickard. He has a long list of offences including breaking and entering progressing to aggravated burglary a couple of years later for which he was given three years jail. He was released just eight months ago.'

'This just get better and better Roy, I suppose though it's too much to hope you have an address for him?' Roy answered with a grin: 'Come on George, do you want me to do all your work for you? As it's for you though I will go and find out.'

'Thanks you're a star Roy.'

Roy went to try and get an address for Rickard and George called Mike back and gave him the news, he said: 'Right I'll be there yesterday. This should show the powers to be that we can manage on our own, eh George?'

'Well yes but I won't tell them that.'

'Fair enough I'll see you in a while.'

George then contacted DCS Shaw who offered to let Francis know of the developments. George arranged to meet up with them the next morning.

Mike arrived as Georges phone rang, it was Roy, he told Carter: 'I have Mr Rickard's last known address.' George asked Roy to wait while he found a pen, when George was ready Roy continued: 'He was last known to live with his widowed mother—Mary Rickard—at twelve Monkton Road, Parkview.'

'Brilliant thanks Roy, I owe you one.' Roy laughed and replied: 'Only one George?'

'Now now don't get greedy Roy.'

'Ok fair enough, let me know how you get on.'

'Oh I will I will.'

George obtained a search warrant then called the team together in the incident room for a quick briefing on the latest developments, after which he organised a four am raid on the Rickard residence. At three thirty George, Mike and two Detective constables who were all armed, boarded two unmarked Police vans and headed for the house. They were backed by six Constables and a WPC.

As they approached the house the drivers switched off the headlights and parked a short distance away, going the rest of the way on foot.

George sent Mike and three officers to watch the back of the house while he and the remainder quietly approached the front door.

George ordered one officer to break the door down with a battering ram and the officers burst into the house shouting: "Armed Police stay where you are".

They worked their way cautiously going from room to room with their guns at the ready. They only found one person in the house though, that was Mrs Rickard. She was curled up in her bed shaking with fear.

George ordered everyone out of the room accept the WPC, she helped the woman put her dressing gown on and comforted her.

The DCI went into the kitchen and made Mrs Rickard a cup of strong sweet tea. He waited while she calmed down a little then apologised for the rude awakening, he told why they were there and asked if her son lived with her. She informed George that he didn't and that she hadn't seen him for quite some time. Since he went to prison in fact for GBH and burglary.

George showed her the warrant and told her that unfortunately her house would have to be searched. He assured her he would insist that everything was put back how it was.

Leaving the WPC with the woman George called Mike and two officers and they commenced the search

George and Mike searched the woman's bedroom but found nothing but, a DC called from the bathroom saying: 'Sir you need to see this.' When George and Mike entered the bathroom the DC told them: 'I pulled the bath panel away and found this hidden behind it.' He was pointing to a small bundle of blue plastic, George remarked: 'That's like the plastic Mr Johnson was wrapped in.' He asked for it to be photographed then he reached in and lifted it out. George ordered another photo and then opened the parcel. Inside he found four men's wallets, three black and one brown. There was also a black lady's purse plus a sum of money in twenty and ten pound notes. Another picture was taken and George took the bundle downstairs where he counted it in front of Mike and a PC. There was eight hundred pounds in twenty pound notes and four hundred in tens.

George opened one black wallet and found three credit cards all in date and a photo of a smiling blond haired woman, the credit cards were issued to David M Wilson. The other two black ones were empty however the brown one contained two credit cards issued separately to the Johnsons. There was also a photo of Mrs Johnson in the wallet.

"Bingo we have the husband's wallet" George yelled. Then said: 'Right lads make sure you leave nothing unturned we are getting close now.'

Leaving the others to continue the search George opened the lady's purse but found it empty.

George took the items found behind the bath to show Mrs Rickard and asked if she was up to answering some questions, he said the WPC would stay with her.

She said: 'I'll try but I don't know much about Shane's business, as I said I haven't seen him for a long time.'

'I understand that Mrs Rickard but we have found these items hidden behind the bath panel which indicates he has been here very recently and he intends to come back some time.'

'What items?'

'Well there is a large sum of money and other items, one of which—a wallet—belongs to a man who was found murdered last Tuesday, there is even a photo of his wife who was murdered four days earlier.'

Murdered! 'What are you talking about? I know Shane is no Angel but there is no way he would get mixed up in something like that.'

'Well I'm afraid he is involved somehow, there is evidence that he was in the vicinity where the woman's body was found, he was also seen in the area where the husband's body was discovered.

Oh my God! 'What am I going to do?'

'I am sorry Mrs Rickard I realise how distressing this must be, however I must show you the items we found, please tell me if you recognise anything, is that ok?'

'I suppose so, yes.' George showed her the photo of Angela Johnson and asked: 'Do you know this woman?'

'No I can't say I do, who is she?'

'She is the murdered woman.'

'I can't believe this.' Mrs Rickard gasped. George continued: 'I'm sorry but I have to do this.' He showed her the photo of the blond woman, she didn't recognise her either.

He then showed her the blue plastic the items were wrapped in and asked if she had seen it before.

She replied: 'It looks like the stuff Shane covered his motorbike with.'

'Is it still here, the bike?'

'As far as I know, it will be in the shed if it is, but I haven't been out there for ages.'

'Can he drive a car Mrs Rickard?'

No! 'He hasn't even passed his test to ride his bike.'

Before he continued with his questions George asked the WPC to go and ask a constable to check the shed for the plastic sheeting.

George gave Mrs Rickard a breather then continued by showing her the money and asked if she was sure she knew nothing about it, he told her: 'There is over a thousand pounds here.'

'No I told you I haven't seen him. anyway Shane was always broke, he was always asking me for money so I can't imagine where that lot has came from.'

'Finally then, have you ever seen these wallets and this purse before?'

'No never.'

George thought for a while then said: 'Ok Mrs Rickard if you haven't seen Shane for so long how was he able to get in and hide these items in your bathroom? You see these two credit cards were only issued six months ago.'

'I honestly don't know, I told you.'

'Does he have a key to the house?'

'He did have but I had the locks changed when he went into prison because I was fed up with him coming and going as he pleased, so no he hasn't.'

'Well he has managed to get in somehow, have you noticed anything odd at all?'

'No I don't think so. She paused for a second then said: 'Hang on though, come to think of it I did come home one day from shopping and I found the back door unlocked and I was certain I had locked it when I went out.'

'When was this?'

'About two weeks ago.'

'Do you keep any spare keys in the house?'

'Yes there should be two back door keys in the kitchen drawer.'

'Would you look and see if they are still there please?' She went to the kitchen and opened the drawer and pulled out a key, she held it up and said: 'There is one missing.'

'Well there's your answer then, does he have any friends or relatives in the area?'

'No family other than me but he did used to knock around with an old school friend I don't know his name or where he lives though. I only saw him once when he called for Shane.'

'Can you give me a description?'

'No I only saw him for a few seconds.'

'Do you have a photograph of Shane?'

'Actually I do have one, it was taken on his eighteenth birthday, he doesn't like his picture being taken and he destroyed all the ones around the house but I had this one in my old purse, he missed that one.'

She went to get the picture but when she came back she said that one was gone too. She said he must have gone through the house when he sneaked in.

George thanked her for looking just then a Constable came in to say there was no motor bike or any sign of the plastic sheeting. George asked: 'Was the shed locked Constable?'

'No sir, the door had been forced open quite recently, there were scratch marks on the catch and they were still shiny where the padlock had been forced off.'

'Ok thank you, would you please tell everyone we are finished here and to make their way back to the vehicles?' He apologised to Mrs Rickard for the intrusion and asked if she would inform him if Shane should turn up. She said: 'Oh you can be sure I will, I want a few words with him myself.' George informed her: 'It would be preferable if you said nothing, it may well just spook him.'

'Ok the Inspector.'

'Goodbye then Mrs Rickard and once again I apologise for the intrusion.'

On his arrival back at the station George called in at the technical department, they were checking the tapes from the store. He asked the chief Technician: 'What have you found Harry?' He told George: 'Your man has been in the shop five times in the last week, he just buys packets of sweets. He was wearing dark trousers, and a lighter coloured coat with the collar up and he had short dark curly hair. I can't specify colours as the tapes are in black and white.'

'Can you see who served him each time?' Harry said: 'Take a look.' George watched the video, he saw Len the manager serve Rickard twice, and Robert Watson served him the other three times.

George thanked Harry and asked him to return the tapes to the store ASAP and to thank the manager.

Mike Harper met George who told him: 'The guy in the videos is definitely Rickard we just have to find out where he is now. Now the picture of him is publicised maybe someone else will come forward.'

'I hope so George, I hope so.'

CHAPTER SIX

Tuesday morning Tilley arrived at work earlier than her usual time, she couldn't wait to tell Lucy and Rob about her dad recognising Rickard. When Lucy walked in Tilley grabbed her arm nearly pulling her off balance. 'Guess what my dad has seen that guy as well.'

'Hang on Tilley let a girl get in the door.' Lucy gasped.

'Sorry but I'm so excited.'

'I gathered that.' Lucy took her coat off and after pouring a cup of coffee, she said: 'Right now tell me what's got you in such a state?'

'You know my dad works in Len's convenience store, well that bloke has been going in there for a few weeks.'

'How did he identify him?'

'He saw my sketch in the paper yesterday and he went to the Police last night.' With that Rob came in, Lucy shouted: 'Quick run or Tilley will pin you against the wall, she has more news.' Rob immediately ran into the gent's toilet.

'You are both so horrible, for that I am going to sit at my desk and not say another word.' Lucy replied: 'Thank goodness.' Then called out to Rob: 'Ok Rob it's safe to come out now.' She laughed then said: 'Joking aside, why don't we go out tonight and have a drink and a bite, then you can tell us everything.'

'Ok why not? It will make a nice change.'

Rob peered around the door pretending to see if it was safe to come out. 'What's going on then?' He asked.

'Well we are all going out tonight for a drink and a meal and Tilley will bring us up to date with her sleuthing.' Bob said: 'I'm not sure if I can, I will have to ring the Missus and see what's on.' After a pause he said: 'Hang on a minute, I can, she goes out Tuesday's it's her yoga night. We have a baby sitter and I normally go to the pub. I'll call her lunchtime and tell her not to cook for me.' Good! Tilley said excited. 'We can go to Simon's pub, it's nice there.'

'Oh yeah got a soft spot for him have we?' Lucy joked and Tilley's face turned crimson. She answered embarrassed: 'No I have not, anyway I'm getting on with my work now.'

Coincidentally later that morning Tilley's phone rang and it was, Simon from the pub. He said: 'Hello can I speak to Miss Watson please?'

'Hello Tilley Watson, how may I help you?'

'Hi Tilley It s Simon from the Junction, I'm ringing to see if you were responsible for that sketch in yesterday's paper?'

'Simon; you shouldn't call me at work you'll get me shot. How did you get this number?'

'I looked it up in the phone book, I'm sorry I just had to know.'

'Well ok yes it was, it's rather spooky you calling though, my workmates and I are coming to your pub tonight so I can fill you in then.'

'Ok that's great, I'll see you then.'

When they left work the three decided to have a meal before going to the pub so they went for a burger then onto the pub.

When they walked in Simon was serving a customer and didn't notice them. Rob told the girls to get a seat and he would fetch the drinks, he asked what they wanted, Tilley wanted a bloody Mary with no ice and Lucy asked for gin and orange with ice. Rob ordered a pint of lager for himself.

Simon said he would take the drinks to them so Rob paid and went and sat down. He turned to Tilley and said: 'Now then Tilley what's this all about?'

Tilley had only just began to speak when Simon brought the drinks over, he then noticed Tilley, he said: 'Hello Tilley nice to see you again, I have been thinking a lot about you lately with all this murder and intrigue going on, that's why I had to call you this morning.'

'Hi Simon, nice to see you too, yes a lot has happened since I last saw you.'

'Aren't you going to introduce me to your friends then?'

'Of course, this is Lucy and Rob, my work colleagues, I won't call them friends they wind me up too much.'
'You know you love it.' Rob said and reached out and shook Simon's hand, Lucy did likewise and said: 'I was wondering what Tilley's fancy man looked like, I must

say I approve.' 'See what they're like Simon, they are like this all the time.' Tilley retaliated. Simon just said: 'With a compliment like that, I'm not complaining.'

'Don't you go encouraging them anyway I thought you were on my side.' He stood up and put his hand on Tilley's shoulder and said: 'I am, look my barman will be in soon and then I will join you if that's ok?'

'No please do.' Rob said it will make a change having another man for support.' Tilley retorted: 'You don't need support you do quite well on your own.' Simon laughed and headed back to the bar.

When the barman had come in Simon joined them and Tilley took them through all the new developments.

The evening went well Tilley was bombarded with friendly jibes and innuendos as usual, however she drunk more than she was used to, so much so when she stood up to leave she fell straight back down again, sparking Lucy to say: 'Oh dear Tilley's a little tipsy.' Tilley was quick to reply: No I'm not! She stood up again and just as fast sat back down once more. Lucy crouched down in front of Tilley and said: 'Look we can't let you go home like this.' Tilley insisted: 'I'm alright I just need some air.' 'That is just what you don't want.' Simon added and the others agreed. Simon continued: 'Let me call you a taxi?' Tilley shook her head. Simon asked why not and she explained: 'I don't want to make a mess in the car, the way I feel that is more than a possibility.'

'In that case you can stay here tonight.'

'Yeah see, I told you so.' Lucy remarked nudging Rob's arm and winking. 'Stop it.' Tilley recanted then said: 'Thank you Simon but I'll be alright, anyway I would still have to go home in the morning to change my clothes for work.'

'That's no problem I'll give you a lift to your apartment in the morning, you can change and I will take you to work and I am not taking no for an answer. I have spare rooms upstairs that I let out and they are all empty. Now say goodnight to your friends and I will go and make up a bed for you.'

Tilley gave in knowing she was in a no win situation, so Rob and Lucy put on their coats and Lucy said to Tilley: 'Now don't do anything I wouldn't.'

Tilley just pointed to the door and said loudly . . . . *GO!!*

CHAPTER SEVEN

The previous evening after his interview Bob Watson arrived home at just past ten o'clock.

Joyce greeted him with a big hug saying: 'Thank goodness you're home I have been worried sick.'

'You are so silly Joyce I have only been gone a couple of hours.'

'I know Bob but I am so scared for you and Tilley, I just hope this man is not involved and it all fades away.'

'Well you may not get your wish love, the DCI said I was very helpful and I may have given them their first real lead.'

'Thank you very much Bob, you certainly know how to cheer a girl up, by the way Tilley phoned earlier to find out how you got on. I told her you would ring her when you came home.'

'I had better give her a call then.'

'Don't be too long love I just want to go to bed although I don't think I will sleep much with all this going on.'

'I know love, look you go up, I won't be long.'

Tilley was just about to ring her dad when her phone rang. Her dad said: 'Hello love.'

'Hello dad how did you get on?'

'Well DCI Carter thinks my information is important.'

'Does that mean you saw the murderer as well?'

'I don't know about that love but it does seem that man is involved.'

'I knew it, wow, this is so exciting.'

'Calm down Tilley, I should tell you your mother is getting very upset about all this and I don't want you or I to get any more involved until we are sure of what's going on.'

'Ok dad but what will happen if we did see the murderer?'

'I don't dare think that far ahead so for your mothers sake keep your enthusiasm to yourself, Look I am going to bed now and I suggest you do the same and think about something else, ok?'

'Yes alright dad, goodnight and give my love to mum.'

'Of course, goodnight and leave the TV off.'

At eleven twenty Wednesday morning, DCI Carter received a phone call, the male voice asked: 'Is that DCI Carter?'

'Yes it is, how can I help?'

'Good morning, I am Deputy Chief Constable Todd from London and District. We haven't met yet because as you probably know I only took up the post in August. However I have been following developments in your double murder investigation and we have a situation connected to the case that needs addressing immediately. I don't wish to discuss this on an unsecure line so I am coming down there today. I will need all your team present including Chief Superintendant Shaw and Francis the profiler. I should be there late afternoon.'

'Ok Sir I will get right onto it.'

George went to Mike harpers office and discussed the pending arrival of the DCC, Mike asked: 'Did he give any clue as to why he is coming? It must be serious to get him out of his warm office and come all this way.'

'No Mike he just said there was a situation of some sort, I hope he is not too late though, I haven't been home since yesterday.'

George mustered the team together in the incident room at three thirty, he and Mike Harper with CS Shaw and Francis all stood at the front facing the assembled team. George asked Superintendant Shaw loud enough for the team to hear if he was up to speed with the latest developments. He said that he was, he said he and Francis had studied the files and were in agreement that although this Shane character was definitely involved he didn't have the profile of a cold hearted killer or to cover his tracks so well. He said Francis was convinced that there was more than one person involved. She based that on the fact that a vehicle of some sort had to have been used to carry the bodies and Rickard only rides a motor bike and who knows how long ago he did that. George said he was sure everyone was in agreement with Francis's comments and asked her: 'Have you anything to add to your profile?' She Replied: 'Well yes, we are looking for at least two characters desperate and clever enough to leave no DNA or finger prints. Admitted a partial print belonging to Shane Rickard was found on a sweet wrapper found at the site Miss Watson saw him on the morning of the woman's murder but, I do not consider him as a murderer he is just a small link in the chain.

I believe by the manner of these murders that they are not their first. It may pay to search for similar cases with same MO.

I would assume they are about Forty to fifty years of age and work . . . . Before she could finish a WPC entered and told George that the DCC had arrived. George apologised to Francis for the interruption and followed the WPC out she told him she had put the DCC in his office. He thanked her and went to his office the DCC stood up and said: 'DCI Carter I presume.'

'That's correct Sir, how do you do? I must say I am a little concerned why you are here.'

'Of course, all will be reviled soon, is your team assembled?'

'Yes Sir they are in the incident room.'

'Ok then let's go and put you all out of your misery.'

George and the DCC entered the incident room amid a lot of chatter and a hush suddenly came over the room. George introduced the DCC to everyone and Superintendant Shaw shook his hand and said: 'Hello nice to meet you again Sir.' George remarked: 'Oh you know each other then?' David Shaw replied: 'Yes I was at the party celebrating Arthurs promotion, Francis was there as well.' George turned to the DCC and said: 'Right now that we are all introduced Francis was in the process of giving us her profile so far, is it alright if she continues?'

'Yes of course carry on Francis.' Francis promised to give the DCC a full copy later then continued: 'Actually I was almost finished, I was about to say I would imagine our suspect or suspects, either works in or knows someone who works in a job that gives them access to a van, or large car which they used to dispose of the bodies. That's about it for now.'

George thanked her and said: 'Ok Sir the floor is yours.'

'Thank you Inspector.' He turned to face the gathering and began: 'Good afternoon everybody, you are now all aware who I am. I have been asked by the Chief Commissioner Dyson to come here and inform you all of a major development in the Johnson's murders. This morning we were contacted by the FBI . . . . This caused a little muttering within the room. George hushed everyone and the DCC continued . . . . It appears MR and MRS Johnson were in actual in fact a Mr and Mrs Parker and they originated from London. They were on holiday in New York and unwittingly were involved in a shooting in which two senior members of a well known and feared crime family was killed in cold blood.

Three Police officers were killed in a multi vehicle pursuit and four were seriously injured, one officer is still on the critical list.

Our victims were in a taxi cab when the shootings occurred which was just coming out of a side street when the cab came face to face with the car the gunmen were in. Both cars collided and Mr Parker was slightly injured, unfortunately for them they saw the gunman's faces.

The driver of the gunman's car was killed outright but the other opened fire on the taxi killing the driver. Mrs Parker dived down between the seats and pulled her husband with her but her husband was shot, fortunately the gunmen ran off and the husband was only injured in his right shoulder.

To protect the Parker's Police reported to the press that they were both killed in the crash because they were able to give a positive identification of the gunmen from mug shots.

The gunmen were arrested the next day and the couple picked them out from an identity parade.

The Parkers agreed to testify in court and a safe house was arranged. The murderers were eventually convicted with the help of the Parkers evidence and were sentenced to life in prison.

The Parkers were given new identities and a new life but they were adamant they came back to this country. The FBI worked with our secret services and gave them a new start and MI5 were supposed to keep an eye on them.'

Mike looked at George when he heard about the new identities with a knowing smile, having suspected a witness protection connection. The DCC asked if anyone had any questions, David Shaw responded asking: 'How long has the Government known that the murder victims were the Parkers?'

'Not very long, once we requested information on the Johnsons internationally, the FBI contacted MI5 as soon as they made the connection. It is obvious that the people behind the shootings traced the Parkers here and somehow found them and took them out.

We have to find this Rickard character he is the only link we have with whoever carried out these atrocities.'

The DCC turned to David Shaw and asked: 'Where are we in the search for him?'

'Well I would rather George Carter fill you in there Sir, he has been here all night with DI Harper, they carried out a raid on Rickard's last known address early this morning.'

'Oh I see, I didn't realise we were that far ahead, what can you tell me Inspector?' George suggested they go to his office so he could bring the DCC up to date then those officers that attended the raid that morning could go home. The DCC agreed and thanked the team for a wonderful job so far.

George and the DCC entered George's office and George invited him to sit down then ordered some coffee, he then commenced his report: 'As David said we raided Shane Rickard's house in the early hours today, following the discovery of his identity from a partial fingerprint on a sweet wrapper. We found that at the site where a young lady—Tilley Watson—thought she saw a suspicious character mulling around on the morning of the woman's murder. Actually there was a similar wrapper found near the woman's body. Miss Watson was able to help composite a descriptive sketch of the man after spotting and following him in Bromworth.' George went on to describe the following developments right up to and after the raid on Rickard's mother's house. The DCC said: 'Very impressive George and to think the powers to be thought you were moving too slow.'

'With respect Sir, we can only move when we have something to move on, and luckily we got a break.'

'I couldn't agree with you more, well done from me anyway. Now this Shane Rickard how do you think he came to have that amount of money stashed away when he always acted as if he never had two penny's to rub together.'

'I don't rightly know Sir but, we are wondering if perhaps being that they were local he was recruited to select a safe dumping site for both body's, he could have been easily tempted with that sort of money. He could also have been forced to physically help with dumping the bodies.'

'That may well be so George we know that he doesn't drive but that chap who saw him in the boat, what was his name?'

'That was Gary Simpson Sir.'

'Yes well, he saw him rowing away from where we think the man's body was put in the water, who's to say he didn't dump him over the side of the boat?'

'I agree Sir we really do have to step up on the search for him. Do you think it would be a good idea to offer a reward for information leading to his arrest?'

'Yes I don't see why not but I will have to consult with the Commissioner. I will have a word when I get back to London. I'll call you when I get a decision. Ok you seem to have things under control here, carry on the good work George there may well be a promotion after all this.'

'Well I can't say that wouldn't be welcome. Thank you Sir.'

'Now keep me up to speed and I will be in touch concerning the reward.'

Six thirty five that evening George heard back from the DCC to say the reward on Rickard had been approved. George called Mike and told him to arrange a press conference for later that evening.

The press conference was set up for nine thirty, local and national press plus TV news staff attended. George and Mike sat facing the gathering. George stood up and informed them of the reason for the conference but insisted there were to be no questions at that stage. He continued: 'Right now ladies and gentlemen, I have a statement.'

"We have had a break in the search for the man in the sketch printed on Tuesday. Acting on information received we have identified the man, he was last known as "Shane Rickard". There is a five thousand pound reward for information leading to his capture. If anyone knows anything however small please contact your local Police station immediately". 'Ladies and gentlemen PLEASE insist that the press or TV are NOT to be contacted as we are dealing with ruthless killers and do not wish to put anyone at risk. Please put it out there ASAP. That's all, thank you ladies and gentlemen.'

Next morning George Carter was in his office when Mike Harper knocked his door. George called him in and said: 'Oh hello Mike I was just going to call you, we have the phone records from the couples house, there was nothing special accept for the two blocked calls. They could have come from the secret service. Trouble is MI5 play their cards close to their chests. I have contacted the Commissioner and he is going to try and get them to work with us, I'm not holding my breath though.'

Mike acknowledged George's information then asked: 'Are the phone records in from the Rickard house?'

'Yes I was just going through them, there were seven calls made in the last month all to the same number in Bromworth. Mrs Rickard said she didn't make them so Shane must have they were made after the date Mrs Rickard said she found the door unlocked. I'm waiting for the address so we can check it out . . . . With that his phone rang, George listened then said: 'Right thanks for letting me know.' He put the receiver down and said: 'That doesn't help us much mike, that number Rickard called is a rented office in Bromworth. The present occupier has only been there for just over a week. We have the name and address of the letting agency though so let's go and have a word with them, we can have a word with other occupants as well.'

'In the meantime George what do you think about asking Mrs Rickard if she can help with a sketch of the guy she saw with Shane?'

'I suppose we could although she did say she didn't get much of a look at him, give her a call and ask her Mike.'

Mike left George and went to his own office and called Mrs Rickard. When she answered Mike said: 'Hello is that Mrs Rickard?'

'Yes it is.'

'Mrs Rickard this is DI Harper, I'm sorry to bother you again but would you consider helping compose a sketch of the young man that called at your house for Shane?'

'I'm not sure I can, as I said yesterday I only caught a glimpse of him.'

'I understand but we would be grateful for anything you can give us, you never know it may be the lead we need to find Shane.'

'Ok I will try do you want me to come to the station?'

'Yes if that's convenient we will send a car for you this afternoon.'

'Yes that would be alright.'

'Good thank you so much, we will pick you up about two o'clock, it shouldn't take too long.'

Mike had only just put the receiver down when the phone rang, it was Steve from Forensics, he told mike: 'We have traced a transaction from one of the credit cards found in Rickard's house it's registered to a David M Wilson. It was used at a guest house called the Conifers on the night before the woman's body was found.'

'Fantastic, where is the guest house?'

'Five minutes drive from where Mrs Johnson was found and not a million miles away from where we found the husband's body. Too much of a coincidence don't you think Mike?'

'Too right Steve, have you got the address?'

'Yes I have faxed it to you.'

'Thanks Steve, I'll go and tell George.'

Mike collected the fax and took it to George, he reacted by saying: 'Things are starting to come together at last. Right Mike you arrange a car to pick up Mrs Rickard then go to the guest house, get as much info as you can on who stayed there recently. I will arrange for someone to meet Mrs Rickard and take her to the sketch artist . . . . by the way Mike the Superintendant and Francis are going back to London tomorrow it seems that the top brass are happy with our handling of the case now.'

'It's a pity they couldn't see that earlier. Anyway I'll be off, I'll let you know what I find out.'

'Oh I nearly forgot Mike, "The National Intelligence squad are sending over two bods to talk to us. 'I'll brief you on that later.'

At the Conifers guest house Mike rang the doorbell, the door was opened by a neatly dressed lady Mike guessed she was about sixty years old.

He showed her his ID and said: 'Good morning Madam I am Detective Inspector Harper from Parkview CID. I am making enquiries into guests who may have stayed here on or about Friday the ninth of October.'

'Oh yes I remember there were, three of them, it is normally very quiet at this time of year so it was unusual to have three guests at the same time. They booked for four nights but stayed only four. Come in Detective, would you like a cup of tea?'

'Thank you, yes that would be nice.' She showed him into the lounge and introduced herself as Mrs Joanne Perkins and invited him to sit down. She excused herself and went to make the tea.

She returned after a minute or so with the guest register for Mike to look at and returned to the kitchen. While she was gone Mike made a note of the name of the three guests observing they were all men. Mrs Perkins returned with a tray of tea and biscuits. She sat down and Mike said to her: 'Right then Mrs Perkins . . . . She interrupted him: 'Oh please call me Joanne?'

'Ok Joanne, I see these guests were all male, did you notice anything odd about them at all?'

'Yes but not right away. You see one man made the booking over the phone and he was the first to arrive at about four thirty. He was aged about forty five I would suppose.'

'Which one was he?' Pointing to the register she declared: 'That one . . . . Wilson—David Miles Wilson. He was American he said he didn't know how long they are going to stay and that he would settle up when they leave. I though he looked a nice man so I trusted him. I showed him to his room and I had just come down the stairs when the other two arrived, one was another American but I am not sure where the other one was from but, it was him that made me wonder if all was not as it should be.'

'Oh and why was that?' Mrs Perkins poured the tea and handed a cup to Mike, pointing to the milk and sugar she said: 'Help yourself and please have some biscuits, I make them myself.' Mike said thank you and took a biscuit and exclaimed: Oh they are very nice! 'Now you were saying.'

'Yes well the second American arrived with the other chap. He didn't look very well at all.'

'The second American what was his name?'

'That was Michael John Franks, he signed them both in explaining that they only arrived in the country from America that day and his pal didn't like flying so he had drugged himself up to help him get through the flight. I wasn't sure though, he didn't talk although he tried but Franks stopped him each time saying he was disorientated with the drugs and that he needed to get him to his room so he could sleep it off.'

'I see his name was Mr Smith.'

'Yes Alan James.' Mike showed her the picture of Shane Rickard and Mr Johnson and asked if they were one of the men. Her eyes widened and exclaimed: Oh my, yes him! She pointed to Mr Johnson's picture and continued: 'That's Mr Smith. I thought there was something wrong because I never saw him again after the day he arrived.'

'When did they check out and how did they pay?'

'Mr Wilson paid by credit card when he left at eight thirty on the Tuesday morning, he paid for the five nights even though they only stayed four. I never saw the other two leave, actually I have the credit card receipt in my records.' Joanne showed Mike the receipt and he noted the number then asked: 'Is anyone in the rooms at present?'

'No as I said it is normally quiet around this time.'

'In that case I'd like our Forensics department to check them over, would that be ok?'

'Yes of course, the rooms have been cleaned though Detective.'

'I understand that but there may be something left behind. Lastly Joanne, would you be willing to come in and give a written statement, I can have you collected in the Morning.'

'Yes of course young man.'

'I don't know about the young man but flattery will get you everywhere.' Mike winked at her and thanked her then said goodbye.

When Mike returned to his car he used his car radio and called the Forensic department and arranged for a team to check the three rooms over, he also gave the technician to check, the credit card numbers Joanne had just given him against the card found at Rickard's mother's house. After a minute the technician came back and told Mike that the numbers were a match.

When Mike reached the station he went straight to DCI Carter's office. George could see that Mike was excited and remarked: 'You look pleased with yourself Mike, lost a penny and found a fiver?'

'Next best thing, there were three men that stayed at the Conifers from four thirty pm on the ninth to eight thirty am the thirteenth. One was Mr Johnson and he was drugged up, the other two were yanks.'

'That's wonderful Mike, well done have you any names or ID's?'

'Yes I got their names but no ID's, the landlady showed me the register but you can bank on them being false. Mrs Perkins—the landlady is coming in tomorrow to make a statement so I will arrange for her to look at some mug shots, although they are American and possibly not in our database.'

'Good work Mike, by the way Mrs Rickard didn't recognise anyone from rogue's gallery but she has helped compile a rough likeness of the guy she saw with Shane, we will just have run with that for now. Well there's not much more we can do today so you go home and in the morning we'll go and visit the estate agents that rented the offices Rickard phoned.'

'Thanks George it will be nice to sleep in my bed, let's hope that we are closer to a major breakthrough.'

'Fingers crossed Mike now off you go see you in the morning. Oh yes Mike, the plaster cast of the tracks that SOCCO made from the tyre tracks near where the husband was found have been identified, they are normally fitted to a Volkswagen van or camper.'

'Well that would be large enough to carry a body or two, don't you think?'

'Very possible Mike, anyway off you go, see you tomorrow.'

CHAPTER EIGHT

Next morning George sent Detective constable Harris to collect Mrs Perkins while he and Mike went to the estate agents.

On arrival at the agents they were greeted by a blond haired young lady. She approached them saying: 'Good morning gentlemen, can I help you?' After both men had shown their ID's George said: 'I am DCI Carter and this is DI Harper from Parkview CID, we are trying to trace who rented one of your offices in Venture Gardens on or about these dates.' The woman looked at the dates and said: 'Ok gentlemen I will go and check.'

She came back a few minutes later with a blue file and said: 'Yes this is the one, it's on the thirteenth floor, number one three six. There are new occupants there now though called Mathews Inc's.' She asked them to take a seat and she would go and get the person who arranged the lease.'

A moment later a young man appeared, he introduced himself as Peter crane and asked how he could help.' George made the introductions and told him what they were there for. He showed them into a small office and closed the door, they all sat down then he informed them: 'Yes I dealt with that it was leased six weeks ago for six months, hang on I will get the records.' He returned with a book and opened it, he said: 'Here you are, the booking was done over the phone and the references were faxed to us, the full payment was made in person by a young man, all in cash and he collected the keys.'

'Was either of these the man?' George showed him the sketch of Shane Rickard, and the man his mother saw him with, Crane shook his head.

'Are you absolutely positive?'

'Yes I swear.'

'Ok, do you know what the office was used for?'

'He said it was going to be an enquiry centre, it was odd though the keys were returned by post just over two weeks ago with no explanation and the contract torn up in the envelope.'

'That's very interesting. We will have to speak to all the occupants in the building.'

'That's fine you can go any time you like.'

'As this is a murder enquiry we would like to go right now if we could?'

'That's no problem Inspector I will be with you in a few moments'

George and Mike returned to their car to wait for Peter Crane, while they waited DCI Carter called the station and arranged for six officers to meet them at the office building.

George and Mike arrived at Venture Gardens and met up with the officers outside. George spoke to them saying: 'Right men we are here to speak to everyone in the building from cleaners to directors, we want information however small about occupiers of room—one three six on the thirteenth floor, they were only there for four weeks and disappeared about three weeks ago. The Di and I will take the thirteenth floor. George gave all the officers copies of the two sketches and told them to show them to everyone, we will meet here in the lobby when we are all finished.'

When Peter Crane arrived George approached him and said: 'Before we go in do you recognise any of these people?' He showed Crane the photos of Mr and Mrs Johnson and the blond woman which was found at Rickard's house. Crane said he didn't recognise any of them. George then gave each of the officers a copy of the three photos to show around the building, he then asked Crane to open the door and they all went in.

It took about an hour for everyone to complete their enquiries. On returning to the lobby Mike and George met up with the officers and George asked: 'What have we got then?'

Each officer individually gave their reports, over all though the operation was not much of a success, George did say that some occupants on the thirteenth floor told him and Mike that there was a man seen entering and leaving the office in question but he never stayed in the office very long, the door was always kept closed and the blinds were always pulled down and the top of the door was frosted glass which restricted the view.

They all said he was not very old or a particularly tidy person. He seemed nervous and kept his head down so his face could not be seen. He always wore a brown overcoat with the collar up and a white baseball cap which meant they could not see the colour of his hair. No one recognised the people in the photos though.

George said to Peter Crane: 'I see there are CCTV cameras spread around inside and outside of the building, have you any tapes?'

'No I'm afraid not the cameras are dummies.' George thanked Crane for his help and ushered the officers back to the cars.

On their return Mike told George he would go and see if Mrs Perkins had recognised anyone in the mug shots, he was told that DC Harris who escorted her was in the canteen so Mike went up there and got a coffee and Joined the DC saying: 'Sorry to interrupt your break Tim.'

'That's alright Mike I'm just snatching a quick coffee.'

'I was wondering whether you had any news for me.'

'Not yet, after taking Mrs Perkins statement I put her in with a room with the mug shots and came here while she was looking at them. Constable Gardener is going to notify me when she is finished. The names in the register were false, however she did say they had a dark green Volkswagen camper van and she took the number.'

'Brilliant Tim that must be the vehicle they used to transport the bodies.'

'How do you work that one out Mike?'

'Well the casts of the tyre tracks in the lane by the river has been identified as belonging to a Volkswagen van or camper.'

'Ok I'll give you that one. I checked the registration number and the camper was reported stolen in London seven weeks ago.'

'Ok Tim, get onto the boys in London and get them to pay a visit to the owner to see he is on the level and check the circumstances of the theft.'

Tim and Mike finished their coffees and went to see how Mrs Perkins was getting on. She had just finished looking at the mug shots and as they approached room she and the Constable came out, Mike asked her? 'Did you recognise anyone Mrs Perkins?'

'Yes I think so one of them does look like one of the yanks.' She pointed at one of the pictures and continued: 'That one there, he looks like MR Wilson accept he has quite long brown hair here but he had short black hair when he stayed at the house, he looks younger in the picture too, I am sure it is him though. I didn't get a good enough look at the other one because he had a baseball hat on and was wearing dark glasses, I wouldn't be able to pick him out even if his picture was in there.'

'Thank you so much Mrs Perkins, you have been a great help.'

'You won't be putting my name in the papers or anything will you?'

'No of course not but, we may require you to attend an identity parade if we apprehend any of these men, you will be behind a two way glass panel though and we will do everything in our power to protect your identity. Although you may be asked to give evidence in court I'm afraid.'

'Oh dear will I? I've never been in a court room before.' Mike put his arm around her shoulder saying: 'There's no need to worry we will go through the whole procedure with you if it is necessary, there will be nothing to worry about I promise.'

Mike asked Tim to get a car to take Mrs Perkins home and went back to see George. He greeted Mike saying: 'Hi Mike Roy called with a report of the search of the guest house, they checked for finger prints but the room had been wiped clean, however they did find two partial prints on a used syringe they found under the bed in Mr Smith/Johnson's room. He is checking them against the data base as well as testing what was in the syringe.'

Mike related to George everything Mrs Perkins had put in her statement and that she recognised the American named Wilson from the mug shots. He also told him that Tim was contacting the MET to have the owner of the stolen VW questioned.

Mike returned to his office leaving George to catch up on some paperwork but he was interrupted by a knock on the door, it was a Constable from the front desk and he had a man with him, he apologised saying: 'Sorry to interrupt Sir but I felt it was important.'

'What is it Constable and who is this?'

'This is Special agent Freeman of the FBI he said it was urgent he spoke to you.'

The FBI! 'Well I never saw that one coming. Show him in Constable.'

When the agent entered the office George introduced himself and invited him to sit down. He asked: 'For what do we owe the pleasure of the FBI in this neck of the woods?'

'Hi Detective, I'm Special Agent Jack Freeman, I am here in connection with your two murders. You see your two victims were put in witness protection because they testified against two members of a powerful crime syndicate in New York and they are now serving life sentences.'

'We do know all that but please go on you've got my attention. What's happened to bring you here?'

'Well the two men that were shot dead were serious drug dealers but, a young guy from over here was also involved although somewhat involuntary. He returned Britain but is being protected by your government.'

'Do you have a name for this guy?'

'His name then was Clive Rees—Parkinson. He was in the middle of his gap year and was in the States but he got into gambling and ended up heavily in debt to a ruthless loan shark. He used the debt to force the kid to sell drugs to the young son of the head of the crime gang. However the loans guy had a score to settle with the crime lord and the drugs were actually pure heroin so the boy died a horrendous death.

Consequently the young Brit wasn't very popular and called on the British embassy to bring him home. His father John Rees—Parker, who ironically is now the Minister for justice somehow managed to get him a position in politics and is now a junior Minister in his cabinet.'

'Has he kept the same name?'

'You will have to ask your security chiefs that one I'm afraid.'

'Is that all you came over here to tell us or are there more problems on the way?'

'Well that depends whether your murders are connected to the New York incident, it would be a major surprise if they weren't though don't you think? It is thought that as the couple at the scene of the shootings were British the gang associated them to the young Brit. The bureau considered it too sensitive an issue to risk using unsecure lines or faxes so here I am.'

'Ok that's all understandable, are you staying over here?'

'No I am flying back tonight but we will be at your service if you should require any further information.'

'Well there is something you may be able to help with.'

'Anything, try me?' George asked if Freeman knew the names of the two Americans, he replied: 'No never heard of them but I will check up on it when I get home, did you think I should have known them?'

'Well yes as they are American, they booked into a guest house with the male victim a few days before he died.'

'Interesting, ok bud I will check it out as soon as I get back, incidentally which, I should be going my flight is in three hours.'

George thanked him and said goodbye.

After Jack had left George called Mike to his office to fill him in on the visit, he told him: 'I deliberately didn't show him the photo of David Wilson because he said he didn't know either of the names but I don't quite believe him, he is holding out on something I am sure. George asked Mike to arrange a news conference for later that afternoon to give them an update regarding the American's suspected involvement he then suggested they go to the canteen for a break. As they walked out they were met by a Detective Sergeant, he told them that the VW was owned by a "Clive Rees—Parker. George thanked him and went with Mike to the canteen.

On their return to George's office there was a brown envelope on his desk, it contained the report of the search of The Conifers, he told Mike: 'It's from Roy Sharpe, he has a hit with the finger prints on the syringe, they belong to a known criminal wanted in New York for assault with a deadly weapon—a tyre wrench, on a motorist during a road rage incident from which he jumped bail thirteen months ago.

The New York boys have faxed over his file with a photograph, Roy compared it with the mug shot of David Miles Wilson and it was him. His real name though is Angelo Mieko Brice.

He has previous convictions over here and in the states for violent crimes. He was in the navy and that's when he collected his record over here, he beat up a British sailor in Portsmouth but the yanks talked the authorities into releasing him into their custody. He was however dishonestly discharged a year later for leaving a Military Policeman crippled for life after a brawl in a bar in Las Vegas while on leave.

He is dangerous so I think we should release his details to the public and warn them not to approach him. I will try and get another reward for information. Roy has also confirmed that the drug in the syringe is the same found in the two bodies.'

George and Mike continued to discuss the latest developments selecting exactly what to release to the media.

The news conference was set up for five forty five. George and Mike entered the room where about twenty members of the local and national press were assembled along with television news representatives.

George and Mike took their seats facing them and George commenced proceedings: 'Good evening everybody, I am Detective Chief Inspector George Carter, this is Detective Inspector Michael Harper. We have invited you all here today to update you with the investigation into the murders of Mr and Mrs Johnson. We will be taking a few questions later.' "We have fresh evidence that Mr Johnson was kept prisoner in a drugged state by at least two men, actually they are Americans. He was held at a guest house the address of which is being withheld.

The names of the Americans are: John Michael Franks and Angelo Mieko Brice.

Brice is already wanted in America for attempted murder, he is dangerous and must not be approached, we have his photo and we will hand it around later. They are known to be driving a green Volkswagen camper van stolen from London prior to the murders". George read the registration out and invited Mike to continue: 'Good evening, "as DCI Carter has already said, the camper van was stolen from London and we now know who the owner is, that is also being withheld at present.

Shane Rickard is still a leading suspect and we would urge the public to report any sightings of him or the

American. If anyone saw or heard anything suspicious or odd no matter how small in or around the areas where the bodies were found on or about the days of the body discoveries, we would like to hear about it. All information will be treated as confidential so nobody will be at risk".

Mike handed back to George: 'Right ladies and Gentlemen we have a few minutes for questions.' Immediately a flurry of hands went up and everyone began shouting out questions all at once. George called them to order and said: 'Calm down everybody, one at a time please?' Pointing to a man who was sitting in the front row he said: 'You go first.' The man stood up and announced: "Stanley Walters—Bromworth Argos" 'How were the couple murdered?'

"They were suffocated with a cushion or pillow after being subdued with a sedative administered by a syringe—needle marks were discovered on both victims". The man sat down and George pointed to a young lady she gave her name as Stephanie Conway of the Parkview Journal. She asked: 'Do you know why they were murdered?' "We have a possible motive but it may hinder our enquiries to announce it at this time. We will however inform everyone when we have more positive evidence".

George said one more please and pointed to a local TV representative in the back row. He said his name was John Porter from Parkview Television Network, he asked: 'What are Americans doing over here murdering English citizens?'

"As I said we are not in a position to say as yet, however we are following up on leads and hope to have answers imminently". 'Ladies and Gentlemen please do not present your pieces in the manner of the last question we do not wish to stir up international conflict on top of everything else.'

Clapping his hands George announced: 'Ok thank you everybody, please report this information sensitively.' Giving them a telephone number to broadcast for people to call in confidence he dismissed them.

Mike and George went to George's office and there was a note from the Deputy Commissioner informing that two agents from the National Intelligence Squad were on their way to discuss the case. Mike remarked: 'All the big guns are coming out of the woodwork for this one but what the heck could NIS want?'

'Good question Mike, it's a strange one'

CHAPTER NINE

Sunday morning Tilley was sitting in her dressing gown eating her breakfast when her phone rang. When she answered she was pleased to hear her dad's voice: 'Hello Tilley have you seen the papers today?'

No! 'Why what's happened?'

'Well nothings actually happened but they have printed your sketch again plus a picture of another suspect. His name is David Miles Wilson and he's American, he is also known as Angelo Mieko Brice. They are also looking for another American called Michael John Franks there's no picture of him though. They think they are driving a green VW camper van.'

'Wow dad that's brilliant does that mean that they have nearly solved the case?'

'I don't think so love they are just appealing for information, I dare say that if they catch either of these men they will be close, do you want me to bring the paper over to you?'

'No thanks dad, you can bet your life Lucy will have it at work tomorrow, I have written the names down anyway. You can give me the registration number of the VW though, if you like?'

'Don't tell me you are going out searching for that now?'

'No but you never know I may see it on my way to work or somewhere.' Reluctantly her father gave her the number and thanking him for phoning her she said: 'Give my love to mum and don't worry I'm not going out with my magnifying glass quite yet.'

'I am pleased to hear that, ok by Tilley, speak to you soon.'

That evening Tilley was cooking spaghetti when her phone rang, a man's voice said: 'Hello is that Miss Watson?' Tilley answered a little tentatively: 'Yes who is that?'

'Miss Watson I am Detective Strong I am part of the team investigating the two murders. We were wondering, could you come down to the station? We have something you may be able to help us with.'

'What right now?'

'Well as soon as you can, it is important to the case.'

'I see, well I am cooking my supper now but I can come down after I've eaten.'

'That'll be fine we will pick you up, what time would you like us to collect you?'

'About eight thirty will be ok.'

'Right we will see you then.' Tilley replaced the receiver and stared into space for a while wondering what the Police wanted then she shook herself back to reality and finished cooking her meal.

Tilley's door buzzer sounded at eight thirty five, she answered saying she would be straight down. When she stepped outside she saw a large black car with the rear widows blacked out, she looked at the windows not sure why they were like that. A dark haired slim young man in a grey suit was standing by the front passenger door, he could see she was a little apprehensive so he told her: 'Don't worry about the windows, this was the only vehicle available tonight, we normally use it to transport prisoners.

Tilley accepted the explanation and the man introduced himself as Detective Strong he then opened the car door and she climbed in he then went around and climbed into the driver's seat and drove off.

They headed towards the common where there were no street lights, suddenly without warning a hand came around from behind clamping around Tilley's mouth and nose. She just about noticed a horrible strong smell then passed out.

The person in the back clambered into the second front passenger seat and asked the driver if he knew where he was going. The driver answered: 'Course I do, I'm not stupid.'

'I'm not so sure about that.' The other man answered continuing: 'Now concentrate on your driving and don't do anything to draw attention to us.' He then held Tilley upright so she appeared to be sitting normally.

They drove to Parkview marshes and then into a deserted industrial estate. Pulling up outside a dingy unlit deserted warehouse the two men pulled Tilley out of the car and carried her up some dusty wooden stairs. Then they took her into a large room with remnants of packing cases and other debris scattered all around.

They lay her on the dirty floor and tied her hands behind her with a white nylon rope, then tied her legs together. After putting a gag on her they went out and locked the door, went downstairs and left locking the outside door.

One of the two men was one of the Americans—Michael Franks. The other was a younger Englishman known as Len. He was recruited by the Americans in a pub in Bromworth, his job as a driver for a car valet company put him in a position to access vehicles that wouldn't be connected to them. He was easily tempted with the offer of a large financial reward if he helped them with no questions asked.

Back in the car they drove to a backstreet hotel just outside town, parking the car in a dimly lit street they went into the hotel and up to a room on the second floor. Inside waiting for them was the other American Angelo Brice alias Wilson. When they entered the room Brice asked: 'Did everything go as planned.' The Englishman replied: 'Sweet as a nut.'

'She's safely hidden I hope?'

'Yeah no one's going to find her there pal.'

'Now let's get one thing clear, I'm not your pal. Now go back to the car and wait until you hear from us.' Len left the room mumbling to himself and slammed the door behind him. Brice remarked angrily: 'That guy sure get's my goat unfortunately though we need him so I'll put up with him for a while, for how much longer though I'm not sure.' Franks agreed then asked: 'What's the next move then?'

'We get the woman in the hotel, she's obviously blabbed to the cops about us staying there, we have to get her out of the way because she can give us just as much grief as the other dame.'

'When are we going to get her?'

'No time like the present, I'll go with that ignorant Brit this time then I'll leave him at the warehouse to baby sit them.'

The two men arrived at the Conifers, the American climbed into the back of the van and as Franks had done he sat behind the front passenger seat concealed by the darkened rear windows.

Len rang the bell and after a while Mrs Perkins opened the door slightly, poking her nose out she asked: 'Who is it?' Len answered: 'I'm Detective Strong Mrs Perkins, could I have a word please?'

'Oh yes of course just a minute.' She took the safety chain off and opened the door in her dressing gown and asked: 'Hello Detective what do you want at this time of night?'

'I'm sorry madam but we have apprehended a man in connection with our enquiries and we think he stayed here, could you attend an identity parade tonight?'

'Oh I don't know it's very short notice.'

'Yes we know, it's just that if he is one of the men he would be the link we are looking for to solve the case.'

'Well as you put it like that then alright but I will have to go and put some clothes on.' Len told her he would wait by the car.'

She came out ten minutes later and Len helped her into the nearside front seat then went around and got into the driver's seat. He drove off but after a few minutes Mrs Perkins noticed they were headed in the opposite direction to the Police station, she immediately told Len. He thought for a moment then said he knew a short cut but, Mrs Perkins told him that she had lived in the area all her life and they were definitely going the wrong way.

Len panicked and called for the American to shut her up, this frightened her and she tried to open the door to get out. Brice pulled her back and clamped his hand around her face holding a chloroform soaked cloth. She struggled and kicked out but was soon subdued.

After he climbed into the front he yelled at Len calling him "a useless bum" and told him to get off the main road and get to the warehouse.

At the warehouse Len unlocked the door and they pulled Mrs Perkins from the car and carried her up to the room where Tilley was laying unconscious. Brice checked her ropes and found them to be loose, he snarled: 'You can't be trusted to do a simple job of tying up an unconscious woman can you?'

'Don't look at me pal there were two of us you know? It's not all my fault.'

'No but you are not exactly a genius either are you?' After retying Tilley's bond's Brice ordered Len. 'Come on give me a hand and try and do it properly this time.' They tied the landlady up in the same manner as Tilley and then tied them both together back to back gagging the landlady.

Brice was an expert with knots from being in the navy and knew that the women weren't going to get out of theirs bonds in a hurry.

The American grabbed Len by the lapels of his coat and said with a sneer: 'Do you think you can stay here and watch these two without making a pig's ear out of it?'

'I'm not stopping here on my own, it's cold and damp and I'm starving. It's not as if they can go anywhere is it?'

'Look I've had it up to here with you, if you want your money then you are staying here, there's some blankets in that chest over there, put one each over the women and you can have the rest. I will send some food and water later for you and them. If all goes to plan they won't be here for more than two or three days.'

'What is the plan exactly?'

'That's not your concern, just watch these two, keep them quiet and keep them out of sight.'

Brice left after making sure Len locked up properly and returned to his hotel. 'How did it go?' Franks asked as his partner entered the room. Brice replied: 'A twenty four caret farce, I don't know how we got lumbered with that useless limey.'

'Don't worry about him it will be over soon and then we can deal with him.'

Brice sent Franks to get some food and water from the all night petrol station down the road and take it the warehouse, he said: 'When you have done that take the car somewhere quiet and torch it, I have put a can of gas in the back along with a bicycle, you can use that to go back to the warehouse. I will pick you up later in the hire car. Take the dark lanes and don't use lights. Put the bike in the VW we will get rid of both eventually. It's safe where it is for the moment.'

When Tilley started coming to, it took several minutes to acclimatise herself to her predicament, when she did she was shocked to find she was gagged and tied up. She also had an awful taste in her mouth. The light was dim and it took several moments more to realise she was tied to someone else.

Terrified she tried frantically to pull herself away but couldn't, she strained to see over her shoulder and just managed to see that the other person was a woman. She realised that the woman was older and that she was also gagged and unconscious.

She thought for a while and tried to make some sense of what was happening, she vaguely recalled being picked up by a Detective then the horrible smell before she passed out.

What she couldn't understand was why and who was this other woman. She started to cry feeling very cold and frightened, she wondered where she was and whether there was anyone around. She started lifting her legs up and stamping them down on the wooden floor. Len heard the noise and thought to himself: "Great that's all I need".

He went to the door and unlocked it, he went inside and grabbed Tilley's legs and held them down telling her to "quit the noise". He then said: 'No one can hear you so stop wasting your energy you are going to need it to survive the next few days.'

He went out and slammed the door locking it, "why did I get involved in all this?" He mumbled to himself.

About an hour passed Before Franks arrived with the food and water, he banged on the door and Len let him in. 'About Time I'm starving give me the food.' Franks told him to wait then finally opened the bag and said: 'Here's pizza's for you and there's some soup in plastic cups for the women. There's some water as well, are they awake yet?'

'The young one is she has already been banging on the floor with her legs.'

'Don't fret about that there's not a soul within miles of here, we staked it out long enough to know that.'

'Maybe so but you don't have to listen to it.'

'All right I'll have a word, give me the soup, I got straws so you don't have to untie their hands to feed them.'

Franks pulled on a mask made out of a white bag with holes for eyes, nose and mouth. He went into the room and Tilley cowered away as best she could. He told her: 'Don't be afraid you won't get hurt as long as you do as you are told, I am going to loosen the gag but if you attempt to make any noise I will put it back on and you can go without food or water. Am I understood?' Tilley nodded gingerly and he untied the gag. The minute her mouth was uncovered she bombarded Franks with questions. She stuttered: 'What am I doing here? Who are you? What do you want with me and who is this woman?'

'Hang on, take a breath why don't yah? You are both here because you know too much and we have to prevent you both from doing for us before we have completed our business and gone home.'

'What business? This is about the murders isn't it? My god you are the murderers, you and that Shane

Rickard.' Franks burst out laughing and saying: Rickard!!!
'Oh no that is the funniest thing I have heard for a long
time. Rickard couldn't kill a worm without vomiting. No
girl, he is just helping us with a few things. Look I have
told you too much already, now drink your soup.' He
held the straw to her lips and she tentatively took some
soup, she instantly spat it all out again saying: Ugh!
'That's disgusting it's cold and thick.'

'Ok fine if you want to starve so be it.' Franks
snatched the cup away snarling: 'You Brits are always
winging.' He began pulling the gag back up but Tilley
begged: 'No, No stop, I'll drink it, I'll drink it.'

'Oh don't do me any favours, I couldn't care less if
you starve or not.'

'Please? I'm sorry.' Franks relented and put the
straw back up to her lips and she reluctantly drunk as
much as she could trying not to gag. Franks then gave
her a drink of water and went to replace the gag but
Tilley pleaded: 'Please don't put that back on? After all
you did say that no one could hear if I screamed It's so
hard to breath with that on, I promise not to make any
noise.'

'Ok but if you make me regret it, you will be very
sorry I can assure you.'

'Thanks but what about her?' Tilley indicated to Mrs
Perkins with her head.

'Well I suppose it wouldn't hurt but I warn you any
noise from either of you . . . . Tilley butted in: 'I promise
we won't.'

'Good and make sure she knows when she wakes
up.'

Before Franks left he told Len: 'Don't stand any nonsense from them, if they start anything put their gags back on.'

'Ok Sir.' Len said sarcastically saluting. Grabbing Len by his arms he snarled: 'You are one sorry son of a bitch. I swear I will have you one day.'

'Promises, Promises.' Len replied. Franks shoved him backwards and stormed out of the room. Len was about to close the door to the woman's dim prison when Tilley asked if he could give them some more light. He replied angrily: 'You'll want duvets and hot chocolate next. Just shut up and don't give me any more grief.'

An hour or so later Mrs Perkins began coming around. Ooh! 'Where am I? Why am I tied up?'

'Shush we are both tied up, don't struggle the ropes are too tight.'

'Who are you? What's happening?'

'We have been kidnapped by the murderers of that Johnson couple, they say we know too much and they plan keeping us here until they have finished what they have to do. They are yanks and they're aware we know things about them and want us out of the way.'

Mrs Perkins shifted around as much as she could and said: 'I can't stay like this, I have arthritis and I am in agony, how did I get here? The last thing I remember was being picked up by a Detective.'

'He's no Detective he's just a no body doing their dirty work for them. I am pretty sure though he could be persuaded to help us.'

Tilley started shouting out: 'Hey you out there, this woman's in a lot of pain.' Len banged on the door telling her to be quiet or the gag will go back on.'

'I'm serious she needs to get up off this floor. You have to help her.' Len came in saying he knew they were going to be trouble. Tilley responded: 'No we're not but she has got arthritis and she is too old to be sitting on a cold hard floor.'

'Look I can't move either of you, they will kill me.'

'Yes and they will kill you if one of us dies, if they are caught and either or both of us die they will never see daylight again. That puts you in a no win situation doesn't it?'

'Yeah considering I don't even know what they are up to.'

'Do you mean you don't know they are murderers?'

Murderers! 'Oh yes nice try, it'll take more than that to phase me though.'

'It's true they killed that couple in Parkview.'

'You're serious aren't you? I knew they were evil but I didn't suspect that.'

'Yes I'm serious, I swear to you.'

'Alright but if you are playing me you will be sorry, as it is I can't do anything right with those two, I'm beginning to think it's not worth the trouble.'

He untied the ropes that held them together, he then loosened the one holding Mrs Perkins arms to her legs and helped her to her feet. He warned her: 'Stay there and don't move.' Not that she could go far tied as she was".

He went out to the other room and returned dragging a wooden chest and turned it upside down and helped her sit on it, putting one of the blankets on it first. He then helped Tilley to turn over onto her other side 'Thank you young man, you are not all bad are you?' Mrs Perkins remarked.

'Don't try to soften me up, any more bother from either of you and you go back to how you were.' He re-tied the ropes and put a blanket over their shoulders. He then said to Mrs Perkins: 'I suppose now you want some food?' He went to pick up the cup of soup but she said: 'No thank you I couldn't stomach anything with what's going on but I would like a drink though.' Len got the water bottle and held it to her lips, she sipped a little and he took the bottle away. Tilley asked him: 'What about going to the bathroom? We will have to go at some stage.'

'Well you can wait until one of them yanks comes back I'm in it deep enough now.' With that he went out and locked the door.

Tilley turned to Mrs Perkins and said: 'I do believe we have got him rattled, by the way I'm Tilley Watson, What's your name?' Mrs Perkins answered: 'Nice to meet you dear, not under very nice circumstances though. I'm Mrs Perkins, I own a guest house—The Conifers and those Yanks stayed at the time of the murders and that poor woman's husband was with them, he was drugged up and they told me that he didn't like flying so he took drugs. The Police found out though that he and his wife were sedated before they were killed, it seems that he could have been murdered in my house that made me go all cold. I picked one of them out from some mug shots and he's a nasty piece of work by all accounts actually there was a picture of him in the papers. Why have they got you here dear?'

'Well it was quite innocent at first really.' Tilley went on to tell Mrs Perkins about her involvement and Mrs Perkins said: 'It's easy to see why they are worried about the two of us.' Tilley then said: 'I'm really worried about my mum and dad they warned me about getting too involved but you can't just sit back and do nothing can you?'

'Certainly not dear, I had no doubts about telling the Police what I knew. How long do you think it will be before you are missed Tilley?'

'Well at first it will be at work but they will probably just think that I am off investigating something. No it will be tomorrow night, well actually it will be tonight now won't it? I'm supposed to ring my parents, what about you? I suppose your husband will report you missing.'

'I'm afraid not my dear, he died nine years ago. No my daily will raise the alarm, she changes the bedding every Monday, even when no one has stayed there I like to change the beds once a week. I usually give her a hand and I never go out until we've done that. It's weird though dear I don't feel scared, what about you love?'

'Surprisingly no, I did when I first woke up but now I am mostly thinking how we can get out of this place.'

Mrs Perkins nodded in agreement then they chatted for a little longer about their situation until they slowly drifted off to sleep.

CHAPTER TEN

When Franks left the warehouse he drove out into the country and found a dark secluded area. Pulling the vehicle over he got out and went around the back and took the bike out, he then grabbed the gas can. Wheeling the bike a few yards away from the van he returned and unscrewed the cap of the can, he poured the petrel all over the inside and outside of the van throwing the empty can into the van he then opened a box of matches and took one out, lighting it he slid it back into the box and waited until the rest of the matches caught alight. He then threw the box into the van and it immediately exploded into flames and the heat was soon unbearable, he then ran to the bike and rode off back to the warehouse.

"Look at that" A young couple were in a car parked off the road under some trees and the girl spotted the glow in the distance. Wow! The young lad cried out. 'What is that?' Just then the girl spotted something twinkling in the moonlight coming quite fast towards them, the girl grabbed her boyfriend down below the dashboard as franks whisked past them.

"The twinkling she had seen was the moonlight reflecting off of the bike's handlebars".

Franks didn't see their car and carried on towards the warehouse. Once he was out of sight the couple came back up and the girl pointing the glow in the distance said: 'I bet that's the car that went past here a while ago and I reckon that bloke set it alight. We ought to report it.'

Her boyfriend agreed so they drove off and found a phone box. The young man phoned the fire brigade and reported the fire but, when he was asked for his name he hung up not wishing to involve himself or his girl.

Two fire engines were dispatched and following protocol the Police were alerted.

When the Police car arrived at the scene the fire was virtually under control. Two officers got out of the car, one of them remarked: 'Someone's made a right mess of that, there's not a lot left.' His partner agreed and said: 'No there's not but I can just about make out the rear number plate though, he made a note of the number then said: 'SOCCO and Forensics will be here soon so let's wait for them.'

While they were waiting the driver called the registration number in. About ten minutes later he received a reply. He was told that the van was reported missing the Thursday evening prior to the women's kidnapping, so he called his duty Detective Inspector:

'Hello Gov we have a hit on the torched van's number plate. It is registered to a Sally Dean it's been missing since Friday evening when it should have been returned to her from a car valet company in Bromworth.'

Later at the scene of the near burnt out van SOCCO found an empty drinks can on the floor in front of the burnt out rear seat, a partly melted syringe was also found down the side of the same seat but there was nothing else recoverable in the vehicle. However they did lift one smudged fingerprint on the outside handle of one of the rear doors.

When Forensics tested the drinks can it was too badly burnt to retrieve any evidence however the finger print from the door handle and one clear print retrieved from the partly melted syringe both came from the AmericaniAngelo Mieko Brice. There was no evidence though that the syringe had been used.

When the results had been handed to the duty Detective Constable he immediately contacted the Parkview serious crime squad passing the information on to George Carter.

Later that morning George Carter received a phone call to say that the two NIS agents had arrived, on his way to meet them he met up with Mike Harper. George suggested Mike go with him, he said: 'Maybe they will give us something to go on.'

'Well I'm now holding my breath George.'

'Ever the optimist, eh Mike?'

'You bet Gov.'

George and mike met the NIS agents at the front desk. George greeted them saying: 'Hello I am DCI George Carter and this is DI Harper, welcome to Parkview.' One of the agents shook George's hand and said: 'Good Morning I am Agent Andrew Simms and this is Paul Henderson. Is there somewhere in private we can talk with no cameras and Microphones?'

'Yes of course, my office.'

'Good can we press on then? We need to complete our business as quickly as possible we are needed back in London.'

Once they were in George's office he locked the door and pulled down all the window blinds, Agent Simms then asked: 'Ok gentlemen what can we do for you?' 'Do you mean to say you haven't been briefed as to why you are here?' George replied.

'Well vaguely, it's something to do with some murder or other we understand.'

A double murder actually! 'Of two people under witness protection who your people were supposed to be monitoring, I must add.'

'Yes well we can't babysit these people, they want anonymity but they also expect to live a normal life, that's not easy, we have too many people in the system. It isn't possible to watch them all I'm afraid.'

'I don't think that is a good enough answer quite frankly. These people as you call them risked their lives to put vicious criminals away and deserved to be protected as you had promised to do. They had only been in the country for about six months and they deserved better treatment than your department gave them.'

'How do you know how long they were here?' The other agent cut in. George retorted: 'It doesn't take genius to work that one out, they only surfaced around then and the husband's elderly parents were booked into their nursing home around the same time. What we want to know is how have these murderers managed to trace them so easily? There must be a leak in your house.'

'Not necessarily, they could have been followed here.'

'Even if that were so there would still have to be an informer somewhere and I am pointing to your organisation. You need to get to London and go through your staff with a fine tooth comb.'

Standing up George announced: 'I think we are done here gentlemen, please let us know when you have found your mole. I will be reporting your "cooperation" to my superiors.' George extended his hand for a handshake but the two agents just turned and walked out without a word. George remarked loud enough for the two agents to hear: 'Nice to know our country is in such good hands, don't you agree George?'

'Absolutely Mike, they aren't getting off the hook that easily though. I'll notify the Chief Constable of their un-cooperative behaviour. They think they are so superior to the Police when in truth they are just minions doing higher ranked individuals dirty work.'

After asking Mike to send an officer to the valet company George called the Chief Constable.

Later Mike was on his way to George's office and met one of the officers that went to the valet company. He told Mike he was on his way to give George his report on their visit there. Mike told him to give it to him and he would hand it to George.

George was on the phone, when he hung up Mike handed him the envelope. George opened it and shouted: "Bingo" 'The driver of the torched car is "Leonard Fisher" it's the same guy who collected the office keys. The car should have been delivered back to the owner, a Mrs Dean on the evening of Thursday the eighth. We have his employment details and a photo from his ID badge found in his locker and we have an address for him. Now we need to know the significance of that office. Take a couple of officers with you and show his picture around the offices, maybe now we have a proper photo someone may recognise him. Also send a team to Fisher's digs, if he isn't there get the landlord to let you in go look around.'

CHAPTER ELEVEN

The night after Tilley's kidnapping her parents were at home, her mum remarked: 'Tilley hasn't called yet, it's nearly ten o'clock, she always phones about nine.' George said: 'Well you know Tilley with all this Police business going on, her mind is all over the place. She's probably in bed now, I'll ring her tomorrow night.'

'Alright love but I worry a lot about her these days.'

'I know love I'm sure she's alright though, go to bed and I will bring you up a nice cup of hot chocolate.'

'Ok you have persuaded me.'

In Tilley's office that morning Lucy was looking at the clock on the wall and was puzzled at Tilley's absence. She remarked: 'Hey Rob it's nine twenty five and Tilley isn't in yet.'

'I know, don't worry though she's probably out stalking some poor bloke or other.' Rob replied laughing.

'Yeah you're probably right but it's not like her, I can't remember her ever being late for work.'

'I can, the day she saw that guy in the bushes.'

'Well yes but that was different.'

'I don't see how, after all we don't know where she is now, do we?'

'I suppose you're right, let's just wait and see.'

As the day went on the topic of conversation was all about Tilley's absence, James her boss quizzed his staff as to whether any of them had any idea why she was not in. No one did of course although Rob's possible explanation was humorously discussed.

Tuesday evening Bob waited until he was sure Tilley should be home and rang her, not getting a reply he said to his wife: 'There's no reply Joyce, I have to admit that I am getting a little worried now.'

'Oh Bob we have to call the Police.'

'Maybe but let's wait another half an hour in case she caught a later train.'

When the hour passed Bob rang Tilley's number again and there was still no reply, he told Joyce he was going to her apartment. She said: 'I'm coming with you.'

'No Joyce you stay here in case she gets in touch.'

'Alright but let me know as soon as you know something.'

'Of course I will love, although I'm sure there's a perfectly reasonable explanation.'

Bob let himself into Tilley's apartment with a spare key Tilley gave her parents to hold. It was clear that she had been home at some stage as the lights were on in the kitchen and the lounge. He could see that she had eaten a meal as the dirty plates etcetera was left in the kitchen sink, something Tilley never did, she was very particular about washing up her dishes. It was obvious the dishes were from at least the night before because there were remnants of spaghetti in the saucepan and it was all dried up. Her handbag was also left on the sofa.

Bob called his wife to tell her what he had found. Trembling she said: 'Oh bob we have to call the Police now, I just know it has to do with this murder business.'

'Don't upset yourself Joyce, look do we have any of her workmates or friends number's we can call in case she is with one of them.'

'No but I am sure she has them in her address book in the little drawer of her telephone table.'

The book was in the drawer but Bob could only find her work phone number, he looked around but found nothing that would help trace where his daughter could be so he decided to try her work number. There was only a recorded message announcing that the office was closed between the hours of five pm and nine am Monday to Friday and was closed at weekends. He was just about to hang up when the message continued giving a number that should be called in emergencies.

Bob called the number and a male voice answered: 'Hello James Cooper.'

'Hello Mr Cooper, my name is bob Watson, my daughter works for your company. I assume it is your company?'

'It is and yes she does work for me, actually I'm glad you have called because she didn't come in today, which is most unusual because she has not had an unscheduled day off in all the time she has worked with us. It is even stranger that she didn't ring in she is just not like that. I even rang her apartment a few times but she didn't answer.'

'Well that's the thing Mr Cooper Tilley is missing.'

'Missing? Oh my Lord you must be worried sick.'

'Yes we are especially Mrs Watson, I take it you are aware of her involvement with the murders of that couple?'

'I do yes do you think it is connected to that?'

'I can't think of any other reason, I am going to the Police before I do though do you have her other colleagues phone numbers or addresses? 'It's just in case she mentioned anything to them that could throw some light on where she may be.'

'Yes but I don't think they will be much help because they were just as mystified as I was when she didn't come in, it's all they have talked about all day'

'Right then Mr Cooper, in that case I'd better hang up and call the Police.'

'I think that would be the best move Mr Watson, please do let me know when you have some news, Tilley is such a lovely girl her colleagues will be very upset.'

'Of course I will and thanks for your help and concern.'

After letting Joyce know Bob went to the Police station. The front desk was manned by a duty officer, he greeted Bob: 'Good evening Sir how can I help?'

'Good evening, my name is Bob Watson I want to report a missing person.'

'Ok Sir, may I ask the name of person in question?'

'It's my daughter—Tilley Watson.'

'How long has she been missing Sir?'

'Since last evening at least and by the state of her apartment she left in a hurry.'

'What do you mean by "the state of her apartment"?'

'Well all of the lights were on and she left her dirty supper things in the sink, she would not do that normally, she is a very tidy person.'

'I am sure she is Sir, I take it you have a key to her apartment?'

'Yes we hold it for her in case she loses hers.'

'When did you go to her apartment Sir?'

'Tonight, I phoned her last night as she was supposed to phone us on Sunday evening but she didn't. I called her this evening and when there was no answer I went there and found the apartment messy and her handbag is still there. I know something has happened to her. I called her boss and he told me that she hadn't turned up for work today.

'Did her boss notice anything odd or different about her the last time he saw her?'

'No I asked that and he said she was her normal self and that was last Friday. I spoke to her on the phone Sunday morning and she seemed fine.'

'I see well we usually only consider a person missing after forty eight hours but I will go and talk to someone. Please wait here Mr Watson.' Bob informed the officer: 'Before you do I think you should know that Tilley is known to your serious crime team because she is a potential witness in the double murder case.'

'Well that explains it, I thought the name was familiar, give me a minute Sir and I will get someone to talk to you, would you like a cup of something?'

'Yes please, a strong coffee would be nice.'

'No problem Sir, please take a seat, someone will be out soon.'

The constable knew that George was in his office Mike was also there they were going over the latest events. The constable knocked on the door and went in. George asked what he wanted and he told him: 'Sorry to disturb you Sir but there is a Mr Watson in reception, he has reported his daughter as missing.'

'How long has she been missing?'

'He says at least since last evening.'

'Ok bring him up and get him some tea.'

'I have already arranged a cup of coffee for him.'

'Good, then make sure it is brought up here.'

The constable brought Bob to Mike's office and George shook his hand as did Mike, he said: 'Very sorry to hear about Tilley, please take a seat and tell all you can from the beginning.' Bob's coffee arrived and after taking a sip he told the two men about Tilley's disappearance.

George and Mike listened intently, George then said: 'Now the last time you spoke to Tilley was when Mr Watson?'

'Sunday morning, we spoke on the phone and she was going to call that night to arrange for her and her mother to go shopping next Saturday. We weren't unduly worried when she didn't call as she is prone to forgetting but, when I couldn't contact her tonight we were worried so I went to her apartment and she wasn't there, in fact she hasn't been there since at least last evening.'

'What makes you believe that?'

'Well there were lights on and dirty dishes in the sink it was obvious that they had been there a long time because the remains of her supper were all dried out. I called her boss and he said she didn't go to work today.'

'Does she have any friends or family she may have gone to?'

'No we are her only family here and she doesn't have any friends outside work, she's a bit of a home bird . . . . Hang on though, thinking about it she has recently befriended the landlord of the Junction pub down by the station. Simon I think his name is.'

'Ok Mr Watson you go home to your wife and leave it to us, we will go and see this Simon and we will be in contact. Forensics will want to go over Tilley's apartment will that be alright.'

'Yes anything to help find her.'

'Ok Mr Watson, we will call with a time.'

When Bob left George called the chief Forensics officer. George asked: 'Hello Barry would you arrange a team to go over an apartment, its Tilley Watson's.'

'Tilley, that's the girl who gave us Rickard isn't it?'

'Yes it is she has gone missing, it seems the last time she was seen was leaving work last Friday evening, although her father spoke to her on the phone on Sunday Morning. We just want to see if anybody has been in her place.'

'Ok George when would you like us to go?'

'In an hour, I will call her father and arrange for him to meet you there and let you in.'

When George hung up Mike suggested doing a house to house enquiry surrounding Tilley's apartment building. George said: 'Good idea Mike, I'll instigate it right now there will be more people at home. You head it up Mike.'

Twenty minutes into the house to house a message came through from a constable reporting that a young boy on his way home from football practice on Sunday evening, noticed a large dark coloured car parked in the road outside Tilley's apartment building.

It was about eight thirty, he couldn't be sure about the time though because he wasn't wearing his watch but he knows he long it takes him to walk home from the sport centre and that seems about right.

George asked for the boy's address and arranged to meet the officer there. The officer was waiting for him with the boy, the officer said: 'This is Gavin Woods Sir.' George said hello to the boy then asked him: 'Are your parents at home lad?'

'My mum is.'

'Good can we speak to her?' The boy took him to his house and opened the door and called his mother, when she came to the door she looked concerned seeing George and the PC standing with Gavin, she said nervously: 'Whatever is the matter? What have you done Gavin?' George reassured her saying: 'Don't worry Madam he isn't in any trouble, quite the opposite actually, let me explain. I am Detective Chief Inspector George Carter.' He showed her his ID and told her why he was there. She said: 'Thank the Lord for that, I suppose you had better come in.' She showed them into the lounge and George asked Gavin: 'Now what did you see Gavin?'

'As I told that copper I walked home from footy practice and when I passed by those flats there was a big dark car parked outside, the two back windows were all blacked out.'

'Did you see anyone hanging around at all?'

'No but I think there was someone standing on the other side of the car because I saw fag smoke coming up over the car.'

'How did you see that in the dark Gavin?'

'It was parked under a lamppost and I could see the smoke in the light.'

'Very good Gavin that's very helpful.' George then said to Gavin's mother: 'I'm sorry for disturbing your evening Mrs Woods, would you be willing to bring Gavin down to the station just to put what Gavin has just told us on record, at your convenience of course.'

'Ok will tomorrow night be alright?'

'Perfectly do you want to be picked up?'

'No I will drive, tomorrow is our fast food night and we go into town anyway.'

'Jolly good, just tell the constable at the desk what you are there for and he will take care of you.'

After they left the house George told the officer to take two other men to the apartment building and search the area outside. He said to collect anything they find there and get it to the lab for testing. He then went and found mike and they went to see Simon at the pub.

At the pub George explained to Simon why they were there, Simon responded saying: 'My God! 'Poor Tilley, I can't believe it, she must be petrified.'

'Simon; by the way what is your surname?'

Collier!

'Ok Mr Collier, when was the last time you saw Miss Watson?'

'Only a few days ago actually, she and two of her colleagues—Lucy and Rob came in one evening, she got a little drunk and stayed in one of the rooms upstairs. I took her back to her apartment the next morning, she changed then I took her to work. That's all I can tell you I'm afraid.'

'So you have been to her apartment then?'

'Yes but not inside, I waited outside in the car.'

'What kind of car do you drive Mr Collier?'

'An old Mini Cooper, it belonged to the previous owner of the Junction and it was passed onto me with the pub.'

'I see and how long have you had this pub?'

'Only nine months, I was running a bar in America for twelve years but I missed the old English pub. I came back eleven months ago and was lucky to find his pub up for sale and bought it.'

'Right Mr Collier Thanks for your time, take my card and if you see her or remember anything, please contact us immediately, day or night.'

'I will but please let me know when you find her?'

'Of course, thank you again and goodbye.'

George and Mike were on the way back to the station and George said: 'Well I am whacked.'

'I bet, likewise here.' George suggested they go to his house and have a drink, Mike replied sternly, NO! 'You come back to mine.'

'Ok Mike a drink's a drink wherever it comes from so take me to it.'

CHAPTER TWELVE

Ten o'clock Tuesday Morning Mike went back to the letting agents and met up with Peter Crane and showed him Fisher's picture and asked: 'Do you recognise this man?' Crane confirmed he did saying: 'Yes he is the man who collected the keys for that office.'

'Are you absolutely sure?'

'Yes Positive.'

'Ok thank you we just needed for you to confirm it now we have his photo, we may well need to talk to you again though.'

'That's fine.'

Mike returned to headquarters and went straight to George's office, he looked anxious so Mike asked what was wrong. George told him: 'Believe it or not Mike we have another missing person.'

'What? Who?

'Mrs Perkins, the landlady of the guesthouse.'

'That's incredible, when?'

'Shortly around the time Tilley was taken presumably, her daily reported it an hour ago. The scenario is the same, lights left on, bed not slept in . . . . Mike butted in asking: 'Why has she taken so long to report it George?'

'She wasn't well Monday and didn't go to work, her husband went to tell Mrs Perkins on his way to work but she didn't answer the door so he put a note through the letterbox. He told his wife that there were lights on in the hall and upstairs but she wasn't unduly concerned as she knew Mrs Perkins got up early, however when she got there at nine o'clock this morning she found her missing and called it in.'

'This is getting serious George, what's going on?'

'Good question George, a Forensic team are on their way over there, let's hope something turns up. Anyway Mike, how did you get on?'

'Oh yes, that Crane chap definitely Identified Fisher as the key collector.'

'Interesting, question now is was it Fisher who Rickard called from his mother's house?'

'It certainly seems so but no one identified him when we were there did they?'

'No that's true, look it's a long shot but why don't you take of copy of the photo to Venture Gardens and show it around, someone May well recognise him from an actual photo, take the sketch of Rickard's mate as well.'

'It's possible I suppose, I'll get to it right away.'

'Thanks Mike, by the way there was nothing found at Tilley's apartment or Fisher's digs maybe will be luckier at the Conifer's.'

Mike Harper took Fisher's and Jenkins photos to the office's, one young man—Sam Stokes—who was not in the building when Mike and the team were there before said that he was sure the man was Jenkins, he said: 'I only ever got a glimpse of him, however one afternoon he was coming in when I was going out and we came face to face. The man looked up momentarily by surprise and then looked down again as fast as he could, I am reasonably sure that it was the same man though.' Mike thanked him and hastily made his way back to the station.

On his return there was a note on his desk requesting he go straight to George Carter's office. Mike complied and knocked on George's door. George called for him to come in telling him to sit down. He asked: 'How did you get on Mike?'

'Hopefully ok, there's a guy there—Sam Stokes—who thinks he bumped into Jenkins once when going into the building.'

'Jenkins? That's a turn up, how sure is he?'

'Not positive but pretty sure.'

'Well it's all we have to go on, ok let's put it out nationally. Now Mike the reason I wanted to see you is, I've heard back from the Chief Constable, he has talked to the boss of those clowns from the NIS and has backed us over our complaint, he said they will look into their behaviour and our claim regarding a mole.'

'Good, a mole has to the answer to how they found the couple so easily. I also think there is something more to this business than just revenge for their testimony they seem to be trying to prevent something coming out. After all why take such a risk killing that couple and kidnapping those two poor women?'

'I totally agree with you, it is my view that this mole is someone high up in the chain, we could even have a government cover up on our hands. By the way Forensics found nothing at the Conifers, they dusted the doorbell for finger prints but a lot of people push that bell like postmen etcetera. The officers did find three cigarette butts in the road outside Tilley's place where Gavin saw the van parked, they are being tested for DNA and prints at this moment.'

'I suppose it's too much to hope there was CCTV at either of the buildings.'

'Afraid so at Tilley's but there is one at the Conifers. Our tech boys have the tape and are looking at it.'

'Great, surely we can get a lead on these characters and start to wind this case up.'

'It's a waiting game now Mike, let's go and have a cup of tea and step down for a while and gather our breath.'

While they drank their tea they mulled over the case, Mike observed: 'We seem to be getting three steps forward and two back at the moment.'

'I know Mike; let's hope that something comes from the tests on the fag butt's . . . . As if by magic a voice replied: "Your wish is my command oh Master". George and Mike looked at each other in amazement then the voice continued: 'We have a hit with fag butts.' The voice belonged to Martin Winter from Forensics, he went on to say: 'The DNA is a match to Fisher and the prints from the rear doors of the torched car belong to the yank—Brice, alias Wilson.' George thanked Martin then turned to Mike and said: 'That links fisher with the kidnapping of Tilley at least but I don't think he or Rickard are more than just gofer's in this business. I am worried though that when they have fulfilled their usefulness, they and the Woman could be disposed of in the same way as the Johnsons. After all we don't know whether the women are alive or not even now. It's a pity that no one has seen anything concrete.'

'Well we do have that lad Gavin; maybe he will remember something else.'

Finishing their tea's they walked back to their relative offices, on the way George advised Mike that he thought it may pay to reinstate the house to house but on a wider scale, he said: 'Someone has some information I am sure of it.' Mike replied: 'Here's hoping George.'

On his return to his office George called the duty Sergeant ordering the extended house to house to commence immediately.

George spent the next hour or so catching up on paperwork, about seven thirty pm he received a fax from a Detective Inspector Larry Taylor of Bromworth central Police station, which read: "A man answering the description of Shane Rickard has been spotted in a pub in Bromworth's west end. The landlord was alerted by a customer last night when he came face to face with the suspect on his way to the toilet. Please contact me on the number below the moment you receive this fax".

George immediately called the DI, he answered: 'Detective Inspector Taylor, can I help you?'

'Hello I'm DCI Carter of Parkview I have just received your fax.'

Ha! 'I'm assuming you were pleased to receive it.'

'Yes thank you, it's good news, what's the situation at the moment Inspector?'

'Well we are watching the pub—"The Dog and Rabbit" also we have men posing as customers. The landlord has said he would give the nod if he turns up.'

'Ok thanks, I'll send DI Harper and DC White and some officers over. Do you know how often he has been in the pub?'

'The landlord says at least three times in the last three days but no one recognised him until last night.'

'Ok thank you Inspector, I will dispatch my men forthwith.'

While George was on the phone Mike came in with the images from the CCTV from the guest house. George replaced the receiver and mike showed him the images, George remarked: 'That looks like Fisher standing by the vehicle. 'Pointing at the nearside rear window he continued: 'Hang on that looks like a face. Take it and ask the lab to enhance it for us, it's not much use as it is. Oh Mike Roy put Rickard's mate's sketch through facial recognition and he got a hit, it's a Christopher Jenkins, he has some digs two miles outside Parkview, uniform are over there at this moment going over the place.'

'That's brilliant, things are moving along, albeit slowly.'

CHAPTER THIRTEEN

The morning after her abduction Tilley was the first one to wake up, she didn't sleep very much what with being tied up and sitting on the hard floor took its toll plus there were creepy crawlies all over the place, not to mention being unsure of her future, Mrs Perkins awoke soon after. Tilley who was moving around trying to get some feeling back in her arms and legs asked Mrs Perkins: 'Are you alright?' Mrs Perkins couldn't fathom where she was for a minute but when she finally remembered she answered: What? 'Oh it's you dear, yes . . . yes . . . I think I'm alright, stiff and in pain, thirsty, hungry and worried but otherwise I'm fine. Listen to me joking around at a time like this, sorry my dear.'

'Don't be sorry, we have to keep our spirits up, now I think it's time we woke our guard up, don't you? On the count of three shout as loud as you can, ready? One, two, three *"HEY YOU OUT THERE, WE NEED TO GO TO THE TOILET"*.

Len came in furious saying they would have their gags put back on when one of the yanks came back. Poppycock; Mrs Perkins responded. 'You are here to watch us and make sure nothing happens to us so, take us to the bathroom now or I will tell the yanks that you have been mistreating us, then you will be for it.'

'How did I end up with you two, you are making my life more hell than it already is.'

'Well treat us right and we will be putty in your hands.' Tilley cut in, adding: 'Now is there a bathroom in this crass place or not?'

'Yes if you can call it that.'

'Good then take Mrs Perkins first and when I have been we can have a drink.'

Reluctantly Len relented he knew he wouldn't get any peace if he didn't.

Untying Mrs Perkins legs he supported her to the bathroom. When they reached the door Len stood there not knowing what to do next. Mrs Perkins didn't let him wonder for long, she said: 'Come on then young man, untie me.'

'Not on your life lady, I don't trust either of you.'

'How on earth do you expect me to manage otherwise, unless you want to come in and help me?' This changed Len's mind, he untied Joanne and said: 'For heaven's sake ok but, I'm staying outside the door and don't even think about trying to get out of the window, it's nailed down and we are two floors up.' Mrs Perkins assured him: 'Don't worry Sonny my days of doing acrobatics are long past.'

When Mrs Perkins re-emerged Len escorted her back to rejoin Tilley. After retying her legs and hands he told Tilley: 'Ok your turn, and as I told your friend, don't try and escape, there's no way out.'

'Ok keep your hair on, I know the situation.'

When Len brought Tilley back and retied her he went into the outer room and brought the cold soup and the water bottle, he offered the soup to the women but Tilley snapped: 'You don't honestly expect us to have that do you?'

'Well I'm sorry but I'm all out of bacon and eggs.' Len replied and snatched it away. He handed them the water and went to leave the room but Tilley stopped him saying: 'There's no need to be funny, after all you wouldn't want it would you?'

No! 'What else do you expect though?'

'Anything but we are not having that gung, isn't that right Mrs "p"?' Mrs Perkins nodded her agreement. Len sighed and said: 'Well you will have to wait until one of them yanks turn up won't you? I haven't had anything either you know.' Tilley had calmed down by then and said: 'I know, I'm sorry, look what is your name?'

'I'm not sure I should tell you that with all that's going on.'

'Well we're all in this together so at least we should all get along.'

'Ok why not? It's Len but that's all I'm telling you.'

'Look Len, we are sorry for treating you so horribly . . . . Tilley glanced at her fellow captive and gave her a sly grin then continued: 'We know you are only doing what those yanks tell you to but we are very hungry and that stuff just makes us want to vomit.'

'Me too, I haven't touched any of it, I've made do with some chocolate I had in my pocket. Trouble is I can't contact them and God knows when one of them will come back, if ever.' Len dare not tell the women he'd had pizza. Tilley reassured him: 'Don't worry Len, by the way I'm Tilley Watson and this is Mrs Perkins.'

Len sat down on a crate and asked the women why the yanks had kidnapped them and the women told him all they knew. Len reacted saying: 'Well that hasn't helped me much, when you said they were murders last night I thought you were trying to wind me up, but now . . . . Tilley cut in: 'Sorry Len but you did ask, hey look maybe we can help each other.'

'What? Help? Help you do what?'

'Well you are in this mess right up to your neck. You don't think they are going to just pay you and let you walk away do you? You know too much which makes you as much a liability as we are. Mrs P knows the two yanks and I can identify Rickard.'

'Rickard, I don't know any Rickard.'

'You don't know him eh? Well he is just another one of their expendable minion's like you, look Len you can help us escape and come with us, we will make sure the Police don't lock you up, after all you didn't know what you were getting mixed up in did you? I know Detective Carter, I am sure I can persuade him to be lenient.'

Len stood up kicking the chest away and stormed: *'I DON'T THINK SO, LOOK I'M GOING BACK OUT THERE AND LOCKING THE DOOR, I DON'T WANT TO HEAR ANOTHER WORD FROM EITHER OF YOU. ARE WE CLEAR?'* Slamming the door and locking it he went downstairs and out into the fresh air, it didn't matter right then that it was raining hard, picking up a stone he hurled it at the side of the building muttering to himself: "Damned women trying to get inside my head, well they hadn't better try that again or I'll finish them, you see if I don't . . . . they are right though, I'm not sure those yanks will want me around after they have finished whatever they're here for. If they think I am taking them with me though and slowing me down they'd better think again.'

Back upstairs Tilley said to Joanne: 'That went well.' Then asked: 'Seriously though what do you think our chances are of getting him on our side?'

'I'm not sure, he is definitely shaky, it shouldn't take much more before he cracks. You are a cunning little minx aren't you dear?'

'I am, I hate saying this but this is all so exciting.'

'I don't think that is the exact words I would use right now my dear, but there.'

Wednesday evening Tilley's parents were having tea, although they couldn't eat much as had been the case since Tilley was kidnapped. Joyce said: 'Tilley has been missing for over forty eight hours and we haven't heard a thing, I think we ought to call that detective Carter to see if they have found out anything yet.' Bob reached across the table and took her hands in his saying: 'I know how you feel love, I'm just as worried but I'm certain they would have called us if there was any news but, if it makes you feel better I will give him a call.'

Bob went into the hall to make the call in case there was some news that he would rather tell he himself then for her to overhear and get the wrong idea. He called the station and was eventually put through to DCI Carter, he said: 'Hello Inspector this is Bob Watson, we were wondering if there was any news at all on Tilley.'

'Oh hello Mr Watson, no nothing to indicate where she is but we do think we have a lead on who actually took her and the vehicle she was probably abducted in. Mr Watson, are you aware that there was another woman taken along with your daughter?'

No! Who? When?

'She is a lady who runs a guest house on the edge of town—"The Conifers"—it's situated close to where the two murders were committed and where the bodies were dumped, we know that the two yanks stayed there during the period of the murders, we also know for sure that the husband was with them. It is obvious he was there against his will and It is more than likely he was murdered at the guest house or shortly after they left. Like Tilley the landlady has seen people involved in the murders.'

'My God, does that mean they could come for me and my boss? After all we identified Rickard as well.'

'I don't think so you only saw Rickard in your store, Tilley actually saw him in the vicinity of the murders and followed him on that Monday. Somehow they have found out that she had helped with the sketch, Mrs Perkins actually came face to face with the suspects and picked out one of the men from some mug shots. They could actually put them away with what they know whereas yours is just circumstantial evidence.'

While George was talking he was unaware that Joyce had heard him react when he heard about the second kidnapping, she asked fretfully: 'Who's coming after you?' George attempted to reassure her and said: 'Nobody Joyce, don't worry, it was just me being daft Detective Carter has assured me I am in no danger. Go and sit down, I'll finish talking to the Detective then I'll tell you everything. He apologised to George saying:

'Joyce is out of her mind with worry with all this I had better go and comfort her.'

'Of course Mr Watson I promise I will contact you immediately we hear anything that helps us find her.'

Bob thanked the Inspector and hung up. He went into the lounge and sat next to Joyce and put his arm around her, he said: 'I'm sorry for worrying you even more than you already are but something the Detective said had me panicking for a bit.'

'Why, what did he say? Nothing about Tilley I hope?'

'No he hasn't any news on her yet . . . . Bob went on to tell Joyce what George had related to him. Joyce responded saying: 'Does that mean her life is in danger? Oh Bob please tell me it isn't?'

'Unfortunately I can't Joyce, I'm sorry but I just can't. No one can say what these cretins will do, we just have to hope and pray that she will be alright. Joyce nodded wiping tears from her eyes, Bob pulled her to him and hugged her and they sat on the sofa staring into nothing.

That evening at eight fifty George Carter received a call from DI Larry Taylor to say Rickard had turned up at the pub. George asked: 'How long has he been there?'

'Only a couple of minutes or so, get here as soon as you can my men will watch him for now.'

'Ok thanks, Di Harper, DC White and some uniforms will be with you ASAP.'

At nine twenty five Mike and the team arrived at the "Dog and Rabbit". Mike liaised with the Sergeant of the local officers who had been watching the pub. The Sergeant told him that Rickard was still inside. Mike thanked him and asked if he would work with his men. The Sergeant willingly agreed. Mike told all his officers to wait out of sight but to cover all escape routes, he then told DC White: 'I'll go in first, give me five minutes then you come in. Ignore me but cautiously try to make contact with the plain clothes boys already in there. He told the Sergeant in charge of the uniformed men to keep a close ear on his radio as he would click it three times when he was about to arrest Rickard giving them time to converge on the door.

Mike entered the pub and was glad that it was fairly quiet. Two men in their late twenties or early thirties were playing pool, while two others were on the fruit machine. Three more people—one man in his fifties Mike guessed and two younger women—were sitting at the bar. He spotted Rickard sitting alone at a table. Behind the bar was a stoutly built man.

Mike stood at the end of the bar where it was quiet and the barman came and asked what He wanted to drink. Mike answered: 'Just a St Clements please.' When the man returned with his drink Mike made sure no one was in earshot and asked quietly: 'Are you the landlord?' Discreetly he showed him his ID and the man nodded slightly and took Mikes money, putting it in the till. He then wrote something on a piece of paper and walked from behind the bar to collect empty glasses, as he walked past Mike he slipped the note into his hand.

Mike waited a minute or so then went into the toilet locked himself in a cubicle and read the note. It said: "Wanted guy at table, your men playing pool"

When Mike returned to the bar DC white had arrived, he was standing close to the man and two women. Mike walked past ignoring him.

White ordered an orange juice and went to watch the pool players, there seemed to be an air of recognition between them and one of the men dropped his cue and White stooped to pick it up, the pool player did the same. The player whispered: 'You from Parkview?' White nodded slightly and picked up the cue handing it to the other man. He nodded his thanks then cautiously informed his partner and continued with their game.

White walked back to the bar and managed to catch Mike's eye, he looked at the pool players and back at Mike, he got the message. White ordered another drink and went to sit close to the door.

After a few minutes Rickard stood up and went to the bar ordering another pint. Mike didn't react immediately instead he let Rickard order his drink. The landlord sensed that Mike was about to make his move so he told Rickard that the barrel had to be changed giving Mike time to prepare. Mike glanced over at White who was watching intently and nodded. Mike looked at the pool players giving them the nod. Mike went to the toilet and making sure no one was in there he pulled the radio from his pocket and gave the prearranged three clicks. The officers on receipt of the notice commenced blocking the door and side entrance to the pub.

Mike returned to the bar and looked at white who guessed his intentions. Standing up he moved to just behind Mike who put his hand on Rickard's left shoulder, when Rickard looked around White grabbed his right arm, he twisted it behind his back then pushed him against the bar. Mike grabbed Rickard's left arm, bending that behind his back.

The two at the pool table rushed over and helped subdue Rickard which was hardly necessary as Rickard was so stunned at the speed of the action he was motionless.

Once the handcuffs were put on Rickard, Mike cautioned him saying: "Shane Rickard; I am arresting you in connection with the murder's of Angela and Andrew Johnson plus two accounts of kidnapping". Mike read him his rights and when he got to the part that stated his right to a solicitor Rickard was insistent that he didn't need one because he hadn't done anything. Mike said that was his choice.

While they were taking him out to the car Rickard continued to protest his innocence saying: 'You're making a big mistake, it's those yanks you want.'

Two uniformed officers had already brought a car to the front of the pub and Rickard was placed in the back seat between two officers and whisked off to the station.

Mike thanked the plain clothed officers from the local station and climbed into his car with DC White.

Mike radioed ahead announcing the arrest, when George Carter heard the news he was delighted and headed to the booking in area to greet Mike. They booked Rickard in taking his processions including his shoe laces and belt and locked him in a holding cell awaiting interview.

George congratulated Mike but he said that it was a joint effort and praised the officers from Bromworth and the men from Parkview. George then said: 'This could be the turning point we need Mike, we'll let him stew for a while then you and I will interview him. I've notified the Chief Constable and we are holding a press conference in the morning but, now I have a couple of phone calls to make.'

George went back to his office and called Tilley's parents. Bob answered: 'Hello, Bob Watson.'

'Hello Mr Watson DCI Carter here, I bet you didn't expect to hear from me so soon did you?'

'No I didn't have you some news?'

'Yes I have, you will pleased to know that we have arrested Shane Rickard.' Bob was ecstatic, he couldn't resist yelling: *'Joyce, Joyce, come here quick.'*

'What, have they found her?'

'Oh Lord, I'm so sorry love I wasn't thinking, no they haven't found her yet but they have Rickard . . . . Sorry Inspector do carry on.'

'No problem Sir, well we arrested him earlier this evening, we will be interviewing him in a while and if he has any information concerning Tilley I will call you immediately.'

'Ok thank you Inspector, thanks for telling us so quickly, cheerio.'

When Bob hung up he apologised to Joyce for getting her hopes up, she was sobbing when she had stopped she bravely suggested Bob call James Cooper so he could tell Tilley's colleagues the next morning.

After talking to Bob George called Mrs Rickard, he said: 'Mrs Rickard this is Detective Inspector George carter, I must tell you we have arrested Shane this evening.'

'Oh my, is he alright, you didn't hurt him did you?'

'No madam he's fine, he's in a holding cell at present but we will interview him shortly and I will let you know when you can see him, it won't be until tomorrow now though.'

'I'll come down there and wait.'

'I don't recommend that Madam, you could be waiting for a long time and the seats in reception are not very comfortable. You will be better waiting until we call you then we will send a car to collect you.'

'Ok then detective I will wait, thank you so much for letting me know.'

After he had hung up George called Mike into his office and arranged for coffee and sandwiches, while they waited for them George said: 'I think we are in for a long night, do you want to go home? I can get someone else to sit in at the interview.'

'Not on your Nellie George, I wouldn't miss that for the world but you have a wife and daughter to think about, you go home I'll head the interview.'

No! 'As you said I wouldn't miss it, I have already called home and said goodnight, they are used to my long hours.'

'Ok George, well we have another step forward, let's hope there are not any steps backwards this time.'

'Let's hope so Mike, let's hope so.'

The coffee and sandwiches arrived and they relaxed for a while. George quipped: 'Are you sure you are fit to do the interview after all you drank at the pub?'

'Oh just about, the coffee will help.' They both laughed then George said: 'Well if you're ready shall we do it?'

'Lead on George, lead on.'

Once everything was set up Rickard was handcuffed and taken to an interview room. George and Mike entered with files on the case. They sat down and in an attempt to unravel Rickard they fiddled and looked through their files and whispering to each other. It seemed to work because Rickard began fidgeting in his chair, telling them to get on with it. George told him to be patient if he wanted it done properly, he said: 'You are in serious trouble Shane, you do realise that don't you?' Rickard just ignored him.

Eventually Mike turned on the tape machine stated: "Informal interview with Shane Malcolm Rickard, the date is the twenty first of October, nineteen eighty three" "The time is twenty three forty two. Present is Detective Chief Inspector George Carter and Detective Inspector Mike Harper. Also present is Police constable Davies".

George began: "Shane Rickard; you are charged with conspiring to commit murder and kidnapping". 'Have you anything to say in your defence?'

No! 'Nothing, not until I get a solicitor anyway.'

'I thought you were innocent and didn't want a solicitor?'

'I am innocent but I know you lot, you will twist everything I say so I want a brief.'

'So be it Shane but you should have told us before we set this interview up, you are wasting your own and our time but it's your decision. I would like to ask you one thing though before we arrange your solicitor do you have any knowledge of the whereabouts of Tilley Watson and or Mrs Joanne Perkins? Before you answer though, be advised that any co-operation will help considerably with your situation.'

'I have never heard of either of those two people so may I have my solicitor now?'

'Fair enough Shane but you will have a wait on your hands it isn't easy getting a duty solicitor at this hour.'

'That's alright I have nowhere I need to be and I'm not saying anything until I get one.'

'Ok Mike, turn the tape off.' Mike stated: "Interview with Shane Rickard suspended at twelve ten am.'

Mike and George left the room, George told the officer to lock the door and leave him in there on his own and to call the duty solicitor. We'll let him stew in there maybe he will be more co-operative, I'll be in my office, let me know when the Solicitor gets here.'

Back in his office George found a message from the Tech lab with an enhanced image of the character in the rear seat of the kidnap car. Although it wasn't much clearer he did recognise the face as Brice. He put the picture in his file to be used in Rickard's interview.

CHAPTER FOURTEEN

After about three hours Franks returned to the warehouse. When he knocked on the door Len looked out through a crack in the frame, seeing it was Franks he opened up. He asked Franks: 'No one followed you here did they?'

'What do you take me for you moron? You look after your side of things and let me do mine. How are our guests, still here are they?'

'Ha Ha very funny, they are cold and starving and so am I.'

'Oh my heart bleeds anyway you have food and water.'

Food! 'That muck isn't food, its thick gung and we won't have any more of it.'

'Oh you're not eh? Well how would you like me to hold you down and pour it down your throat.'

'Yeah right in your dreams, just try it yank. You act all big but I bet you would cringe if someone turned on you.'

'You think so do you? Well lucky for you we still need you for a little longer otherwise I would happily show you.'

'Yeah ok anything you say.'

'Well as it happens I have some food here and more water, turn that down and you all starve.'

Franks threw a plastic bag containing sandwiches and two bottles of water at Len, Franks then picked up a mask and went into the room where Tilley and Joanne were held. He saw the women had been moved and yelled at Len: '*WHAT'S THIS, WHO TOLD YOU TO INTERFERE WITH THEIR ROPES*?'

'If I hadn't they would be in no condition to last out here and they had to go to the toilet.' Franks replied, a little calmer: 'That's our decision to make not yours.'

'Ok you stay here then, I have had enough of you crazy yanks I know you murdered that couple but you aren't killing me, I'm off.' Len ran over to the wall and picked up a lid from a crate and hurled it at Franks but it just missed him, Len ran out and down the stairs but Franks grabbed the lid and hurled it down at Len hitting him on the back and he fell hitting is head on the wall.

Franks ran down and roughly dragged Len back up the stairs not caring that Len's head was banging against the wall as he did so. What he didn't realise though, was that his mask was pulled off in the struggle.

'*LEAVE HIM ALONE YOU BRUTE.*' Joanne screamed out at Franks, then she recognised him and blurted out: 'That's the one called Franks, he was at my house.'

Franks ignored Joanne and pushed Len down onto the floor next to the women, he snatched up a rope and tied Len's feet together and then his hands behind his back. Len was groggy and Tilley shouted at Franks:

'Who is going to guard us now you pig? One of you two murderers will have to do it now.'

'Stop with the murder talk, I suppose it was you two who put that into his head. You will be very sorry for that and that you've seen my face this changes things for you interfering women.' Tilley blasted him saying: 'Yes we did tell him, it's true isn't it? He has the right to know what he's mixed up in.'

'Yeah and look what good it's done him? Typical, you women just can't keep your traps shut. Right I am putting your gags back on and you can starve and die of thirst for all I care.'

He pulled the gags back on and put one on Len, he gave Len a whack on his head and growled: 'You have pushed your luck too far this time you lousy Limey, you've done for them two now.'

Franks left the warehouse and went back to the hotel. He burst through the door slamming it behind him. 'Come in Michael. Why don't you?' Brice said sarcastically.

'Don't start with the mouth I've it up to here, that darned limey defied us and loosened those women's ropes, when I called him over it he tried to hit me with a crate lid and tried to escape. I put an end to that so I did now he is tied up with the women. They have been poisoning his mind about the murders so now he knows the score. We will have to take it in turns to watch them now.'

Damn it! 'I knew I should have handled it in the first place.'

'Oh now you don't trust me, is that it? Ok well how about I walk out and leave it all to you, would that suit?

After all me and those limey's have done all the dirty work for you so far, I'd like to see you cope all on your own.'

Franks went to walk out but Brice called him back . . . . 'Take no notice of me Buddy, this is all getting out of hand, as soon as we have heard from the boys up top we can shut up shop here and go back home.'

'Alleluia to that.' Franks replied and put his hand out and said: 'I suppose that means you trust me again.'

'Of course I do Bud' I never doubted you.'

Two hours after Rickard's interview was suspended the duty solicitor turned up. After being briefed by the charge officer and reading the arrest notes the Duty Sergeant took him to see Rickard in his cell, the solicitor said he wasn't going to speak to his client in the call, he wanted privacy. The Sergeant said: 'Ok let's go.' Taking Rickard by an arm he took them to a small room and locked them in.

Once inside the Solicitor introduced himself as Dennis Cole and switched on a mini tape recorder, he commenced asking: 'Now Mr Rickard, or shall I call you Shane? Rickard just said: "Whatever". The Solicitor continued: 'Ok then Shane, tell me everything from the beginning.'

'Well I was in a pub one night "The Junction" by Parkview station. I was drinking my pint when this yank came in and stood next to me. He didn't say anything straight away but eventually he asked me if I was a local. I asked if he meant a local in the pub or the area, he said either. He then held his hand out and told me his name.'

'What was that?'

'Wilson, David I think.'

'Do you remember when this was?'

'I'm not sure, about seven or eight days before that woman was murdered on the common.'

'What woman was that?'

'Dunno, I don't take notice of the news, I just remember reading about it somewhere. He said he had been over here for about four weeks. I wasn't bothered whether I spoke to him or not but decided to as the pub was quiet and I was bored.'

'What did you talk about Shane?'

'Nothing special at first then he asked if I had a job which I didn't and then asked where I lived. I asked why he wanted to know but he said "No reason it's not important". He was asking a lot of questions so I thought I would do the same. I asked what he was doing in England and he said he was here with another yank on business. I asked what business but he said he couldn't say but, if I wanted to earn some money with no questions he may have something. If I'd known how it was going to turn out though I'd have told him to shove it.'

'Apart from the obvious, how has it turned out?'

Disastrous! 'He wanted me to find a safe place to dump something large and it had to be out of the public eye. I asked what it was but he told me it was not my concern. I wasn't sure about it but I was skint and owed money all over the place so I bit the bullet. I then asked if this "thing" was heavy and he said "fairly" so I started looking around the next day. I tried one place . . . . The solicitor butted in and asked: 'Where was that?'

'On the edge of the common, it was dark and off the road but I couldn't get far enough into the bushes.

I found a plastic milk crate and threw it in to see how deep it was but it only went down a few feet. I did find a perfect spot though, about a quarter of a mile further up and I met him in the pub and gave him directions. He told me he didn't need directions as I was driving but I told him I didn't drive. He wasn't happy but I told him he should have asked that in the first place, that's when I discovered how mean he could be.'

'How was that?'

'He snarled at me with an evil look in his eyes and grabbed my lapels and said I had too much lip then walked out.

Three days later he met me and wanted me to find another place to "lose something" he said the river would be good but with access for a vehicle to get near the water's edge.

I "borrowed" a boat that was moored in the marina and found a suitable site, there was a dirt track leading down to the river which was wide enough for a car or van to go down, and no buildings anywhere nearby.

I waited until about four o'clock Tuesday morning and took the boat back to the marina. I had just passed the track and was going around a bend when I heard a splash coming from behind me. I looked back but couldn't see anything but I did hear the noise of and engine coming from the area of the track, I just continued rowing. Next day when I heard about the bloke's body in the river I panicked and kept low for a while, I got bored though so I started going to The Dog and Gun.' Rickard continued to explain how it all led to his arrest.

The solicitor told Rickard: 'Right, you are in a lot of trouble but if you co-operate with the Police you may well get a lighter sentence.' Rickard though about it for a while but eventually he consented to co-operate.

Cole went to see DCI Carter and informed him that Rickard was willing to tell all he knew and that he was ready to be formally interviewed.

George set up the interview for seven o'clock that morning. Mike entered the room and George was already there, Rickard and his brief were also present. Mike sat down and George introduced him to the solicitor then George opened a file and asked if everyone was ready. That was confirmed and the interview commenced.

Starting the tape Mike stated: "Formal interview of Shane Malcolm Rickard. The date is Thursday the twenty first October, Ninety eighty three. Time is four twenty five am.

Present is Detective Chief Inspector George Carter and Detective Inspector Michael Harper. Also present is Dennis Arnold Cole, solicitor for Shane Rickard and Police Constable Davies. Preliminaries over George commenced the interview: "As you know you are charged with two counts of murder and two counts of kidnapping, you are also charged with handling stolen goods". 'What have you to say?' Rickard looked at Cole and he nodded, Rickard then said: 'I have nothing to do with any murders or kidnapping, although I do know now, that is why they used me.'

'What do you mean by that Shane?'

'Well I know that dead woman was dumped in the same place I found for that yank, the bloke's body was found in the river close to the area I also found for him . . . . Gesturing towards the solicitor with his head,

Rickard continued: I know nothing more than what I told him.'

'What would that be then Mr Cole?' Cole related to George what Shane had said about the boat and hearing a splash and the engine noise.

George resumed the questions asking: 'So you know nothing personally about the bodies or the kidnappings?'

No! 'How many times do I have to tell you? I don't even know who has been kidnapped.'

'Ok Shane but we have to be sure. Now tell us about the Americans?'

'I only met one, Wilson. As I told matey here I met him in a pub in Parkview and he made it his business to befriend me but I made it clear that wasn't going to happen but, that didn't stop him offering me money to find somewhere to "lose something" as he put it

'How much did he offer you?'

'Two grand, I needed it as I owe money everywhere. I had no idea at the time though what he wanted to "lose" but I am sure now it was the bodies.'

'Ok, let's talk about the money we found at your mothers along with wallets and other items.'

'You found that lot? That's the money he gave me, well what's left of it that is.'

'How did you get the wallets, purse and credit cards?'

'He gave me them to dispose of but I kept them to bargain with in case they went back on their word and didn't pay me of it all went pear shaped.'

'Well it has certainly done that but, continue to co-operate and I will speak to the judge. Now what can you tell me about phone calls made from your mother's house to a rented office in Bromworth?'

'Well firstly I didn't know it was an office, the yank gave me the number and told me to ring it a few times and wait until it was answered, leave it for a few seconds then hang up.'

'Did you recognise the voice on the other end?'

'No, nobody spoke, they just waited until I hung up, I just did what Wilson said and asked no questions.'

'Well then Shane, what would you say if I told you that the guy on the other end was no other than your blond haired Pal, Chris Jenkins?'

'Jenkins? 'I went to school with him, we've had the odd pint together but that's all but he knows nothing about any of this. He was with me one night when I met Wilson but as far as I know they never spoke to each other, unless they did when I went to the Gent's.'

'Well we do have a witness that puts him in that office so it sure looks like they know each other. Now then Shane do you know the names: Tilley Watson, Joanne Perkins or David Franks?'

No! Wait a minute though, isn't Franks the bloke mentioned in the paper with Wilson?'

'Yes that's right, so Wilson never mentioned Franks then?'

No never!

'Ok then Shane that's all for now but we will be speaking to you again. By the way your mother wants to come and see you.'

Oh no!! 'I don't believe it, she'll only want to bend my ear about how I turned out etcetera, etcetera, I don't want to see her.'

'You may be interested to know she is very upset and worried about you, I am having her picked up and brought in so I suggest you see her, you need all the support you can get at the moment, also the court may bail you into your mother's care otherwise you will wait in jail until your trial and that could be months.' Rickard remained silent so George told the constable to take him back to his cell. Mike spoke for the tape: 'Interview suspended at seven forty seven am".

George and Mike stayed in the room and spoke briefly to Rickard's solicitor then they went to George's office, George said: 'That wasn't very fruitful Mike.'

'No not very much, all it has done really is to eliminate Rickard and his mate as serious suspects but, at least they are two less to worry about. The office situation is a strange one though it doesn't seem to have any purpose or connection with the murders other than the link with the yanks.'

'You're right Mike, I thought grabbing Rickard was a turning point but all we can do him for is receiving stolen goods and possibly aiding and abetting, it puts us no closer to knowing where these poor women are.'

CHAPTER FIFTEEN

Meanwhile that morning Bob and Joyce Watson were talking: 'I'm frantic with worry Bob.' Joyce sobbed: 'I can't bear not knowing if she is actually alive or not. What are we to do, why didn't she listen to us and drop the whole thing?'

'Well darling that's just Tilley isn't it, when she gets her teeth into something . . . . Joyce stopped Bob: 'I know I know, but you didn't help by going to the Police making matters worse.'

'Oh Joyce surely you are not blaming me for her kidnapping are you? I only told them that bloke had been in the store what else could I have done?'

'Oh I just don't know what to think anymore, I'm going back to bed and don't bother me unless you have some good news.' Joyce rushed up the stairs sobbing her heart out. Bob sat down on the sofa with his head in his hands murmuring over and over: 'Tilley, Tilley, Tilley.'

Joyce had only been upstairs for ten minutes when the phone rang, Bob snatched up the receiver thinking it was some good news, it was DCI Carter and he said:

'Hello Mr Watson, as you know we arrested Shane Rickard last night, well unfortunately he has no idea where Tilley is or in fact who she is' Bob asked: 'Can you believe him?' At that Joyce rushed down the stairs blurting out: 'Is it Tilley? Is she alright?'

'It's DCI Carter love but Rickard knows nothing about Tilley.'

'Here let me talk to him.' She snatched the receiver from him saying: 'What's this about Rickard, he must know where she is can't you torture him or something? I want my daughter back.'

'I know you do Mrs Watson but he knows nothing I can assure you, we do have a lead though on another suspect and we hope to arrest him today but for now that's all I can tell you I'm afraid.'

Joyce burst into tears and virtually threw the receiver at Bob, he told George: 'I am so sorry Inspector but she is inconsolable right now, I am so worried about her.'

'That's understandable, I'm just sorry I can't give you the news you want but, we are working twenty four seven and will not rest until we have found her. Now go and comfort your wife, if you wish we do have a victim support representative you and your wife could talk to, just let me know and I will arrange it. Anyway I will let you get back to her and I will let you know immediately I have some positive news for you. Take care Sir, I will be in touch.'

'Thank you Detective we do appreciate what you are doing but please make it good news next time you call.'

After Franks left the warehouse Tilley and her two fellow captives didn't move for a while but, Len eventually shuffled around the best he could and pushed himself backwards to get close to the women. He was hoping to get close enough to loosen one of their ropes or for them to loosen his.

Tilley guessed his intentions and did the same, gesturing to Joanne to follow suit. They ended up back to back. Len stretched his fingers out and found Tilley's hands, they both pushed back with their feet and Len managed to feel the knots of her ties.

He tried in vain to loosen the knots so he tried the same on Mrs P, again with no luck. All the moving about caused Tilley's gag to loosen, she shook her head vigorously and soon the gag slipped down and she said: 'Len Is there anything close to you that you could possibly reach with your feet to cut these ropes with?' He looked around as best he could and at first saw nothing but, then he noticed that poking out from under a blanket was a small piece of metal attached to a small fragment of wood broken off from the crate lid he threw at Franks.

He tried but couldn't reach it with his feet, looking back at Tilley he gestured with his head that he wanted all three of them to shuffle towards it together. Nodding in agreement Tilley made sure Joanne was ready she started counting one, two, three then they all shuffled together until Len was close enough to lift his feet and drop them onto the metal and he began dragging it close to him, the problem now was how were they to pick it up to enable them to cut the ropes. They rested for a while and then Tilley thought of a plan, she said: 'Look if we put our backs together and push back with our legs we may be able to stand up, then we could position ourselves around the metal and sit down again with it in the middle of us. One of us could then hold it and the others rub their ropes up and down on it and cut them.

Len and Mrs Perkins considered the idea and decided it was the only way, so they agreed.

It took a lot of effort to stand up, especially for Joanne but eventually they were on their feet and although after a struggle managed to work their way around the wood and metal.

After a rest they had to decide how they were going to pick the metal and who was going to do it. Len said he would try so they each shuffled their bodies forward until they were virtually laying out flat, allowing Len to grab the wooden end, then shuffled themselves back up and they were ready.

It was obvious that Joanne would not have the mobility to move her arms up and down so Tilley told Len to concentrate on her hands then she could untie him and Joanne. After a lot of effort and a few small cuts to Tilley's hands Len eventually cut through Tilley's bonds.

Once she was free she used the metal and cut through the rope on her legs then cut Joanne's hands free.

Mrs Perkins took the metal from Tilley and cut her legs free, pulling her gag down she yelled in delight: I'm free! I'm free! 'Oh that is such a relief.' She struggled to her feet and went over to Len and pulled his gag down and he blasted: 'Ok you old bat enough with the self indulgence, get me out of these pigging ropes.' Tilley said angrily to Len: 'That's no way to talk to an old lady, especially as she holds your freedom in her hands.' Len was quick to reply: 'Yeah and who did all the work getting the ruddy metal close enough to cut your ropes?' Tilley retorted: 'Our ropes? I suppose yours will just miraculously fall off? You are so selfish. I think we ought to leave him here. What do you say Joanne?'

'I thoroughly agree dear and now I'm off to the loo.'

'Ooh yes and I am coming with you.' Len responded saying: 'Hey come on you two, cut me free I'm in pain here.' Tilley responded saying: 'Only if you are you going to apologise to Joanne for being rude?'

'I suppose so I'm sorry lady, now please cut me free?'

'Ok but not until we come back.' Tilley replied and taking Joanne's hand they walked out stiffly but giggling.

Len was not amused and shouted: ***"YOU WAIT YOU TWO ARE DEAD".***

Tilley and Joanne returned from the bathroom after freshening themselves up and Len soon balled at them to cut him loose. Tilley said to him: 'Well that depends on what you intend to do when you are free. I mean are you going to help us escape or are you going continue being selfish and leave us here.'

'I promise I will help you, they have a VW camper hidden out back and I can drive us all out of here,' Mrs Perkins and Tilley looked at Teach other with a big grin on their faces when they heard about the VW and Tilley asked: 'Is that the car they brought us here in?'

'No that was another car, I stole that for them.' Tilley said: 'Alright I will cut you free but you go back on your word and I will tell the Police that you were in it from the start with the yanks, do you hear me?' Len sighed and replied; 'Yes I hear you, now get these damned ropes off . . . . Please?'

While Tilley cut Len free Joanne went to fetch what was left of the food and water after which Len took the women to where the camper was hidden under a canvas sheet. They uncovered the camper and Tilley warned Len: 'This thing had better work because if you are trying it on you will be sorry.'

'I am fully aware of that girl I can assure you.' He slid the driver's door open and climbed in, pulling the sun visor down and retrieving the keys. He put the key in the ignition and turned it but the engine wouldn't start. Tilley Growled: 'I warned you Len and I meant every word,'

'Alright, alright give me a chance it's old and temperamental, like you women.'

'Stop the insults and get this thing started, it's not hard to see why those yanks don't like you.'

'Well at this moment I'm thinking I should have taken my chances with them instead of lumbering myself with you two.'

'He's very ungrateful isn't he dear?' Joanne piped up. 'Very.' Tilley replied.

On his way into work Thursday morning Mike passed the front desk, the duty Sergeant called him and said: 'Morning Mike I have just come off the phone, a woman who lives next to Jenkins digs recognised his picture in the paper this morning. She said that as far as she knew he still lived there because she saw him go in the front door yesterday afternoon. Mike thanked him and went straight to George's office. George asked Mike to take a plain clothes officer with him and go and check it out.

Mike arrived at the digs and pushed the manager's buzzer, a man answered: 'Hello who is it?'

'Hello I'm Detective Inspector Harper from Parkview Police. Can I have a word with you please?'

'Yes of course come in.' Mike heard the door latch click and pushed it open. The manager lived on the ground floor of a seedy building which was long overdue a lick of paint.

The manager introduced himself as "Harry Turnbull". Mike said: 'I'm here in connection with the search that was done of one of your tenants a few days earlier this week.'

'Oh yes Mr Jenkins, how can I help?'

'Has he been back since the search?'

'Yes he came back that night, he asked what had to his room and I told him, I asked if he was in any trouble and he said no it is just that he was seen with a guy who had been done for selling drugs. He said that the Police had spoken to him and he was in the clear.'

'Do you know if he is in at the moment?'

'No he isn't he left with some guy about an hour ago, what do you want with him.'

'I'm sorry Mr Turnbull but I am not at liberty to say.' Mike showed him the pictures of the Americans and Rickard and asked if he had seen any of them with Jenkins. Pointing at Franks, Turnbull said: 'Him. I don't know the others though.'

'Has he been here often?'

'Yes about four times as far as I know, I don't go out much as I suffer from Agoraphobia so I see most of who comes and goes. I don't know his name though.'

'Have you noticed whether he has a vehicle at all, if so what make?'

'He has yes but he changes cars often though.' Mike showed Turnbull photo's of Mr and Mrs Johnson but he didn't recognise them apart from seeing them in the papers. Mike then asked: 'Do you know of any regular haunts where Jenkins hangs out?'

'I know he uses a greasy spoon down York Street, that's probably where he is now actually.'

'Well thank you that is very helpful Mr Turnbull, we may need to speak to you again though but goodbye for now.'

Once they were outside Mike told the PC that they were going to the cafe and hopefully catch Jenkins by surprise.

They reached the cafe and Mike tried to look through the window but Jenkins wasn't in view so he decided to go in. He told the Constable: 'I will try and radio the situation to you but if I can't I'll come back out and we'll decide a strategy, now stay alert.'

On entering the cafe Mike looked around cautiously, there were only a few customers but Jenkins wasn't one of them so he sat at a table and put the photos of Franks and Jenkins face up on the table with his own ID alongside.

When the waitress came over he asked for a cup of tea and cautiously pointed to his ID and the pictures, the girl looked around and wrote on her note pad and handed it to Mike as if it was the bill. She had written

"Young one in toilet". Mike nodded and she went to put his order in.

Mike waited for Jenkins to come back and watched him, fortunately he sat back down at his table and ordered another coffee, Mike went to the toilet and it was empty so he took the chance and radioed the PC: "Suspect inside, I will follow him out and apprehend him, keep an eye on the door and assist as necessary".

Mike returned to his table and his tea arrived, the waitress pretended to wipe the table and getting close to Mike's ear she said: 'I will spill his tea in his lap then you can nab him.'

Mike nodded but was a little apprehensive as he had devised the other plan with the PC. Not wanting to alert Jenkins though he decided to go with the waitress's idea.

A few moments went by before Jenkins coffee was taken to him, Mike put his cup down and watched intently as the waitress approached Jenkins, he left his table and approached Jenkins from the left as the waitress went to his right she leant over and tilted the saucer and the cup slid into Jenkins lap. At the same time Mike grabbed his left arm and forcing Jenkins to his feet he bent him over the table. It was over so quickly Jenkins didn't have time to resist or say anything.

Mike asked the girl to go and call the PC in. He held Jenkins down and showed him his ID and told him he was under arrest and why, while Mike was reading Jenkins his rights the Constable came rushing in. By this time all but two of the customers had fled the cafe, one of them almost crashing into the PC as he approached the door.

Jenkins recovered and began protesting his innocence. Mike told him he would get plenty of time to have his say. Taking him by his right arm the PC put the Handcuffs, he and Mike then took him to their car.

On the way out Mike thanked the waitress for her assistance saying he would be in touch if he needed a statement from her. He and the PC climbed into the car and returned to the station and booked Jenkins in.

After the custody Sergeant had booked Jenkins in he was taken to a holding cell, the Sergeant asked Mike whether he should call a duty solicitor for Jenkins, Mike asked: 'Has he said anything?'

'No, apart from saying he hadn't done anything. Actually he seems to still be in a state of shock.'

'May as well then Serge, he isn't going to give us anything yet.'

When Mike returned to his office he found a message from George, which read: "Mike I have gone to London, we have a breakthrough with our mole theory, back tonight". Mike thought to himself "a good day all round maybe".

CHAPTER SIXTEEN

It was nearly twenty minutes past nine that evening before George returned from London. He immediately went to Mike's office as he was keen to tell him what he had discovered. Mike; he blurted out: 'WE were right there is a mole, not in the security department though, in the government.' Mike sat up straight and said: 'Tell me more.' George sat down and said: 'Do you remember the junior Minister that owns the stolen VW camper? Well it seems he knows our yanks.'

'That means he must have let them take the VW and he must have a hand in the goings on here surely.'

'It certainly looks that way Mike but there is to be no move on him until all the pieces are put together here and in the states, anyway I will go into it in more depth later.'

'Well that's your news George do you want to hear about mine now?'

'You're not going to upstage me now are you Mike?'

'Not quite but close, I have arrested Jenkins.' Mike announced proudly and went on to fill George in on the circumstances of the arrest. George replied: 'Well done Mike, you are getting good at these arrests I see I will have to watch my step, you'll have my job next.'

'Hardly but it is satisfying to get another link in the chain even though it may only be a weak one.'

'I couldn't agree with you more Mike, let's get a coffee and we can discuss our day.'

While they were drinking their coffee George suggested pitching Rickard and Jenkins against each other, saying that they were giving each other up. Mike agreed it was a good plan.

Once he had received the news that a solicitor had spoken to Jenkins George set up a formal interview for twenty three fifteen.

The interview commenced and George gave Mike the lead, he began: 'Christopher John Jenkins, do you know why you were arrested today?'

'Sort of, I suppose it's about that office aint it.'

'Well you tell us, what was that office all about?'

'I don't really know, I met a yank in a pub and he wanted me to arrange the lease then stay in the office and take phone calls but not to say anything, just wait a few seconds and hang up.'

'You do know we have your mate Shane in custody don't you?'

'Shane, what Shane Rickard?'

'That's the one he has been quite helpful he actually gave you up.'

'Yeah I know your game Ricky didn't know what I was doing. I used to meet the yank secretly after I met him one night when he was with Shane in a pub. He arranged for another yank to meet me at my flat, his name was Franks.'

'Rickard knew alright, it was him that called you at that office, he has been working with the other yank—Brice—for a long time.' Ok now Christopher, I want you to look at some pictures and tell me if you recognise anybody.' Mike showed Jenkins pictures of the Johnson couple and Tilley and Joanne. Jenkins looked and said: No! 'I've never seen any of them before.'

'Are you sure because those two people there . . . . Mike pointed to the Johnsons . . . were murdered by those yanks and the two women have been kidnapped, we believe also by the yanks because they could identify them. That puts you and Rickard right in the middle of all this.'

'I told you I don't know any of them, I swear.'

Mike looked at George and shrugged his shoulders hinting that they were getting nowhere and George nodded in agreement. Mike then said to Jenkins: 'Ok Christopher, I think we are done here for now but we will talk to you again.' Mike announced for the tape that the interview was suspended at twenty three fifty three.

Mike and George stayed in the room after Jenkins had been taken away and the solicitor had left. Well! George exclaimed: 'Well not much from him either accept he can give us a description of Franks.'

'Yeah it's not the best result ever but one more suspect in the bag, I'll set up the sketch guy with him in the morning, I don't know about you George but I'm starving, how about going for something to eat?'

'Spot on Mike, let's go but I'm buying.'

They sat in the canteen after they had eaten and they were having a coffee and sitting in silence for a while. George was the first to speak: 'I'm sorry I had to go to London without notifying you but it happened so fast. The Chief Constable called me to say he had classified information regarding the case and said I should go straight up there.'

No! 'Don't be sorry George, what is the situation?'

'Well this Junior Minister was in America during his gap year. As we know he then got himself in heavy debt through gambling and started selling drugs. He sold some bad gear to the son of the crime family who died. He absconded back to London under an assumed name and his father got him a job in Westminster. We also know that the Johnsons were innocently connected to him, hence their murders.'

'I said there was more to the deaths than their testimony in court. We also now know how the yanks got hold of the VW. We really do have to find these poor women.'

'Absolutely Mike, incidentally the CC told me that those clowns from NIS have been reprimanded and told to co-operate with us in future. Ok then Mike I think we may as well go home, thanks for everything today, I'll see you tomorrow.'

When Len finally got the VW started Tilley opened the warehouse doors and he reversed it out. The women climbed in and anxious to get away Len stamped on the throttle. He sped off swinging around the first corner of the building and then the second reaching the front of the warehouse, he turned the third corner and as he did so he met another car head on. Len stamped on the brakes and swerved to miss the car but caught the offside front wing and bounced off hitting a metal post of a notice board.

The other car was driven by Brice who was not wearing a seatbelt and he was thrown forward but the airbag inflated preventing his head from hitting the steering wheel. Len on the other hand as not so lucky because in his rush to escape he hadn't shut the driver's door, also he was not wearing a seatbelt and he was ejected out of the van hitting the ground with his head cutting it open and injuring his left leg. Tilley and Joanne were wearing their belts but were still shaken up.

When both vehicles came to rest it took time for everyone to come to their senses, Brice was the first to clamber out of his car and looking around suddenly realised the other vehicle was the VW. He rushed over before Len or the women could react, pulled out a gun and pointed at the women. "You" He shouted at Len: 'Get up slowly or I will kill them both.' Len answered weakly: 'I can't get up. "He was holding his leg and blood was running from his head" 'I think my leg is broken.'

Leg! 'I ought to break your flaming neck you scum. Right you two out of the car slowly, believe me I will not hesitate to shoot anyone who doesn't do as I say.'

Tilley undid her belt and helped Joanne undo hers as she was shaking with fear just staring at the gun. Helping her out of the van Tilley sneered at Brice and snarled: 'You wouldn't dare shoot us because that would finish it for you and that vile partner of yours.'

'You think you know it all don't you Girlie? I bet it was you who concocted all this escape malarkey, how did you get free anyhow? You were all tied tight, I know because I tied you.'

'Well you underestimated us didn't you pig?'

'Enough with the mouth now get him up and all of you inside.'

The women reached down to Len and took one arm each, they tried lifting him but were unable to as he could not put any weight on his injured leg. Brice kept shouting: 'Come on come on put your backs into it, what are you waiting for?' Tilley came right back at Brice angrily saying: 'Instead of barking orders come and help we are not strong enough to lift him.'

'You got yourselves into this and you can get yourselves out of it, I'm done with you lot.'

'You fat lazy slob.' Tilley growled back: 'Come on Joanne one more try and if we still can't manage it he will have to help us or we stay where we are.'

Tilley asked Len to push as much as he could with his good leg as the women put his arms around their necks. Tilley counted—one, two, three and they lifted him with all of their strength. Len pushed down hard on his good leg groaning with pain but eventually stood unsteadily supported by the women. They helped him into the warehouse and Tilley turned to Brice and said: 'He can't go upstairs he will have to stay down here.' He responded saying: 'You are all staying down here and going somewhere different, I'm not going through all this again. Now bring him over here.' They struggled but managed to get Len over to where Brice wanted him, Brice forced Len down sitting him against a pillar. Brice then made the women sit down against pillars at each end of the building tying their hands behind the pillars and their legs together, gagging them. He then returned to Len tying him in the same manner as the women then kicked Len twice in his injured leg making Len cry out in agony. Brice then gagged Len and pointing his gun individually at the three of them and warned: 'Right you sad lot behave yourselves and you may just get out of all this with your lives.'

Brice went outside and locking the door and went back to his car not sure if it was still drivable. He checked it over finding the left front wing was touching the wheel. He managed to pull it out far enough away he also had to cut the airbag away so he could see to drive. This all done he got in and drove back to the hotel.

'What's eating you?' Franks asked as his partner burst through the door, slamming it behind him.

'That bunch of losers, they only found a way out of their ropes and were about to drive off in the VW but fortunately they slammed into me as I arrived and that sunk their canoe for them.'

'What have you done with them?'

'Don't worry they are all back inside tied up separately and I have put their gags back on.'

'Have they damaged the vehicles?'

'The car is drivable but the VW is wrecked and that gives us problems, we'll need something to carry that lot away with and as if that's not enough that loser Fisher has injured his leg and can't walk, we need a rethink.'

'I thought our people back home were working on getting us out of here. We need to get rid of those millstones before they drop us in it, especially that young dame, why don't you get in contact and hurry them up?'

'I wish it was that simple but they are unreachable, I suppose I could contact our go between and see if he could hurry them up.'

DCI Carter arrived in his office at eight thirty Friday morning and called a constable to get him a coffee. He asked if DI Harper was in and was told that he was but had gone to arrange for Jenkins to help produce a sketch of Franks. Mike had met the duty custody Sergeant at the cells and asked: 'How is our latest guest this morning Serge?'

'Very quiet Mike, he didn't eat his breakfast but he has had a mug of tea.'

'Well I'm taking him to the sketch boys to get an image of that Franks character, I wouldn't be surprised if he isn't let out on bail later today his part in all this seems very superficial, if he helps with this sketch and is willing to identify him officially then he will probably just get a suspected sentence.'

'What about Rickard? We will be running out of time soon, if we don't charge him with something we will have to let him go.'

'That's all under control Jim, The Crown Prosecution Service is contacting us this morning with the charges, I assume he will be charged with aiding and abetting, kidnapping plus possession of stolen goods, then he'll go for his preliminary hearing and be moved to prison awaiting trial. Right then get our friend out and I'll take him upstairs.'

The custody Sergeant opened the cell door and Mike said to Jenkins: 'Come on then my lad we want you to assist our sketch artist.'

'What for I can't draw?'

'Don't worry he does the sketching you just give him the description.'

'What do you want me to describe?'

'Franks.'

'Oh yeah and what do I get out of it?'

'Well if we catch him and you identify him you'll probably just get a suspended sentence but, if you are not helpful then I'm sure we can find something to charge you with.'

'You don't give me much choice then do you?'

'Not a lot, no.'

'Does this mean I can go home then?'

'We will look into that later, let's just see how you get on today and we will have a word with your brief, it all depends on you Chris.'

Mike escorted Jenkins to the artist's room leaving a constable outside, Mike then went to the canteen for a coffee.

While he was drinking his coffee he listened to the canteen radio, he listened intently as a local newsreader announced: "There have been no further developments in the double murder enquiry. A man was arrested yesterday but at present his identity is being withheld. This follows the arrest of Shane Rickard earlier this week. Rickard is expected to be charged later today. The Americans "Wilson and Brice" are still at large and the reward for their capture still stands".

Mike finished his coffee and went to George's office, he knocked on George's door and George said: 'Oh hi Mike I understand you have been busy this morning, you do want my job don't you?'

'No you're safe for the moment, there's too much going on at present I'll wait until it quiet's down a bit then you may have to worry.'

'Thank goodness for that, I was getting worried for a minute.' Mike laughed then related to George about taking Jenkins to the artist. George answered: 'Ok we'll wait for an hour or so then go and see the result, oh yes Mike I've heard back from the CPS, Rickard's Charges are as we expected. His Solicitor is coming in later and I dare say they will want a deal.'

'They have nothing to bargain with though have they George?'

'Well that depends whether we can fool them into thinking we know more than we do or he is holding something back otherwise he doesn't.

We will struggle to prove the kidnap charge though if God forbid we don't find those poor women alive. I just can't believe no one saw anything the night they were taken. The house to house turned nothing up accept that nipper seeing the car . . . . Tell you what Mike, get a team to phone all the guest houses, B&B's and hotels within a ten mile radius of the kidnap areas, ask if there are or have been any American's or anyone acting weird or suspicious staying there recently. Call me if anything turns up.'

Later that morning Shane Rickard was taken to a room where his solicitor and George were waiting, a constable stood outside. The solicitor briefed Rickard on the charges but he repeated his denial of knowing anything about the kidnappings or that he actually helped in any murders. George then spoke: Shane; you are to appear in court tomorrow morning at ten thirty, it is a preliminary hearing to have the charges read and to hear your plea. CPS and your barrister will argue whether bail will be given. I must warn you though I don't think you will get bail in which case you will be taken from court to a prison where you will be detained until trial. Do you understand all I have said?'

'Yes I think so but you said that if I was cooperative you would help me.'

'What I actually said was that we would have a word with the judge, which we will do as soon as we know who it is to be. Now if there's nothing else you can tell me then you can go back to your cell.'

'No I have told you all I know.' George acknowledged Rickard then told the Constable to escort Rickard to his cell. George shook the solicitor's hand and said: 'See you in court.'

When George stepped outside Mike was waiting, he was obviously anxious about something, he rushed over and put his hand on George's back guiding him out of the solicitor's earshot. He spoke in a low voice telling George: 'A woman is at the front desk, she says she saw a large black car with darkened rear windows parked outside Tilley's apartment building on the Saturday morning before she was taken.'

'Why has she taken so long to come forward?'

'Well apparently she was going on a camping holiday to Wales with her family and was driving past the building, the car was parked facing her at a narrow part of the road and she couldn't pass. The driver was standing behind the car and as he walked around to the driver's door she saw his face full on, he smiled in an apologetic manner but then just as quickly looked away keeping his head down hiding his face. He moved the car and she drove on. However she came home yesterday and was catching up with the newspapers and read about the kidnappings and saw the picture of Fisher. She swears that he was the driver of the black car. He was wearing a light grey suit with a black tie.'

'Nice one Mike, get someone to take a statement and show her the photo of Fisher just to be sure and tell her we will probably be speaking to her again. What is her name?'

'Grace Chalmers.'

'Right take some uniforms and go back and knock on every door in the area, someone else must have seen the car parked there they were obviously casing the area. What mystifies me how did they find out about Tilley and where she lived?'

At twelve fifteen Mike and the officer's commenced knocking on doors, they weren't having much success until an elderly man walked down the street walking a dog. Mike approached him and asked if he lived in the area, he said he lived at number twenty eight. Asked if he saw the car in question he replied saying that he had, he said that it was parked outside of the apartments on the Friday night prior to the women's kidnapping at about five fifteen but was gone when he returned about twenty minutes later. It was also there on the Saturday morning but was gone in the afternoon. Mike asked if he saw anybody in or near the vehicle, he said he hadn't. Mike made a note of his name and address and thanked him for his information. The man walked away but paused and came back, he called to Mike and said: Actually! 'On reflection I did see a man standing on the other side of the road, he was about twenty or so and wearing a grey suit. He was looking up at the windows of the building but with his back to me so I was unable to see his face.'

Mike thanked him once again and called the officer's to return to the station.

On returning to the station DI Harper went straight to George Carter's office, he told him what the man and woman had said. George replied: 'Ok so they were staking the building out, we can assume then that they did the same at The Conifers considering what we saw on the CCTV footage, there's no point doing a house to house there though it is too isolated but, send a couple of officers with the yanks and Fisher's picture's to the daily's house, ask if she saw either of them or the car hanging around the Conifers at anytime leading up to the kidnappings.'

On George's suggestion Mike sent a Constable and a WPC to question the daily, she said that she doesn't work weekends but, she did remember seeing a large black car parked down the road from the guest house when she left to go home at four fifteen on the Friday before.

CHAPTER SEVENTEEN

Tilley and the others were left alone for the rest of that Thursday and most of Friday. They were all becoming fatigued having not had a drink or food for so long, not to mention needing the toilet. They tried hard in their individual ways to attempt wriggling free but Brice had tied them all so tight this time.

Little did they know though that later that afternoon the situation was going to improve, all three were worn out trying to loosen their ties when both Tilley and Len heard a noise from outside, dreading that it was Brice or Franks they kept still and silent but nobody came in. They listened intently for a while but heard nothing else, after a minute or so though they heard voices, they sounded young and right outside the warehouse door.

They were tied in such a way they were unable to lift their legs and bang on the floor so Tilley started calling out as loud as she could through her gagged mouth. Len soon joined in but there was no response. They continued for as long as they could but had to give up as their mouths and throats were so dry.

Joanne had no idea what was going on as she had heard nothing however when after a rest Tilley and Len restarted their efforts to be heard, she joined in.

Outside there were two young boys who had been riding their bikes around the deserted trading estate and come across the wreckage of the VW. Boys being boys they couldn't resist taking things off of the vehicle. One of the boys suddenly stopped what he was doing and said: 'Scott; listen, what's that noise?'

'What noise?'

'Listen can't you hear it? It's coming from inside there.' The boy was pointing at the warehouse. 'You're nuts I can't hear anything.' Scott told his mate. "There it is again". The first boy said: surely you heard that?'

'You're right Todd I heard that, come on.' Scott started running towards the warehouse door followed by Todd. They reached the door and tried to open it.

Tilley heard them and looked sideways at Len, she looked back at the door and then back at Len. He nodded and with one more effort they shouted again.

The boys heard them clearly this time and tried to open the door but realised it was locked. They thought for a while then Todd ran back to the VW and looked around, he found a tyre wrench in the back of the van which had a tyre lever on one end.

He ran back to the door and attempted to lever the door off its hinges. He wasn't getting very far but then Scott noticed a gap between the door and the frame. He told Todd to put the lever part of the wrench between that and together they pulled back with all their might, after a few more attempts the frame split right down the middle and they were able to wrench the door open.

When they finally opened the door wide it was difficult to see inside because of the gloom of the warehouse. Once their eyes became adjusted they were shocked at what they saw and Todd blurted out: "He's tied up".

And her! Scott added pointing at Mrs Perkins. Looking around he then saw Tilley and pointing, said: 'There's another one over there.' He and Scott went over to Len because they could see he was injured and Todd pulled down his gag. Before he could say anything Len begged them to untie him as he was in such agony with his leg. 'Who are you? Why are you all tied up?' Todd asked. Len told them: 'We have been kidnapped by violent killers, untie us please we have to get out of here before they come back.' Todd and Scott looked at each other not knowing what to think. Len continued: 'Haven't you seen the papers or the news about the murders of them two people in Fairview?' Scott said: 'Yeah but how are we to know that you are not the murderers?' He grabbed Todd's arm and pulled him away from Len.

'No they are witnesses . . . . Len said gesturing towards the women with his head . . . . and the killers have kidnapped them because they can identify them. We are harmless, come on untie us, look at that old lady does she look like a murderer, she is over sixty for God's sake.'

'I don't know Todd what should we do?'

'I reckon we should call the old Bill, he could be lying . . . . Len interrupted Todd: 'Look it will take you ages to reach a phone and by that time the yanks could come back, then we will all be killed.' Todd thought then said: 'You did say that you read about the murders Scott and that bloke doesn't sound like a yank, let's see what the women say.' Todd went over to Tilley and pulled her gag down. She immediately blurted out: 'I'm not American either I was kidnapped from my flat. I'm the one that identified that Rickard in the papers and that old lady over there owns a guesthouse, those yanks and the dead man stayed at her place the night before the woman was murdered. I swear, please help us get away before the yanks get back.' Todd pulled Scott outside to figure it all out, Scott half believed their stories but Todd still thought there was something weird about it all.

While they were mulling it over Scott remembered something, he said: 'Hey Todd, do you remember Woody at school? He told the cops about seeing that car that was parked outside the place the girl was taken from.'

'Yeah I do remember that.' Todd said. Scott added: 'Well I know that place my auntie lives there, I need another look at that young one.' They went back inside and Scott went over to Tilley and looked closely at her. "I do know her". Tilley was a little baffled but when she looked at Scott again she said excitedly: 'Of course you are Mrs Talbot's nephew, we have met a couple of times when you have visited her.' Scott then said: 'Come on Todd let's untie them, they are telling the truth.' When they tried to untie their ropes however they couldn't undo the knots. Len remembered the piece of metal they used to cut through their ropes when they got free the first time, it was upstairs and he told the boys about it.

Scott ran upstairs and retrieved the piece of box lid with the metal attached. He ran back down and started to cut through Len's ropes, it took a while but eventually he cut through the ropes holding Len's hands, he then began to work on his legs. 'Careful that leg is broken.' Len told the boys and suggested Scott cut the ropes on the side of his good leg.

The boys did that and once the ropes were cut they tried to get him to his feet but he said sharply: No! 'Untie the women I can't stand up.'

After the women were free Tilley slowly got to their feet and she hugged the boys. 'Thank you, thank you, you have saved our lives, how did you find us?' The boys explained as they and Tilley were helping Joanne to get to her feet, she was in pain with her hips and her legs had gone dead.

Eventually the feeling returned to Joanne's legs and she managed to climb the stairs to the bathroom. Tilley had gone outside and was breathing in the fresh air deeply. She shielded her eyes from the bright sunlight and looked around, shortly after the boys followed her out and Scott asked Tilley: 'How are you going to get away with that man's bad leg?'

'That is a good question? How far is the town from here?'

'It's about two and a half miles from here, isn't it Todd?'

'Yeah I suppose.' Joanne then appeared with the remaining trickle of the water and took it over to Tilley. 'You boys are little saviours.' She said and attempted to hug them, after being hugged by Tilley though they shied away from her protesting: "It wasn't cool". Tilley and Joanne giggled then just as quickly returned to feeling grim at the situation. 'What are we going to do now Tilley?' Joanne asked then said: 'I'm petrified at the thought of what will happen next.'

'I feel exactly the same way Joanne I can't stop thinking about my mum and dad, my dad's quite tough but my mum must be going out of her mind. Oh well come on we must see to Len he must stand up or he won't be able to move his good leg, he's going to slow us down enough as it is.'

'Yes you're right but after his outburst the other night threatening to leave without us, I've a good mind to leave him here.'

'I know how you feel but I just think he is as worried and confused as we are, he's no more than a frightened pussy cat.'

'Well he's not curling up on my lap.' Joanne joked as Tilley put her arm around her shoulder and they walked back into the warehouse chuckling. The two boys looked at each other and Scott put his finger to his temple indicating they were bonkers.

On returning to the warehouse the women were astonished to find Len was missing. The women looked at each other and Tilley asked 'Where is he? He didn't come outside I'm positive of that, the question I'm asking myself though is how has he managed to get up not to mention disappear? He couldn't walk on his own let alone go upstairs.'

With that they heard a noise from the rear of the building but dismissed it as the boys rummaging around the VW until they appeared in the doorway. 'Quickly go upstairs the Yanks are back.' Tilley yelled at them. The boys ran upstairs and hid as best they could, the women crept towards where the noise was coming from, they were relieved but angry to discover it was Len, he explained that he had pulled himself up with the help of the wall and found a piece of the broken doorframe and used it as a crutch. Tilley was still angry, she blasted him: 'You scared the living daylights out of us you idiot, why didn't you call out when we came in the door?'

'I didn't hear you, calm down girls.'

'To think we were defending you a minute ago.' Joanne added: 'Leave him here to face the yanks I say.'

Me too! Tilley said turning to walk away. Len blurted out: 'Ok I'm sorry, alright?'

'Well we have to work together Len if we are going to get away.'

'I know but what are we going to do?—Tilley interrupted Len shouting: 'It's alright boys come on down.' Tilley then said: 'The town is about two and half miles away and we have no transport so I think we should find somewhere to hide and send the boys back on their bikes to get the Police.' Len said that may work but they couldn't go far with his leg.' Tilley told him: 'No but I reckon they are more likely to look for us in the direction of the town so we have to go the other way and the boys can tell the Police which way we have gone.'

'That's not a bad plan, what do you think granny?'

'You are too cheeky for your own good young man but I will overlook it considering the situation. Yes I do think it's a good plan but we should get going before it's too late. Now boys are you going to help us?' Too right! Scott said excitedly, I can't wait to tell our mates in school.'

'That's brilliant thanks boys.' Tilley then said: 'Ok you two ride as if your life depends on it and it's possible it might.' Todd and Scott looked at each other and Tilley realised what she had said, she put her arms around them saying: 'Sorry boys that was thoughtless of me but I just wanted to point out the danger of the situation we are all in, we will not let them hurt you though we promise don't we?' Tilley looked at Len and Joanne urging them to support her which they did and the boys looked relieved. She continued: 'Well as I was saying, when you get to the Police station ask to speak to DCI Carter or DI Harper but, if they are not available just tell whoever you talk to that you have found Tilley Watson and Mrs Perkins, we are going in that direction.' Tilley was pointing at a small hill that was to the east of the warehouse. She added: 'They will most definitely assume we went to town and that should buy us some time. Is there a shortcut you can take to town because they could catch up with you if they should come back?' Todd answered: 'Yes we can cut across the bridge over the river, no cars can go that way.'

Brilliant! 'We will keep a look out for the Police and signal to them somehow. Now get going but before you do you must disguise your bike tracks in the mud so they won't know you were here.'

The boys dealt with bike tracks and set off, Tilley and co headed towards the hill which wasn't very steep so Len used the makeshift crutch to support his injured leg while Tilley and Joanne took turns to support him on his left side. At the top were some rocks and trees, a number of the rocks were just high enough to hide behind but low enough to get a good all round view.

When the boys reached the Police station they ran up to the front desk breathing heavily and Todd blurted out: *WE F—F—FOUND THEM!* The desk sergeant told them to settle down then asked: 'Now then found who?' Todd continued a little slower: 'Those people that were kidnapped, they're out at the old trading estate, we have to speak to someone called Carter a Detective I think . . . . Scott interrupted: 'DCI Carter or DI Harper.'

'Alright big head, yeah that's right who he said.' The Sergeant said: 'Alright lads take a seat and I will see if they are here.' The Sergeant called George's office and he was there, he told George: 'Hello its Sergeant Thomas sir there are two young lads here saying they have found the kidnapped women.'

'WHAT? WHERE? Hang on I'm coming down.' George ran down the stairs and rushed into the reception area startling the boys. George apologised to them and sat down next to Scott. He introduced himself and asked: 'Now about these kidnapped women, you say you have found them, where are they? Are they alive?'

'Yeah Todd replied, the bloke has a broken leg though.'

'What bloke? We know nothing about any bloke.'

'His name is Len but we don't know his other name.'

'Are you sure? Do you know the women's names?' Scott answered: 'Tilley something and an old lady—Joanne I think.' George looked at Todd and he nodded.

'Ok boys, now can you tell us where they are?' Todd answered: 'We can do better than that we can show you, we have to hurry though there's some yanks after them.'

George told the Sergeant to call Mike Harper down and contact the armed response team.

Minutes passed and Mike arrived and George briefed him: 'I've called the "ART" but we have to move fast before the yanks get there and it's almost dark.' He turned to the boys and said: 'It will be too dangerous to let you show us, just tell us where they are and how close we can get to them without being seen.' The boys told George where the three were adding: 'The road goes past the warehouse but there is a farm gate to a field a little way before the warehouse, you should get all your cars in there and they will be hidden by bushes and trees. You won't be able to get any further than that though without being seen. They've gone up a hill to the east but they will be looking out for you.'

The boys directed the Police to the scene and George thanked them and arranged for them to have a drink. He then said: 'Ok Sergeant I want as many men as possible in or out of uniform ready to go in ten minutes. They are all to wear helmets and flak jackets I also want helmets and flak jackets for the DI and myself.

As soon as everyone was assembled George briefed them on the situation warning: "These yanks are armed and very dangerous so nobody and I mean nobody take any chances, you only move on my word, three people's lives are at risk as well as your own so no heroics whatever the circumstances. Am I understood?'

Once George was satisfied he had pressed his point home he ordered them all to check their radios were all working and tuned in to the same channel, he then gave the order to proceed.

Meanwhile Len and the women had finally reached the top of the hill, Len was exhausted as were the women after struggling to support him all the way to the top. Finding a suitable spot they sat down and Tilley gave Len a sip of the water. Earlier they had attempted to top the bottle up from the bathroom tap but the water was a dirty green colour so they dismissed it.

When Len had his sip Tilley handed it to Joanne who in turn handed it back to Tilley but she declined as there was only a small amount to go round. Food was also scarce they only had a half of the cold pizza and two packets of crisps which they discovered Len had ferreted away secretly. They had ribbed him but forgave him.

Tilley said that she and Joanne would take turns to watch out for any movement, Tilley took the first watch and positioned herself behind a rock just high enough to be able to look down and peek over the top but still hidden from below.

After what seemed like hours Joanne came to relieve Tilley saying: 'Come on girl it's my turn now, you have been up here for an hour.'

'Is that all? I'm alright you go and rest up. It's almost dark and then we will need two pairs of eyes.'

'Well if you're sure . . . . Tilley interrupted her saying: 'Wait a minute, what is that? Look over there—yes it's a car.'

Tilley strained her eyes and saw that it was a blue car coming from the east. She bobbed down and said to Joanne: "It's the yank's that's the car we crashed into". Tilley popped her head up again and kept an eye on the car as it stopped outside the warehouse. She saw Franks and Brice get out of the car, she heard Franks yell out: 'WHAT THE HELL? THE DOOR'S ARE OPEN.' Tilley and Joanne kept down low as Franks and Brice ran over to the open door, Franks lost no time balling Brice out: 'You idiot, you called me for allowing them to get out, what have you to say now, eh? You said you had taken care of them and we wouldn't give us any more trouble, I've a good mind to break your jaw.' As he raised his right arm they heard the sound of engines coming from the side of the building. Running to peer around the corner they saw to their horror the Police vehicles that were just entering the field.

George and Mike who were in the first car jumped out and directed the others into the field. Tilley heard them and looked up warily, she saw the two yanks were creeping back to their car and without thinking stood up and began screaming: "OVER HERE, OVER HERE IT'S THE YANKS". George just about heard her and looked over to where the shout came from and saw Tilley standing up waving her arms around frantically pointing at the yanks but by then they were almost at their car. 'Come on.' George yelled at Mike and they jumped back into their car, George signalled with his hand for the ART to go on ahead and everyone else followed.

In his panic Brice slipped and fell just as he was about to reach the car, Franks ignored him jumping in the car and starting the engine as the ART vehicle skidded to a halt. The officers clambered out and some ran over to the car but Franks managed to drive off. The rest of the team went after Brice he ran into the warehouse and tried to close the damaged doors but couldn't, so he grabbed a lump of wood and attempted in vain to fend the officers off and was soon overpowered.

Tilley meanwhile had ran down the hill and reached a bend in a part of the road that Franks had to take, she picked up a large boulder intending to lob it at the windscreen as the car reached her hoping to force Franks to stop, as he appeared around the bend however, in her haste and with the boulder being heavy Tilley fell forward rolling into the car's path. Franks jammed on his brakes and before she could recover he leapt out and grabbed her from behind, dragged her to the car and bungled her into the boot.

George had driven after Franks and was about twenty yards behind him, Franks pulled out his gun and fired at them, one bullet shattered the windscreen forcing George to swerve and plough into a metal post, luckily neither officers were injured.

Franks got back in his car and screeched off, the Sergeant in charge of the ART ordered some officers back into the van and sped off after Franks but it soon became obvious he was out of sight and could have taken various tracks back to the main road, so they were forced to abandon the chase and return to where George and Mike were being helped out of their car by two uniformed officers

George recovered and put out an all point Broadcast on Franks and his car informing that he had a hostage. He had caught a part of the number plate which he reported as well as the make and colour.

Leaving the stricken car George, mike and everyone else made their way back to the warehouse. Brice was sitting in a car handcuffed and guarded by two officers Len and Joanne were sitting in another car exhausted, Joanne asked the detective's: 'Where is Tilley? I saw her rundown the hill but then I lost sight of her.'

'Unfortunately she was recaptured by Franks.' Mike told her. Joanne put her hands to her mouth in horror on hearing that. George went over to Brice and formally arrested him after reading him his rights. As Brice turned to walk away he yelled: 'Do you know what you have done? You dumb Limey cop, you have really stuffed up.' George ignored him and thanked all of his men telling them to get back into their vehicles and return to the station. George and Mike however had to go back in one of the other vehicles, Mike remarked on their way back: 'Tilley eh? She maybe a little foolish but we probably wouldn't have caught either of them if not for her. You don't think he will harm her though do you George?'

'No I don't think so she is a good bargaining point for him, but then again you just don't know, he is a hot head. What do you think Brice meant when he said? "Knowing what we have done?"

'No idea George, just hot air probably.'

CHAPTER EIGHTEEN

Franks drove until he was sure the Police were shaken off and found a quiet place to pull over. Tilley had continuously banged on the boot lid screaming and shouting from the moment she was bundled into it.

Franks opened the boot and Tilley immediately attempted to get out but he was ready for her and pushed her back, holding her down, he pulled his gun out and held it against her head warning her: 'You make one more sound and I will not hesitate to pull the trigger, you three limeys have just used up all my patience, now shut up, keep still and you may survive.'

Even Tilley with all her bravery knew not to push him in that mood so she just nodded her head. Franks found some rags in the boot and tied her hands and feet together and gagged her, he then shut the boot lid and drove on to his hotel he knew he couldn't take Tilley in with him but he had to retrieve his and Brice's belongings. As he turned into the street though he saw two Police car's outside the hotel.

Unbeknown to Franks the owner of the hotel had called the Police because he recognised Brice earlier as they left to head for the warehouse, he and his wife had been on holiday for three weeks and not seen an English newspaper until they came home the day before. The Police had already questioned the relief manager as to why he didn't recognised the Americans, he explained that he hardly ever watched television or read newspapers, he preferred reading books.

To avoid being seen Franks reversed around a corner and quickly left the area. He headed out into the country in the opposite direction of the warehouse in case the Police were still searching the area.

After driving for a half hour or so he came across an old derelict cottage which was semi demolished through age and decided to hold up there for the night. He got out and opened the boot and roughly heaved Tilley out, in doing so Tilley's arm scraped along the edge of the boot lid grazing it as well as hitting her head, cutting her above the left eyebrow.

Brice carried her into the only room that had a ceiling of any kind and laid her on her side and removed her gag, he put his finger to her lips warning her: 'Remember what I told not a sound.'

'I promise but can I have some water, there's a bottle in the boot I saw it when you dumped me in there.'

'It's all me with you Brit's well you will have to wait, I have more important things to worry about.' He knew that the Police would be going through his and Brice's hotel rooms and would find undeniable evidence which pointed directly to them as being the murderers. This would include phials of the sedative used to subdue the Johnson's".

Franks growled at Tilley: 'You and your dumb limey pales have really stuffed up our operation, two or three more days and we would have finished our business but you couldn't resist being heroes could you?

Franks went out to the car and brought the water in, he opened the bottle in front of Tilley's face and offered it up to her lips, she leaned forward to take a sip but he snatched the bottle away taking a large gulp himself. "You are a mean filthy pig". She howled at him and started crying, between sobs she told him: 'I hope you get caught and rot in prison.'

'Oh you do, do yah? Well in that case you won't want to drink out of the same bottle as a filthy pig.' He tipped the bottle and let the water start to trickle out. Tilley soon realised her mistake and begged him: 'No please, I'm sorry, I'm so frightened and worried about my mum and dad, please give me some water? I won't mouth off again.'

Franks grunted: 'Just shut up and get some sleep I have to think what to do next.'

Back at the Police station Brice went through the booking in procedure and was then taken to an interview room by two Constables. One Constable removed the handcuffs and told him to sit down he then pulled Brice's arms around the back of the chair and replaced the cuffs.

Brice had to wait while George Carter and Mike Harper prepared to interview him informally, when the two Detectives eventually entered the room Brice growled: 'It's about time. If you think leaving me here on my own was going to intimidate me then think again it's been tried before by tougher cookies than you and they didn't break me so go on do your worst.'

George and Mike ignored Brice they just looked at each other and grinned. George then began: 'Ok Mr Brice, or shall I call you Angelo? We just want to ask you some questions, where's the intimidation in that?'

'Very funny, well I am not answering any questions without a lawyer.'

Ok but when we booked you in you kept shouting that you were innocent and that you had done nothing so why would you need a lawyer? Anyway we just want to clear up a few points but we will not be recording our little chat, I would advise you though if you're cooperative it would go in your favour.'

'If you're not recording then how do I know if I am cooperative, you will keep your word?'

'You don't you will just have to trust us.'

'Yeah, do I look I was born yesterday? I want it taped.'

'So be it.'

Mike looked at George and grinned at George's crafty tactics. George asked Mike to start the tape. Once the tape was started George asked: 'Are you Angelo Mieko Brice, alias David Miles Wilson?' Brice just said: 'No comment.'

'Are you an acquaintance of John Michael Franks?'

'No comment.'

'I thought you were going to cooperative but it seems I was wrong . . . . Turn the tape off Mike it appears our friend here wants the full force of the law thrown at him.'

Mike moved to switch the recorder off but Brice relented and blurted out: 'Ok Ok ask your damned questions.' George said: 'That's more like it, now once again, are you Angelo Mieko Brice . . . . before George could finish Brice cut in: 'Yeah yeah I am and the alias.'

'Do you know John Michael Franks and with his help murder: Mrs Johnson on the ninth of October and Mr Johnson her husband approximately three days later, then dispose of their bodies?'

'No I didn't murder anyone, Franks did both of them, I helped get rid of the bodies but that was all.'

'That was all? You do realise that is enough on its own to send you down for life as an accomplice conspiring in two murders, then there's the kidnapping's and you have been identified by one of the victims as being one of the abductors.'

'Ok yes but I'm not saying anymore without a lawyer.'

'Fine, stop the tape mike.' George told the two constables to take Brice to a holding cell then went back to his office and called a duty Solicitor.

From the warehouse Joanne was taken to the Police station and Len was taken to hospital.

While George was supervising Brice's booking in Mike took Joanne to a warm room and arranged for a hot cup of tea and some sandwiches. Mike asked her if she was alright and did she wish to see a doctor before he debriefed her, she answered: 'No dear I'm fine, I've survived two world wars so I'm sure I can get over this.'

'Well I must say you and Miss Watson seems to have given your captors a run for their money.'

'Thanks to Tilley, how is she? Did she get away from that Brute?'

'It doesn't look like it I'm afraid, unfortunately he has given us the slip for the moment but there will be a full blown manhunt out looking for him soon but, we have found where they were holding up, the place is being searched at this moment.'

'Good show, I am sure she will be ok, she is very strong willed, we wouldn't have escaped without her she is a clever little minx.'

'She sure is, now Mrs Perkins.'

'Oh Joanne please?'

'Ok Joanne, do you think you can identify your kidnappers?'

'Well I didn't know at the time but I found out later that Brice was in the back of the car, he put a rag or something over my mouth and nose, there must have been chloroform or something on it. The other one was Len he pretended to be a Policeman and lured me out to the car in fact it was Len who told me it was Brice in the car. He was tricked by those yanks by offering him a big reward if he got them a vehicle. He did help to get us out though, that's how he got his bad leg and head.'

'I was going to ask about his injuries, what happened?'

'He was fed up with the way they treated him he and tried to run off but that Franks threw a crate lid at him and he fell down the stairs hitting his head. His leg was injured when he crashed into Brice's car with the camper van. Don't be too hard on him.'

'We'll do our best, thanks Mrs Perkins . . . . sorry Joanne I will arrange a car to take you home.'

'Have you told Tilley's mum and dad? She was so worried about them.'

'That is my next move Joanne now you go home and have a nice long sleep, we'll talk again soon.'

'I will young man and thank you for coming so quickly to find us.'

Mike saw Mrs Perkins to the door and a Constable escorted her to an unmarked car. Mike returned to his office and telephoned Tilley's parents, Joyce answered and Mike said: 'Hello Mrs Watson its detective Inspector Harper is Mr Watson there?'

'No he has popped out, is there news of Tilley? Please tell me she's alright.'

'I have got some news yes but, wouldn't you rather your husband was with you?'

No! 'Tell me please?'

'As you wish, well earlier today Tilley and two others managed to escape from where they were being held. Two young boys happened across them accidently and aided in their escape. They turned up at the station and directed us to where they were hiding. Unfortunately the yanks appeared just before we arrived. When we did get there Tilley called out pointing at the yanks but the one called Franks managed to get into his car and drive off.'

'What about Tilley, where is she.'

'Well typically she tried to stop Franks but she fell over and he stopped bungled her into the car and got away.'

'Why is she so intent on putting herself in danger like this? I just don't know where she gets it from, I really don't. Thank you for letting us know detective, please call as soon as you have any news at all? How are the others did they harm them in any way?'

'The young man has a broken leg and head wound but they came from an earlier escape attempt which failed. Mrs Perkins is fine though apart from being very tired and thirsty and Tilley was ok but I don't know whether she was hurt when she fell.'

'Who is this young man? I thought it was only Tilley and the landlady that was kidnapped.'

'Yes it was, he helped in the kidnaps but came down on the side of the girls and was injured for his efforts.'

'Oh dear this is such a dreadful business, when Tilley comes back home I will be insisting that she lives a boring life in future.'

'Yes well good luck with that Madam rather you than me.'

'I know what you mean but I couldn't take another upset like this.'

'I'm sure Mrs Watson, I'm just sorry I couldn't bring you any better news but I am certain we will find her soon. We have a manhunt in progress and we have located where the two yanks were held up, so keep your fingers crossed and we will be in touch with better news soon I'm sure.'

Mike hung up and went to find George who was on his way to his own office, they met in the corridor and Mike told him he had informed Tilley's mother and of what Joanne Perkins had told him. Mike asked George what he intended doing with Jenkins. George told him: 'I haven't decided yet I will wait until I find out what that office played in all this, by the way Mike a solicitor has arrived and is with Brice at this moment so hopefully we can formally interview him soon.'

'Good I hope he will be more cooperative his time.'

It was about an hour or so before George received confirmation that the solicitor had finished talking to Brice and he was ready to be formally interviewed.

Brice was taken to an interview room accompanied by his solicitor and two Police officers, George and Mike followed soon after. When everyone was ready Mike switched on the tape and announced: "Formal interview of Angelo Mieko Brice. The date is Saturday the twenty third of October and time is ten minutes past midnight. Present are Detective Chief Inspector Carter and Detective Inspector Harper. Also present is Mr Brice's solicitor Andrew Brown". When Mike had completed the announcement George began: 'Ok, for the tape, is your name Angelo Mieko Brice?'

'Yes.'

'What is your date of birth?'

'July tenth nineteen forty.'

'Mr Brice, you have been arrested and detained in connection with the murders of Mr and Mrs Johnson and the Kidnappings of Miss Tilley Watson and Mrs Joanne Perkins. What have you to say in your defence?'

'I've murdered nobody Franks did them but I did help in dumping the bodies and the kidnappings.'

'Why was that couple murdered?'

'We don't know the where or why's, we just follow orders.'

'Ok who gave you your orders?'

'I don't know either we are contacted by our source, he gets the orders and contacts us.'

'Who is your source and where is he?' Brice's solicitor butted in to ask how his client would benefit from his cooperation. George assured him Brice could get a lighter sentence if his information led to finding and the arrest of Franks and the safe return of Tilley.

The solicitor whispered to Brice advising he cooperate fully. George continued: 'I repeat who is your source and where can we find him?'

'He owns a bar just outside the rail depot, we never know names he just calls us or we call him, the bar is called: "The Junction". George looked at Mike at hearing this and he acknowledged George with a nod. George continued: 'Ok Mr Brice—can I call you Angelo?'

'Knock yourself out.'

'Ok Angelo, you are doing fine, now what can you tell me about Shane Rickard, what is his involvement in all this?'

'Oh him, he was just too greedy for his own good, he couldn't wait to get his sweaty hands on the dough so he, he found the dump sites and stowed some gear for us.'

'So he had no physical contact with or knowledge of the bodies?'

'No.'

'What about the office, what was that all about?'

'That was just to give you limey cops something to think about to keep you off our backs to give us time to finish what we had to do. It didn't work so we pulled out.'

'Among the gear that Rickard "stowed" for you we found wallets and a woman's purse as well as credit cards along with a large sum of cash. Where did that all come from?'

'We only gave him one wallet and some credit cards to hold, the wallet was the dead guys and the credit cards we lifted at the airport, accept for one and that was mine. We were going to use the cards for any expenses so they couldn't be traced back to us but they were all but maxed out so we had to use mine. He must have lifted the other wallets and purse himself. I assume the cash was the bung we gave him.'

'Did Rickard find the warehouse the women were held at, and why were they taken?'

No! 'Fisher found that for us and he "borrowed" the car we used to take the women. We took them because they knew too much and we needed to take them out of the game before they stuffed the whole thing up for us, we need not have bothered though, they did that anyway.

The bar owner told us where to find the young one because he took her home one morning after she got stewed in his bar.'

'Now you have mentioned "your business" what is your "business"? We know that the dead couple were witnesses to a shooting in New York and were in witness protection. How did you find them and why kill them after the shooters were found and jailed? There seems to no logic in that at all.'

'As I said earlier we only follow orders, we were just told where to go and what to do.'

'Ok, finally we have found your last hide out so Franks won't be going back there, where will he go?' Brice shrugged his shoulders and said: No idea! 'We don't know much about this God forsaken place he does has an area chart in his car though so he will probably get that young broad to read it for him.'

'Ok Angelo we will call it that for now, you will be taken back to your cell but we will talk again soon.'

Brice was helped to his feet by the Constables but as he was taken away he called out to George: 'Don't forget I was Cooperative.'

Mike and George stayed in the room and discussed the interview, Mike said: 'Well that was very interesting, he sung like the proverbial canary.'

'That's for sure, we now know that office is worth no more interest but we need to put twenty four seven surveillance on the junction, Franks could be heading there, set that up now will you please Mike? I will arrange for Jenkins to be released on bail.'

'Right away George, I'll put two men in an unmarked car on for hour shifts.'

'Thanks Mike, I think we have earned a rest, go home after you have done that, I think we are in for a busy time from now on.'

'Thanks George that's one order I will enjoy obeying.'

CHAPTER NINETEEN

At the first light of dawn Franks who had not slept at all went and shook Tilley. She immediately reacted: 'Don't worry I'm awake, you don't think I could sleep in this cold damp hole do you?'

'That makes two of us lady all I have thought about is what I do next. If I don't finish this job then I'm a dead man and if I do there's still no guarantee I will live anyway.'

'What is your job?'

'I don't know, I will have to find my contact, they may cancel it though with Brice in the hole, he is sure to sing at the top of his voice to save his skin. If they do go ahead it will not be easy to complete with you in tow. I don't know maybe I should just run while I've got the chance.'

'Why not just let me go? At least you could move faster without holding you back, maybe I could give you directions if you tell me where you need to be.'

'Maybe, look I will go and find some breakfast then I will decide.'

Franks drove off and Tilley immediately attempted to loosen her ties. She sat upright and pushed her hands against the stone wall and began rubbing them up and down, before she could get anywhere though Franks came back, he was panicking and said: 'There are cops everywhere, we have to leave the car here and go across country. You know this area, which way is the rail depot?' Tilley didn't answer she just asked: 'Where's breakfast?'

BREAKFAST! 'You didn't expect me to look for breakfast with cops swarming all over the place did you? Look we have to go across country I need you to take me to the rail depot, we will have to eat later.'

'Ok I'll try although I'm not sure where we are but, I know the train station is in the west.'

'There's an area chart in the car.' Franks told her.

'Ok untie me and let me see the map.'

'Very clever, I untie you and you run at the first opportunity.'

'Alright don't panic you only have to untie my hands so I can hold the map.' Franks untied her hands and shoved the map at her, she studied it for a while and looked at the sky and saw the sun was coming up behind them, pointing she said: 'That way I think.' She was pointing straight ahead, Franks snatched the map from her and retied her hands, he warned her: 'YOU had better be right, I'm in a no win situation so I will not hesitate to see to you if you cross me.'

'I told you I only think that is the right way I'm no geography expert.'

'Well we will soon find out, I am untying your legs but I am putting a tie around your waist so don't get any fancy ideas, before I do though I have to take care of the car.'

Franks unscrewed the petrol cap and fed a long piece of rag into the tank soaking it with petrol. Before he removed it he went to the rear of the car and broke off a bushy piece of a shrub and used it as a brush to wipe away the footprints and tyre marks in the dirt, he then returned to the car removing the rag from the tank. He trickled petrol over the inside of the car and fed the rag back into the tank then pulled it out just far enough to light it, he lit a match and ignited the end of the rag.

Franks ran over to Tilley and roughly pulled her away into some long grass, as he did the car burst into flames and almost immediately exploded. Franks then attached a longer rag to Tilley's waist and pulled her to her feet and led her in the direction she suggested, with one more look at the car to see that it was burning to his satisfaction they set off through the shrubbery to find their way to the train station.

It took two hours but eventually Tilley and Franks came to an open area with a road running adjacent to it. They didn't need to go that way but Tilley was cunningly attempting to get Franks out in the open, hoping there would be people around and give her a chance to draw attention to her plight. Franks fell for the plan for a while but he saw her desperately looking around and realised her ploy.

Very Good! He grunted at her and yanked at the rag around her waist pulling her back into the cover of the shrubbery. Tilley said: 'I'm sorry you can't blame a girl for trying though can you? Anyway tell me, why are you so keen to reach the train station? I mean are you running? Because if you are why drag me along? As I said before you would move a lot faster without me'

'I aint running I need to see my contact and you're going to get me there, then I will decide your fate, now where do we go?'

'Well we have to go through those trees ahead and that should lead us to the goods yard at the other side of the station, its quiet there and we should be able to get through the goods yard to the platform.'

'I don't need the platform I need to get outside to the pub as you limey's call it.'

'What the Junction? I know that place, I have a friend there.'

'Oh you do, do Yah? Well I know someone there too and he is going to help me decide my next move.'

'You do know that if you take me in there I will be recognised and you're finished don't you?'

'I'll just have to take that chance, won't I? Now shut up and get walking.'

Fifteen minutes later they reached the goods yard. Tilley pointed the way and Franks pulled her to him and said: 'I am untying you but don't get any ideas, I have my gun pointing at you from inside my pocket.' She could clearly see the outline of the gun and was scared as she guided Franks through the goods yard. It was Saturday and Tilley knew the station would be quiet, she told Franks this then said: 'It will be easier to go through to the platform then we can walk out through the exit. The pub will be closed though and you won't get in yet, Can't we get some breakfast? The station cafe is open and I promise I won't make any trouble. Please? I am starving and thirsty.'

'Don't bother your pretty little head about the place being closed, now come on and quit stalling we will have some food soon, you'll see.'

Tilley was puzzled but went along with Franks as she was quickly running out of resistance and the image of the gun was permanently stamped on her mind.

They reached the pub and Franks took the lead, he guided Tilley to the side of the pub and they reached the yard at the rear. He pushed Tilley up the five steps to a rear door on which Franks commenced banging with his fist. Tilley couldn't resist asking: 'What are you doing? My friend Simon owns this pub he'll know about you and Brice, he'll shop you.'

She had only just finished speaking when the door opened and Simon poked his head out, he gasped at seeing the two of them together, he babbled: 'What the hell are you doing? She knows me you've done for us all.'

'Shut your mouth and let us in, we have some thinking to do.' Simon opened the door and ushered them in looking around making sure no one had seen them. He went in and slammed and locked the door and immediately questioned Franks: 'Why in God's name have you come here?' He turned to Tilley who was looking absolutely shocked and said: 'I'm so sorry Tilley. I can't understand how you have ended up here with him.'

Tilley was crying she choked back the tears and said: 'I can't believe you are mixed up in all this, you seemed like a lovely fellow.' Simon put his hand on her arm but she pulled away saying: 'Get off me you traitor.'

Franks said sarcastically: 'Ok you love birds when you have finished, I suppose you know Brice is in jail due to your sweetheart here, the old woman and Fisher are probably blabbing to the cops right now as well.'

'No I don't, how has all this happened? I thought you had them well hidden . . . . Tilley butted in sobbing: 'Yeah but they didn't reckon on our guts, it takes better men than them to hold us down.' Franks went to hit Tilley with the back of his hand but Simon grabbed it and twisted it behind him. Franks protested: 'Ok let go she aint worth it, she's dead now anyway.'

'Oh no she isn't, she will stay here until you finish the job.'

'Have you lost your mind, or are you going to get your hands dirty and earn your keep?'

'I have been doing and here is your last job, the Minister's son is giving a speech at a college in Parkview tomorrow afternoon. It is at the end of a private drive with only one way in and out. You have to take him out, I will drive you there and I have a high powered rifle so all you have to do is find a good spot and when he gets out of his car finish it, then you can get out and go home and so can Tilley.'

'You have lost your mind she can identify us you dumb limey, no she has to go too.'

'I can identify you as well does that mean I am going to die?'

No! 'Unfortunately I need you to get me out of this hellhole, otherwise yes you would.'

'Well you have two options then, you leave Tilley to me or you can go now and take your chances with the Police but you won't get far though without my help.'

'You don't leave me much choice then do you, go on keep your little sweetheart I hope you will be very happy together.'

Simon left the bar, Franks was still holding the rag which was tied to Tilley, he proceeded to tie her to a chair as Simon came back with a coffee pot, he told Franks: 'There's no need for that I will take her upstairs and lock her in a guest room.' Franks replied: 'Oh yeah why not, she can jump out of a window then we will all be finished.'

No she can't! 'I have a room right at the top in the attic and it is a long drop from there, so there's no problem.'

'Well then it's on your head, take her out of my sight I've had as much as I can take of her.'

'And her of you too no doubt and I can't blame her, now have some coffee and after I've taken her upstairs I will cook some breakfast.'

As Simon was taken Tilley up to the room he tried to apologise to her again but she ignored him so he stopped her with both hands on her shoulders and said: 'Now look Tilley I can understand you hating me, I hate myself but I am not a bad guy, I was forced to help them because when I was in the states I got drunk and knocked down and killed a woman with my car and foolishly drove off. As luck would have Brice witnessed it and followed me, he blackmailed me into helping them and I had no way out. Trust me Tilley and somehow I am going to let you escape tonight and you can go to the Police and stop the shooting tomorrow and get him arrested.'

'Oh Simon I knew you weren't bad, I'm so sorry for all the things I said to you.'

'You had every right, I betrayed you, I should have been a man and told them to go to hell.'

Simon showed her to her room and told her: 'Stay here tonight, I will bring you some food up shortly but in the meantime why don't you have a shower and freshen yourself up, there's an on suite bathroom in the room and there is a robe on the back of the bathroom door and I will fetch some clean towels.'

Simon made sure Tilley had everything she needed then he went downstairs, Franks said in his customary sarcastic way: "Girlie all nice and comfy then is she?'

'Shut it Franks you are heading for a big fall.'

'Not by your hand limey, go and get that food and stop whining.' Simon was seething but managed to keep his cool and bit the bullet, he went into the kitchen and slammed the door, he knew he only had to suffer Franks for a little longer and then he and Tilley would be free of him and Brice for good.

CHAPTER TWENTY

Later that afternoon Franks had gone to a guest room for a sleep, this gave Simon a chance to creep up to Tilley and tell her his plan. He told her: 'As you heard the last target for Brice and Franks is giving a speech to some law students of all people tomorrow. I am supposed to arrange for Franks to kill him and then arrange his flight home but, I'm sick of the worry because I had no idea at first they were involved in murder and I am devastated that you have been caught up in it all. Now here is the key to this door, wait until Franks and I are in bed and then creep down the stairs. There is a door that takes you out to the side ally and I will leave it unlocked. Once out into the road turn right towards the station and there is a phone box, call the Police from there and when they arrive give them this, it's a map with the collage circled. He should arrive about two thirty, I was supposed to get Franks there before that so he could get in a good position, I'll take him and I will do what I can to give the Police an idea of where he is.' Tilley asked: 'How about you though Simon? You are going to get caught as well.'

'I know that Tilley and I don't care anymore I just want you safe and for this all to be over.'

'That is so brave but, don't worry I will tell them how much you have helped, I am sure you will get a light sentence.'

'Well whatever the sentence it can't be as bad as what I have been carrying around with me all these years. Thanks for your concern but I don't deserve it, now get some sleep and I will bring you some coffee and sandwiches later.'

Tilley lay on her bed and it wasn't long before she dropped off to sleep. She was in a deep sleep when Simon knocked the door, he called out: 'It's me Simon, are you decent?' Tilley assured him that she was and opened the door. Simon brought in a tray of coffee and some sandwiches. He sat for a few minutes then said: 'Franks and I are going to bed in a minute, give us an hour or so then slip out.' He put his arm around her adding: 'Be careful I don't want you getting hurt. I like you Tilley I just wish we could have met under different circumstances, I would like to think that you and I could get together if and when I get out of prison.'

'Oh don't Simon, I am welling up here but yes I think I would like that too, now go before you see me in tears.'

Tilley ate her sandwiches and after drinking the coffee she put her clothes on and prepared herself for the scariest part of her adventure. She knew that if Franks discovered her, herself and Simon would almost certainly be killed.

She waited until she was sure it was safe and unlocked the door. She crept down the stairs and went out into the ally. The Police surveillance car was parked about twenty yards away but Tilley couldn't see that as it was parked in the shadows. DCI Carter and a DC were in the car and the DC spotted Tilley. He sat bolt upright and spouted out: 'Hey Gove someone has just come out from the ally beside the pub.' He pointed to Tilley and George said: 'I think that's a woman, come on let's go.' They quietly got out of the car and quickly but cautiously closed in on the figure. Tilley had just reached the phone box and was about to lift the receiver when the door was wrenched open, Tilley thinking that Franks had caught her screamed and cowered down covering her head with her arm. It was then that George recognised Tilley and said. 'Miss Watson is that you?' Tilley couldn't believe what she heard and said stuttering: 'Y-Y-Yes, who? Oh it's you detective, oh my God, how did you find me?'

'Well technically we didn't, look forget that for now, how are you, are you hurt?'

'No only my pride, why are you her though?'

'We have had a watch on the Junction ever since Brice gave your friend Simon up, I'm sorry he has let you down, I know you liked him.'

'None of this is his fault though . . . . She was about to enlighten George to the circumstances surrounding Simon's involvement when he stopped saying: 'Hang on Tilley let's get you away from here before someone sees us.'

George and the DC walked Tilley to their car, as soon as they were at the car Tilley immediately continued her defence of Simon, she then said: 'Look Franks is in there and he has a gun.'

'Right we had better get some back up. Now tell me Tilley, what exactly is the situation in there?' Tilley told George about the plot to kill the Minister's son and Simon's plan for the Police to catch Franks before he carried out the shooting. George said: 'Well it does look like he is trying to make up for his involvement but I don't think we need to wait until this afternoon we can finish this here and now, it should be easy to take them by surprise. Please excuse me Tilley I must contact control.'

George called control and announced: 'I need a team of armed response officers immediately at the Junction pub in Fairview, no sirens or lights. Please alert DI Harper that Tilley Watson is safe and under our protection. Request that he notifies Miss Watson's parents and then tell him to attend here ASAP.' Control responded instantly to George's call and carried out his instructions.

When Mike Harper called Tilley's parents, Mr Watson answered: 'Hello who is it?'

'Hello Mr Watson sorry to disturb you at this hour . . . . Mike couldn't finish his sentence before Bob butted in: 'Why are calling? Is it Tilley, is she alright?'

'She's fine sir we have her.' Joyce was halfway down the stairs and Bob relayed the news to her. She ran down the last few stairs and grabbed Bob's arm uttering: 'How is she, tell me she's alright?'

'She's alright love, she's alright.' Mike explained where she was and that she would soon be taken to the station. Bob thanked Mike for the news and asked: 'When can we see her?'

'Very soon there is a car on its way now to collect her. I can also tell you we are hopefully about to detain John Franks and Simon so this nightmare should soon be over and your Tilley has played a vital role, she is some brave girl.'

'Well that's not the words my wife and I would use exactly but thank you anyway detective, thank you.'

'Ok Mr Watson I had better go, you and your wife have some celebrating to do, Goodnight and relax its all over.'

Mike hung up and went down and called for a uniformed officer to accompany him then he drove off following the armed response wagon.

George had radioed the Sergeant in charge telling him to watch for a torch light flashing, saying: 'As soon as you see that turn off your lights and stop where you are.

The van arrived and George went and spoke to the Sergeant: 'We have an armed man in that pub.' George pointed then continued: 'I want the building surrounded in silence, I will need two men to accompany DI Harper and I he is on his way, I will also require two pistols, two helmets and flak jackets.'

A few minutes late George spotted headlights in the distance, he announced to the Sergeant: 'This is probably the Di now but be on guard in case it's not.' The Sergeant called his men to conceal themselves in the bushes and shadows and watched the car, telling them to move only when ordered.

Mike spotted the van and pulled up behind it. George seeing that it was Mike called the officers to "stand down". Mike approached George and said: 'Ready to shoot me eh George? I don't want your job that bad, he joked.' When the Constable got out Mike told George that he was there to take Tilley to the station. George went over to tell Tilley but she protested: NO! 'I'm staying here until I know Simon is safe.'

'I know how you feel Tilley but I cannot put you in danger, it's more than my job's worth, you go back with the Constable, your parents know you are safe and they are anxious to see you. Before you go though can you give me the layout inside and where the two men are sleeping?'

'Ok I only know where Simon's room is though I didn't see Franks after Simon took me upstairs.' George told Tilley not to worry and after she gave him the layout she reluctantly went with the Constable and he drove her off back to the station.

George Carter did a radio check with all the attending officers then asked The Sergeant to get his men in position.

George and Mike slipped into their bullet proof vests and put their helmets on. After checking their pistols they put on night vision goggles and slowly approached the Junction with the two ART officers.

They eventually reached the path leading to the side entrance and then the side door. George quietly opened the door and listened, hearing nothing he signalled for the two officers to go ahead and they all slowly climbed the stairs to the room where Tilley had told him Simon was sleeping. George put his fingers to his lips and turned to the officers holding his hands out with the palms flat towards them. They acknowledged the sign and stopped where they were. George reached out gripping the door knob gently and turned it. The door opened and when it was opened wide enough he stepped inside gingerly looking around. He spotted Simon who was sitting up in his bed staring at the door it was obvious he was petrified. George pointed his gun at Simon and beckoned him with his finger to join him. Simon relieved that it was not Franks climbed out of bed and crept over to George. Mike whispered to Simon: 'What room is Franks in?'

'The room right at the end on the left.' Simon whispered then continued: 'Be careful though there is a fire escape door in that room on the west wall.' George whispered to mike: 'Put handcuffs on him and take him down, get one of the ART men to take him to a car then send two others to cover the fire escape.'

Mike carried out George's orders and was soon back upstairs. They all crept quietly along the passageway towards Frank's room. Standing at the left hand side of the door George signalled Mike to take the right side. George signalled to two officers to open the door slowly and they entered the room looking around with the aid of the night vision goggles but there was no sign of Franks. George and mike followed them in and they checked the room, one of the officers then noticed a light coming from under the door to the en-suite bathroom. They waited until the heard the flushing of the cistern then George and Mike stood on either side of the door with the ART officers standing about ten feet away facing the door with their search lamps ready.

As Franks opened the door and stepped into the room the officers switched on their lamps blinding him and shouted: "ARMED POLICE, STAY WHERE YOU ARE". This gave Mike and George time to grab each of his arms and force him to the floor. The ART officers immediately swooped on Franks and handcuffed him.

It happened so fast Franks couldn't react verbally or otherwise however when he did recover he struggled violently calling them all foul names and swearing revenge. Needless to say he was ignored and read his rights.

Franks was eventually taken downstairs out into the damp early morning air and frogmarched to the ART van and left guarded by two armed officers.

'That went smoother than I anticipated. George remarked to Mike. He continued: 'I think we've cracked it, don't you?'

'I do hope you're right George, if I spend any more time away from my apartment I won't be able to open the door for all the junk mail, what about this minister character though how are we with him?'

'I'll have to contact the Assistant Chief Commissioner and let them deal with him as he is wanted in the states for his drug dealing there and we will obviously want him to answer for his dealings with the murders here as well. I think we will let the powers to be play tug of wall with him. I hope we can keep him over here though but, it would be just like the yanks to let us do the dirty work and then take all the glory. Ok Mike call control and get SOCCO and Forensics here, I want this place turned inside out. ok let's get these two back to the unit, if there's any space left for them that is, if there wasn't after the run around this lot has given us, I would lock them in my garage.' Mike laughed saying: 'Sure George I'm on it.' George said as an afterthought: 'You take Simon in my car and I'll go back with Franks in the ART vehicle.'

As Mike took Simon out of the van he told George: 'Watch out for that yank, he is losing it.' George replied: 'Well I can assure he's already lost it—his freedom that is.'

CHAPTER TWENTY ONE

It was three fifteen am when Tilley and the constable arrived at the Police station. The PC showed Tilley to a warm room and offered her a hot drink. She answered: 'Oh yes please, I would love a hot chocolate, I would also like to use the bathroom so I could freshen myself up, I must look a mess.'

'If you don't mind me saying so miss, I think you look very nice especially after what you have gone through.'

'My you are a flatterer I will have to keep an eye on you, seriously though you are very kind thank you, now where is the ladies?'

'Oh yes sorry miss, come I will show you.'

Meanwhile Franks had arrived at the station and was marched straight to the booking in desk. Two armed officers guarded him and when the process was completed he was taken to a holding cell.

George and Mike however headed for the canteen for a hot drink and to take in all that had happened in the last twenty four hours. Phew! Mike exclaimed as he sat down with a black coffee. 'I wouldn't say no to a double scotch in this.'

'Oh yes me too, I can't believe I will actually be sleeping in my bed tonight, that's if the Missus hasn't changed the locks. Still you have a spare room Mike so you may have a lodger.'

'I don't think you could afford the rent George.' Nothing more was said for a while, then Mike said: 'Well George I reckon everyone in this station deserves a little appreciation for this outcome, don't you think?'

'I do Mike and I will make sure they get it, I must admit though I was tempted to ask for some support a couple of times lately.'

'Well we had it, and Tilley Watson is her name.'

'That's for sure she is definitely a force to be reckoned with, speaking of which I think we ought to go and reunite her with her parents before we debrief her, then she can go home, she has some washing up to do.' Mike laughed heartedly it was obvious they were relieved the whole matter was over with.

Tilley returned from the ladies and the constable went and fetched her hot chocolate. She had just about finished drinking it when Mike came in and said: 'Well miss, sorry Tilley, it's all over, your parents are downstairs waiting for you but first I would like to thank you on behalf of everybody here for all your resilience and assistance. I'm not saying we encourage the public getting involved like you but I can honestly say we would not have caught those yanks without your help. I am also sure that we would not have given that place you saw Rickard on that fatal Friday morning, a second look. It was only because of your insistence that we did, and the sweet wrappers found there was a big lead to Rickard's arrest. I would like to be the first to shake your hand in thanks then I will take you to your parents.

Meanwhile George went to his office and called Tilley's boss, James Cooper's, there was no answer so he left a message giving him the good news. He then met Mr and Mrs Watson and escorted them to a visitor's room to wait for Tilley.

Ten minutes later Tilley was taken to the room, Mike left her outside the door and Tilley opened the door gingerly not knowing what mood her parents were in and what they were going to say, she need not have worried, they rushed over and threw both of their arms around her almost smothering her, she said in a muffled voice: 'Ok Ok let a girl breath.' They pulled away and after wiping tears away from their faces they took her by the hands and they all sat down. It was then that they bombarded her with the whys and what ifs. She told them that she was sorry for all the worry and upset they had endured then said: 'I am still sure I did the right thing, DI Harper said that it was almost entirely my help that Franks and Brice were caught and to Rickard's arrest.' Her mum responded saying: 'That is all well and good but you have to promise us you will never ever put us through anything like this again. We don't need his worry at our age.'

'Oh mum—dad I would never deliberately put myself in that situation, unfortunately things just escalated but, yes I do promise I will stay in and live a boring life from now on, anyway I think I've had enough excitement for a while.'

'I should think so my girl, now DCI Carter wants to talk to you so we are going to have a cup or tea, when you are finished you are coming home with us and having a nice long bath then I will cook you a big breakfast, I bet you haven't had much to eat for quite a while.'

'You must be joking, we had a banquet every night, that's why we had to escape otherwise we would have looked like Billy Bunter.'

'Yes well just the same we will see you later, by for now darling it's wonderful to have you home in one piece.'

'I'm sort of glad to be back as well, seriously though I am very happy to be home, I love you both so much.'

George arrived and took Tilley to an interview room he told her he would not keep her long then commenced her debrief.

Tilley told him about the kidnapping as well as hers and Joanne's days at the hands of the Americans. She also told him how in the end Leonard Fisher helped them escape. She asked George: 'How are they both? She was wonderful considering her age and condition.'

'Joanne has gone home and Len is in hospital under guard. His leg isn't broken but he has damaged his kneecap and his calf muscle. Once he is well enough he will be moved to a prison hospital where he will be processed for trial. Considering his hand in your escape though, he should be looked upon leniently.' She then asked: 'How is Simon? He isn't hurt is he? Can I see him?'

No! 'He isn't hurt but you can't see him until he has been questioned and charged. He has been asking about you so maybe something good may have come from all this.' Tilley ignored George's hint and asked: 'When will he be charged?'

'Later this morning probably, Brice will be dealt with first as Simon only aided and abetted.' Tilley reminded George: 'He was blackmailed into helping them and he did help us escape.'

'I know and I fully understand but he has to be formally charged and go to court, don't worry though I will be sure to put in a good word.'

'I appreciate that detective, I'm so glad it's over I thought those yanks were going to kill us, at least that Franks anyway, he was frightening.'

'Well with yours and all the other evidence they will be going to prison for a very long time and you will be largely instrumental in that.'

'Will I have to go to court?'

'That will depend on how they plea at their respective bail hearings but if you do your evidence can be heard from behind a screen as can your father's. Right Tilley that's about it I think, I expect your parents are anxious to get you home.'

'Yes they are bless them, thank you for finding us detective,'

No! 'Thank YOU Tilley, I hope your life is a little less exciting from now on though, goodbye and please give my respects to your parents?'

'I will goodbye and thanks once again.'

At nine o'clock that morning Detective Constable Ross knocked on DCI Carter's door. George was updating the files on the murders and he called for the DC to go in. He entered and announced: 'Good morning Sir there is a DCI Phillips from Bromworth serious crime headquarters, he says he must speak to you immediately . . . . Before he could finish a lean red haired man pushed past the DC walking right up to George's desk. George was surprised to say the least, he stood up and challenged the intruder: 'Excuse me what do you mean by barging into my office like this?' George looked at the DC, he nodded and mouthed: "Sorry". George thanked him and said: 'I will deal with this now, please close the door?' The Dc left the room and George turned to the DCI who had already made himself comfortable in George's chair, George was furious and immediately ordered the DCI out of his chair and asked what was going on. The DCI told George that he was from Bromworth Central and the two Americans had to be transferred to Bromworth because they were "Class A Criminals" and must be detained in a more secure facility.'

'Oh yes, and on who's say so?'

'The Chief Constable's actually!'

'Well nobody has said anything to me and until they do those prisoners stay where they are.'

'Well I am telling you now so, if you would arrange to have them brought out I have a secure vehicle with armed officers waiting down stairs.'

'I am very sorry but you will have a long wait because if the CC wants them moved he will have to tell me himself. Hell man he only telephoned me this morning congratulating me and my officers on the arrests, I'm sure he would have said something then, so it looks as if you have had a wasted trip DCI Phillips, please shut the door on your way out.'

'Look I am under orders to collect those men and I am going nowhere until I do.'

'That's your choice but you can wait in your vehicle, I hope it has a good heater.'

George stood up and opened the door and said angrily: 'Now please vacate my office I have some work to do?' The DCI leapt out of his chair and stormed out yelling as he went: 'You haven't heard the last of me, I will be back.'

'You will? Then please knock the door next time and wait to be invited in, now goodbye.'

George was understandably furious and slammed the door, he returned to his desk and immediately called the Chief Constable 'Good morning Sir DCI Carter here at Parkview, I have just had a DCI Phillips from Bromworth here, wanting to take the two yanks to his nick, he says that you ordered it.'

'Yes that's right George I've been meaning to call you but everything's manic here, we arrested the junior Minister this morning and all hell has broken loose. The FBI has demanded we hand him over to them but Whitehall is adamant he stays here.'

'That's all well and good Sir but my team have worked themselves into the ground on this investigation and we have a wonderful result, now you want to take it away from them, well I think that is very unfair, we have more than proved we are capable of looking after them.'

'I'm not denying that George but if the FBI don't get their way with this minister we think they will make a move on the yanks and Bromworth have more men than Parkview to guard them, it will only be a temporary measure. As you said you and your team have worked hard on the case so you can all go home and rest up, we will see what happens and I will be in touch.'

'I'm sorry Sir but I am furious that you have taken the pleasure away from my team and thrown it in the dirt.' George slammed the phone down and called Mike to break the news, he responded saying: 'I can't believe that, just as we think it is all over they hit us with this.'

'Yes its hell Mike but I'm not taking it lying down I'm calling the Chief Commissioner and put the ball in his court. One thing's for sure those yanks are going nowhere until I hear back from him. Let's take the opportunity and do an informal interview of Franks, we'll see if he wants to lawyer up then once he has a brief maybe we can delay the transfer, especially if he "sings" for us. At the very least Bromworth would have to work with us once he has started talking.'

'Very shrewd George I must say.'

Earlier that morning when Tilley left George she found her parents in the canteen, they were just about to leave and they met at the door, they all went downstairs and out into the car park. Now I do feel free! Tilley exclaimed and took a long intake of air, she held it in for a few seconds then breathed out, she said: Lovely! 'This is the first time since they took me that I have enjoyed just breathing.' Her mum replied linking Tilley's arm with hers: 'My poor darling I can't even imagine what you and that poor old lady went through, I honestly believed I would never see you alive again.'

'Oh come on mum you don't really believe I would of let them prevent me from sitting on my new sofa do you?'

'Always joking even at a time like this, I just don't know where you get it from.'

'It must be the milkman I reckon, what do you say dad?'

'You didn't get your good looks from any milkman I can assure you. Now come on girl in the car, you have some crawling to do.'

At eleven fifteen am Franks was taken by two uniformed officers to an interview room. He was handcuffed behind his back but, when they entered the room one officer unlocked the cuffs and pulling Franks arms around to his front relocked them and sat him down in the chair. George and Mike observed him for a while from the other side of a two way mirror. He seemed to be calm so George decided to commence the interview. As George had hoped Franks did ask for a solicitor hopefully impeding the immediate transfer of Franks and Brice.

After a few minutes the solicitor arrived, he introduced himself as: Lawrence Grant and sat next to Franks, they had already spoken so George commenced the interview.

Mike went through the process with the tape machine then George began: 'John Michael Franks before we start I need to know your real name.'

'I am John Michael Franks.'

'Ok Mr franks are you aware of your rights?'

'Yeah I know my rights, I'm an American citizen and you have no right to detain me.'

'Well I beg to differ Mr Franks, you have been arrested on suspicion of committing two murders and two kidnappings on British soil, that gives us every right to detain and punish you, also unless you carry a British firearms certificate you have contravened the firearm act by discharging a firearm in a public place. Do you have a valid certificate Mr Franks?'

'You know I don't, I haven't been in this dump long enough.'

'In that case you are in very serious trouble so I advise you to be as cooperative as you can or you will be locked away for a very long time, if not for life. Now tell me who ordered you and your accomplice to murder in cold blood two British citizens? Two people I might add who were no threat to anyone.'

Franks leaned over and consulted with his solicitor as to whether he should give this information and was informed that it would not do any harm. He then answered the question: 'Ok, we were given our orders from the bar steward at the bar you found me in.'

'Where did he get the orders from and how did he get mixed up in this?'

'He received faxes from the states, our people used the bar steward because they had something on him, I don't know what but he sure danced to their tune so it's big.'

'Ok then, what do you know about a junior minister in our government, what did he have to do with this business?'

'Why are you asking me? Brice was the man in charge over here he must have told you everything.'

'Well no, actually he has been too busy giving us everything on you, he told us that you killed the couple and kidnapped the women. He only admits to helping you dump the bodies and recruiting Rickard, Fisher and Jenkins.'

'He's a lying bum he is in this just as deep as me.'

'Does that mean you are admitting to the murders because if you are I suggest you talk to Mr Grant here we will give you some time to talk.'

Mike announced the suspension of the interview for the tape and switched the machine off.

George and Mike went to George's office. George remarked: 'That didn't go too bad, I'm hoping his brief can persuade him to confess then we have a hold on him. While we are waiting lets go and tell Brice that Franks is passing the buck, he may confess to his part in things and then we have him as well. I am also going to call the Chief Commissioner and see what he has to say.

George and Mike went to Brice's cell, the custody Sergeant opened the door and they went in, Brice was sitting on his bunk, George and Mike positioned themselves on each side of Brice and sat down, they looked at Brice for a few seconds then George asked: 'How are you Angelo? Are you comfortable? How's the food?'

'You Brits are so funny, I'm splitting my sides, when am I getting out of here, I heard you've nabbed Franks so by now you know there's nothing to hold me for.'

On the contrary! 'That's not what he says, he reckons you are as guilty as him in fact he is singing like a bird, things look bad for the both of you. You should have a word with your brief ASAP because the first one to speak up will get a deal, the sooner one of you confesses his part in everything the sooner he will get out of his cell and be transferred to Five star Accommodation.' Brice's face lit up like a light and immediately asked for his solicitor.

When George returned to his office he decided to call the Chief Commissioner, when he answered George asked him if there was any news regarding the yanks transfer, he told George: 'Not exactly and, I do sympathise with you, after all we trusted you and your team to run the investigation and you proved it was the right move, it was a tremendous result and I believe you could take care of these men, it's just the FBI, they cannot be trusted. The government insist on keeping them here but we fear that they will try to nab when we aren't looking. Look, give me a little more time I will see what I can do. What is the situation with them at this moment George?'

'Well we are in the middle of interviewing Franks at the moment, we have just suspended it while he talks to his brief, we think he will open up when we resume. We have also had another word with Brice and somehow he has gotten the idea that Franks is ratting on HIM, so he has asked to see his solicitor too. I am almost certain we will have a confession from both of them by the end of the day.'

'Very sneaky George, look I am going to stick my neck out here, I will insist that you keep them there, and Bromworth can send some armed reinforcements to help guard them until they have had their bail hearings. We will have another think then.'

'Thank you Sir my team will be very happy, I will be in touch.'

'Ok just don't let me down, congratulate all your team for me, you are the talk of the force.'

'Thanks once again Sir, goodbye for now.'

George instantly called Mike with the good news, Mike said: "Yes" Loudly, then much calmer said: 'That's one up for us George, I would love to be a fly on the wall when that DCI Phillips gets the order, incidentally Franks solicitor said they are ready to resume the interview.'
'Ok let's do it Mike.'

When the interview recommenced Franks confessed to the murders and assisting with the disposing of the bodies. He also admitted to kidnapping Tilley but not Mrs Perkins. He also confessed to his part of unlawful detention of the women and Len as well as illegal possession and discharging of a firearm endangering the public.' His solicitor asked for leniency in view of his cooperation. George promised to have a word with the judge.
The interview was terminated and George and Mike went to find out whether Brice was ready for another interview but the Custody Sergeant told them that he was coming in that afternoon.

CHAPTER TWENTY TWO

When Tilley and her parents got home to their house Tilley threw her coat off and collapse on their settee giving out a loud sigh of relief. Am I glad that's all over? I just can't believe how it all snowballed since seeing Rickard that morning. I definitely intend keeping my nose out things in the future.' Her mum and dad looked at each other and her mum replied: My God! 'Am I hearing things? 'I never thought I would ever hear those words coming from your lips, I just hope and pray you mean it. Now as you are not hungry I will make a nice cup of tea . . . . Tilley stopped her in her tracks saying: 'Not hungry? 'I could eat a horse that has been dead ten years.'

'Sorry love I have run out of rotting horses you will have settle with a fry up instead.'

'Now that sounds great mum'. Her dad chipped in. He continued: 'I will go and open a nice bottle of wine.'

'Oh I don't know about that dad, I am just about ready to fall over now, heaven knows what wine will do to me.'

'Well you're not going to work tomorrow are you? You can stay in bed and sleep it off? Now what do you prefer, red or white?'

'Oh white please, I have seen enough of the red stuff to last a lifetime.' Her mum added sternly: 'Yes and thank your lucky stars none of it was yours.'

Her dad opened the wine pouring out three glasses, when her mum brought the food in Bob handed her and Tilley a glass each then raised his saying: 'Thank the Lord that our dear daughter has been returned to us unharmed, accept maybe for her pride.' Tilley laughed and her mum added: 'Here—Here welcome home Tilley we love you and we really did think we had lost you forever.' They all took a sip and Tilley said: 'You can't get rid of me that easy I can assure you of that, now let's eat before it goes cold.'

Later that afternoon the desk Sergeant called George informing him that Brice's solicitor had arrived and he was in his cell talking to him. George called Mike to his office and told him. Mike said: 'Good, keep your fingers and toes crossed and let's hope his brief can persuade him to "fess up" his part in it all. This could wind up an historic day for Parkview Police headquarters and I wouldn't be at all surprised if there weren't promotions incoming for a few of us.'

'Funny you should say that because I have just heard that there are and you are definitely one of them Mike.' George extended his hand and added: 'Let me be the first to congratulate you—"DCI Harper"

'Are you being serious? I admit I would dearly welcome promotion but I couldn't take your job George, you have worked so relentlessly throughout this investigation and your family has hardly seen you. No, I will turn it down if they offer it to me.'

'Hold on Mike, take a breath who said anything about taking my job, I've been made Detective Chief Superintendant so stop worrying and enjoy the moment.'

'That's different, how fantastic? It couldn't be more deserved. Your promotion is great too George. Seriously though, let me be the first to congratulate you, does this mean you are leaving us, I didn't think there was a position for a DCS here.'

'You're right there isn't but I am staying. After our success with the case the boys at the top have had a rethink and decided to upgrade this station to a serious crime unit and that calls for a DCS. They are going to build a larger station and merge us with Bromworth and I will be senior officer. And by the way Mike don't you dare call me Sir whenever we are alone.'

'Ok Sir.' Mike joked and saluted him, then said: 'That means you will be DCI Phillips boss, wow bring it on.'

'That's right I will and I intend to break the news to him personally but not before we all go to the pub tonight and celebrate.'

'That sounds just the ticket. Why don't we go and see if Brice is ready to play ball?'

'Yes let's, the sooner we wind this all up the sooner we can go and let our hair down and as you are the new DCI you can lead up.'

George and Mike headed for Brice's cell but was met by the duty Sergeant, he told them: 'I was just coming to fetch you two six officers have arrived from Bromworth how do you want to use them?' George replied: 'I think we will leave that to you Serge as long as Brice and Franks stay with us.' The Sergeant then told George: 'Brice's solicitor wants to talk to regarding his evidence I have put him in the meeting room. Oh and congratulations are in order I believe?'

'Yes well, thanks Serge we'll be on our way.'

On reaching the meeting room they come across Brice's solicitor going over his paperwork, George and Mike sat opposite him and George said: 'Good afternoon what is the situation with your client?'

'Well I have had an intensive chat with Mr Brice and put to him the advantages of confessing, unfortunately he is still not very forthcoming with whether he intends to or not so we will have to wait and see. I am giving him a few minutes then I am going back to see him.'

'Ok well we're going for a sandwich and a coffee you can find us in the canteen when you have spoken to him.'

When the solicitor returned to Brice's cell Brice told him that he would confess and the solicitor said he would go and inform the detectives. The solicitor knocked on the cell door to alert the custody Sergeant that he was ready to leave and the Sergeant unlocked the door but, as the door was opening Brice rushed at the solicitor slamming him against the door forcing it outwards, trapping the Sergeant behind it. Brice fell on top of the Solicitor but very quickly he pulled himself up yanking him by his lapels to his feet, he then put his arm around the solicitor's throat and squeezed tightly until the Solicitor became light headed.

The Sergeant began to get up but and reached to take his firearm from its holster. Brice though warned him not to anything stupid because he could snap the solicitor's neck with one jolt, he told the Sergeant to give him the keys to the cell and the outside door of the custody suite and his gun, the Sergeant knew he had no option but to concede.

Once Brice had the keys and the gun he forced the solicitor into the cell and locked him in, the Sergeant warned Brice: 'You won't get anywhere there are armed Police everywhere.'

"In truth there were no other officers around because Brice was fortunate to have chosen a time when they were changing shifts and the duty Sergeant had not yet deployed the Bromworth officers".

Angrily Brice put the gun to the Sergeant's head telling him to shut up and take him to Simon's cell. Moving cautiously along the corridor with the Sergeant in front they reached Simon's cell. Brice ordered the Sergeant to open the door, when the door was opened Brice ordered Simon out and pushed the Sergeant into the cell. He locked the door and told Simon to say nothing and to do exactly as he was told or he would kill him.

Brice forced Simon in front of him and they made their way to the outside door. Brice gave Simon the key and told him to open the door. Once it was open Brice told him to check that there was no one about. Simon cautiously poked his head around the door and looked about and said that it was all clear so Brice pushed him out into the yard and locked the door. He threw the keys up onto the flat roof and pushing the gun into

Simon's back he ordered him to lead him somewhere safe to hide out until he decided on his next move.

Meanwhile George and Mike were sitting in the canteen waiting for the solicitor to join them when a Constable rushed in and told them about the escape. George slammed the table with his hand making a cup and a plate jump off and smash on the floor and yelled out loud: 'HOW CAN THIS HAPPEN FOR PETE'S SAKE, THERE WERE ARMED OFFICER'S ON GUARD.' The PC sheepishly told George: 'Well actually there wasn't Sir.' He went on to explain the situation to George, he snapped: 'Right I will have words with him when this foul up is resolved. Ok Constable, have all Armed Response personnel and as many uniformed men as possible gathered outside immediately.'

The Constable left as did George and Mike, they rushed to the custody suite where paramedics were treating the solicitor and the custody Sergeant. George asked how they were and was told that the Sergeant had a nasty bump on the back of his head and was a little groggy and the solicitor was in shock and had a bruised and sore throat. He said they were going to hospital as a precaution but they didn't seem to be seriously injured.

George thanked the paramedics and apologised to the solicitor for what happened, he and Mike then headed off to arrange the manhunt for Brice and Simon.

Before he did so he thought he ought to warn Tilley and Mrs Perkins in case Brice went after them. He tried Tilley's number but couldn't get a reply, he remembered then that she was going to her parents and assumed that she was still there.

He called their number and Mrs Watson answered, George asked to speak to Tilley. Tilley's mum called her and told her: 'It's that detective Carter he wants to speak to you. Tilley took the receiver and said: 'Hello Tilley here.' George said: 'Hello Tilley I don't wish to worry you after what you have been through but Brice has escaped from custody and is on the run with a gun, he has taken Simon with him.'

'Tilley froze on the spot and gasped: 'Oh my God you don't think he will come for me do you?'

'Well we are not taking any chances, we have alerted the hospital where Len Fisher is and we have alerted Mrs Perkins.'

'Oh my yes I had forgotten about poor Len, what about Simon is he in danger?'

'We are not sure of anything right now hopefully he is just using him to help him get away. We are sending armed officers to watch your parents house, you are staying there I presume, you aren't going home yet are you?'

'I don't really know, I don't want to put my parents in danger but I would rather not be on my own either, I will discuss it with them and let you know what I decide.'

'Ok Tilley I had better go and organise the manhunt, I will speak o you later.'

When Tilley hung up she looked at her mother, she had her hands up to her face and asked warily: 'What in heaven's name is wrong now?' Tilley explained what George had told her and her mum said: 'Well you have really dug a big hole for yourself this time haven't you my girl?' Yes! Her dad agreed then said: 'Why you couldn't leave well alone, I don't know.' He stormed out of the room slamming the door behind him. 'Oh dear I think I have upset him.' Tilley said sheepishly, her mother replied sharply: 'Are you surprised? We have just endured over two weeks of hell and now this. Does this mean we are prisoners in our home now until these men are caught or God forbid, they come here for you?'

'You don't have to worry about Simon he is as much a victim of circumstances as I was.'

'Oh that cheers me up no end, just a mad man with a gun to worry about now then, I'm sorry but I am with your father on this one.'

Her mum leapt out of her chair and as her husband had done she slammed the door and stormed upstairs. Tilley sat stunned for a while then just burst into tears burbling: "This is the end even if I am the only witness to anything in future I am walking away."

CHAPTER TWENTY THREE

Brice and Simon managed to get outside of town unnoticed which was lucky because they were still wearing the overalls they were wearing while in custody. They found some woods and held up there for a while. Ten or so minutes passed then Brice grabbed Simon by the lapels of his overalls and growled: 'You are getting me out of this stinking country you know who to call and tell them to move it or you will pay.' Simon was scared because he didn't know the number off by heart, he told Brice: 'I left the number at the pub, there was no time to take anything and the cops will have everything by now.'

'You stupid limey you should have memorised the number.'

'Oh so I'm a psychic now am I, how was I to know you stupid yank's would stuff up? No I am finished with this, kill me if you want but you are on your own.'

'Ok I will have to go and get your girlfriend to persuade you.'

'You leave her alone she can't help you.'

'Well it's up to you but I won't hesitate then maybe you will change your mind when I put my gun to her head.'

'Ok ok I will see what I can do, that number should be the last number I dialled on the phone, If I can get in the pub then maybe I can get it. We will need transport though, or we are going to be noticed in these clothes.'

'Good now you are seeing sense, leave the transport to me just get me to the road.'

With Simon's help they made it to the road and Brice positioned himself behind one of the trees that lined the road waiting for a car to appear. He didn't have to wait long, a white van approached and Brice waited until it came closer then rushed out standing in the road facing the van pointing his gun. The van slowed right down and Brice indicated with his gun for the driver to pull over. When the van stopped Brice ordered the driver out and directed him to go over to him. Brice asked whether there was anyone else in the van and the driver nervously shook his head. Brice called Simon over and forced him into the driver's seat then opened the back door, he forced the driver to get in the back and climbed in behind him pulling the door's shut, he told Simon to get them to the bar and not to draw any attention to them.

It was early evening when they neared the Junction. Simon turned down the dimly lit street and stopped the van. He advised Brice it would be safer if he went into the pub alone but Brice was not having any of it, he said he didn't trust him not to run. 'I'm not that stupid.'

Simon told him, he continued: 'If I run you will only go after Tilley so don't panic, I will be back as long as there are no Police about.'

'Well if you don't it won't only be your girlfriend you have to worry about, our friend here will pay as well.'

'You yanks are real pieces of work aren't you?'

'Ok enough with the mouth just get going and don't be all night.'

Simon asked the driver if he had a torch in the van he said he did, it was in the glove compartment. Simon found the torch then looked around checking there wasn't anyone around, he then left the van and went into the alley to the rear of the pub. There were no lights on inside easing Simon's mind knowing that the Police had left although Police incident tape still encircled the building.

He reached the back door and found it locked, he shielded his eyes then using the torch he smashed the window. He waited looking around in case someone heard the glass breaking, once he was sure it was safe he put his arm through and found the key in the lock. He turned the key and opened the door.

He went in and with the aid of the torch made his way to his office, all the contents of the drawers and cupboards was turned out onto the floor so he knew the Police would have all the paperwork referring to the yanks and their operation. Simon lifted the receiver and was relieved to find the phone had not been disconnected. He pressed the redial button heard the ringing tone, after a while an American voice said Hello. Simon asked: 'Is that the bus depot?'

"That was the code that Simon had to give each time he called".

After a pause the voice replied: 'Who is this?' Simon's replied using his code word "Bar Service." The voice asked: 'What is the situation? We know that our friends are inconvenienced.'

'One is, one available to return, we require relevant documents.'

The reply ensured that the required documents would be despatched with urgency to a pre-arranged destination which originally was the pub but Simon advised the voice that it was no longer a "safe destination". He said: 'The alternative choice should now be used.' The alternative choice was a PO Box at the local Post Office in Bromworth.' He was assured that this would be arranged imminently.

Simon hung up and went to his bedroom to see if the Police had left any clothes there and was pleased to find that they had. He grabbed some for himself and Brice he also collected some food and water.

He left the pub taking care not to be seen, when he reached the van Brice growled: 'About time you are playing with people's lives.'

'For Pete's sake Brice you really ought to learn to be patient, look I have food and water and some clothes although I don't know why I bothered.' Simon threw the clothes at Brice and told him that they should get out into the country and get out of the overalls and they should also let the driver go explaining: 'He will only attract Police into the area.' Brice replied sarcastically: 'For once you are using your head, ok let's get going.

They drove a few miles towards the countryside and stopped to let the driver out, they were

Just outside a small village. Using small tree branches and foliage they covered the van leaving just enough space to allow them to climb into the back, Simon had reversed the van into the spot so the back doors were hidden from view. They climbed back into the van and sorted through the clothes each finding something suitable. Once they had dressed Brice grabbed the bag of food and water. Simon had put in bread, fruit, two cooked chicken legs and biscuits. Brice began stuffing food into his mouth while drinking water from the bottles at the same time. Simon watched for a while then had to remark: 'You're so disgusting, Tilley was right when she called you pigs.' Brice wiped the excess food from his overflowing mouth and raised his arm threatening to strike Simon, Simon responded saying: 'That's right violence and verbal abuse that's all you know.' Simon reached out and took the remaining chicken leg and some bread, picking up a bottle of water he opened the rear doors and went out to eat in peace.'

The next morning they finished the bread and water and ate some biscuits neither saying anything.

Once they had finished they uncovered the van and Simon drove to Bromworth using back roads and tracks, they parked about a quarter of a mile from the Post Office and Simon walked the rest of the way.

He entered the Post Office gingerly looking around but thankfully there were no other customers, he asked the clerk whether there was anything in the PO Box and gave the clerk the number. The clerk said there was a parcel but he required ID. Simon froze for a moment then told him that he had forgotten his ID but he thought that as he gave him the PO Box number that would be all that was required.

The clerk however informed him that he could not release the item without some form of ID.

Simon was petrified that Brice would lose it and kill him however he apologised to the clerk saying he would fetch his ID.

In fact he had decided to run for it hoping he could get far enough away before Brice realised he had gone, unbeknown to Simon though Brice had followed him being the untrusting man he was and spotted Simon heading in the wrong direction.

He ran up behind Simon before he could get going and grabbed the back of his coat collar, Brice shoved Simon against a wall and snarled: 'Where do you think you're going you yellow limey, Where's the paperwork?'

'There isn't any I can't get it without ID, so you are stuck here.'

'Oh I am, am I?' He put his gun to Simon's head and growled: 'THIS is the only ID we need now take me to where my papers are.'

'If you keep poking guns into people's faces all you are going to get is back in jail. You must be good at picking people's pockets so why not do what you do best and find some ID?'

Brice looked at Simon for a while then said: 'That's not a bad idea for a limey.' He patted Simon on his back and said: 'Now watch and learn.'

Brice went out into the street and walked about, soon he spotted a man walking towards him in a black suit and carrying a briefcase. He walked towards the man and as they passed each other Brice deliberately bumped into him, as he did he slid his hand inside the man's jacket and took his wallet from his inside pocket. He apologised to the man and walked away.

Brice made his way back to Simon and said: 'Smooth eh Limey?' Simon didn't react so Brice thrust the wallet into Simon's hand and snarled: 'Now go and get my blasted paperwork.'

Simon looked through the wallet and there was a hundred pounds in cash and four credit cards. Brice reached out and grabbed the cash and cards saying he would need money to get back home. Simon said he would also need money to get away so Brice gave him back fifty pounds and said he would use the cards.

Simon searched further through the wallet and found a credit card statement and a letter from the man's bank. Simon told Brice that he could use them as ID but, he would need the card that matched the statement. Brice reluctantly threw the card at Simon and he set off for the Post Office.

When he walked into the Post Office he was apprehensive as there was four people queuing but he bit the bullet and stood in line. When his turn came the Clerk recognised him and asked if he had ID. Simon told him that he had and gave the man the credit card the man said that he should have something with his address on so Simon gave him the statement and the bank letter. This satisfied the Clerk and went and collected the package handing it to Simon.

Simon walked outside taking a long deep breath as he did. He returned to the alley and gave Brice the package, he growled: 'About time now get me to the rail depot and let me get a train to the airport and get out of this dump. Simon asked what Airport he was going to and was told "Heathrow".

As they approached the rail station Simon told Brice it would be safer to go through the goods yard as Tilley had done with Franks, he then told Brice: 'Now get out of the van and out of my life.' Brice had other ideas though, he said: 'Do you really think our boys were born yesterday? You are coming with me as security until I get back on home soil.'

'You're mad I can't come with you, I have no passport or anything.'

'That's what you think, there are papers for you as well and you had better look through them when you are on the train and get used to your new name—Mr Terrence Stuart, oh and I am Jack Forbes.'

Back at Mr and Mrs Watsons home Tilley was very angry at herself for upsetting her parents again. She wept for a while then decided to go out and get some fresh air and give her parents a chance to calm down.

She decided to go and see if she could give a hand with the search of the two men, she called a taxi and went outside to wait.

The taxi arrived and as she climbed in she asked the driver to take her to the Police station. The driver could see that she had been crying, knowing the destination he asked if everything was alright. Tilley told him that she didn't wish to discuss it. The driver told her that he heard all sorts of stories and wouldn't be shocked. Tilley told him she would rather not talk about it and the driver respected her wishes and said no more.

At the Police station Tilley paid the driver and went inside, she approached the front desk and asked the duty officer if she could to speak to DCI Carter or DI Harper. The officer informed her that they were both tied up, he asked Tilley her name and with what connection she wished to speak to them and Tilley told him. The officer paused for a while then said: 'Tilley Watson, you are the girl who was kidnapped? Ok please take seat and I will fetch the duty Detective Constable to speak to you.

Tilley sat down and waited, minutes passed then a DC Banks arrived, he invited Tilley to the meeting room and asked what he could do for her, she told him: 'Well I feel so hopeless sitting at home and Simon the Junction landlord is my friend so, I wondered if I could help in any way with the search. Maybe I could go on TV or something and appeal to him to give himself up, after all he is not a bad man, he was forced to help them.'

'I don't think that would help Miss as he is probably held up somewhere away from TV's and such. Actually Miss, do you know where he may have gone to stay out of the limelight?'

'No I have only met him in the pub but wherever he is I'm sure that he would do his best to get away or get recognised.'

'Well then in that case miss I don't think there is anything you can do, I suggest you go home, we will let you know as soon as we have some news.'

'What about if I went and saw Len Fisher in hospital, would that be alright? I promise I won't help him escape or anything.'

'I don't think him escaping is a problem, not with his injuries anyway. I'm not sure though whether you would be allowed in as he is under heavy guard.'

'Couldn't you call someone at the hospital and talk to whoever is in charge there?'

'I don't know miss, look give me a minute I will see what I can do.' The DC left and after a few minutes he returned saying: 'That will be fine miss but we will take you in an unmarked car.'

'That's ok I think I would be a little wary going on my own anyway.'

'That's settled then, stay here and someone will fetch you when the car is ready.'

'Thank you Detective.'

The DC left Tilley and a few minutes later a plain clothed officer opened the door and told her the car was ready. He showed her to the door at the rear of the station where another plain clothed man waited by the car, he opened the rear nearside door and she got in. The two officers sat in the front and they drove off.

On arrival at the hospital Tilley was escorted up the steps to the entrance by the two officers. Inside she was met by two armed officers, one a WPC. The WPC searched Tilley and when she was satisfied that Tilley was unarmed she was escorted by two armed male officers to Fishers private ward.

Len was sitting up in bed looking very grim but when he spotted Tilley he perked up quickly saying: 'Tilley; My God what are you doing here, are you alright?'

'Yes I'm fine I was just wondering how you were.'

'I'm alright under the circumstances but I'm due to be taken to a holding cell at the station soon.'

'Well don't worry, Mrs "P'" and I have put a good word in for you, so you shouldn't be treated too harshly.'

'Thanks Tilley I appreciate it but I don't deserve it.'

'Len; do you know Brice is on the run and has taken my friend Simon with him.'

WHAT! 'That's all I need, he isn't coming here is he? Who is this Simon anyway?'

'He is the landlord of a pub in Fairview but he was also the yanks contact with their people in the states. I didn't find out until Franks made me take him to the pub, they had blackmailed Simon to help them but he helped me escape from the pub and gave the Police some useful information I hope Brice doesn't hurt him. There are armed Police outside my parents house and Mrs Perkins in case he comes after us.'

'Do your parents know you are here?'

No! 'They are very angry with because they have been drawn into everything but I dare say they will calm down, I hope. Is there anything I can get you, some food or something?'

'Well I could do with some chocolate, and a cold fizzy drink would be great.'

Tilley advised the guards where she was going and an armed officer was assigned to escort her.

On her return Len wasn't in his room, she asked a guard where he was and he told her he had gone for an X-Ray. She waited for twenty minutes for Len to return when he did he was in a wheelchair being pushed by a Nurse accompanied by an armed guard.

The Nurse helped Len back into his bed and after she had left he told Tilley: 'I am sure that X-Ray is my ticket out of here, the Doc said yesterday that my leg was mending well and I would soon be going to the nick to wait for my bait hearing.'

'Oh dear Len what a mess, it seems like years since I first saw that Rickard bloke, and now I wish I hadn't. My mum and dad were so right to try and make me drop it but I am too stubborn for my own good sometimes, I have promised them though that this is the last time I ever get involved in anything and I mean it.'

'And is that why you are here now, not getting involved?' Tilley told him to shut up and lightly punched his arm, Len let out a yell: '"MY LEG—MY LEG". Two armed guards instantly rushed into the room yelling: "ARMED POLICE STAY WHHER YOU ARE". Tilley cowered down beside the bed but Len shouted: 'It's ok I'm fine, I'm fine.' He apologised to the guards for not thinking, they left but not before telling what they thought of him. After they had closed the door Tilley stood up and pretended she was going to punch him again but Len retaliated by pretending he was going to shout out again, so Tilley changed her mind. Len opened the chocolate and gave some to Tilley while she opened the bottle of drink and poured some in his plastic beaker.

About a half an hour later a nurse came in to do Len's OB'S so Tilley said she should go. Len thanked her for the visit and told her he felt much better and that she should be a Nurse. Tilley replied laughing: 'No thank you, I can't stand the sight of blood.'

CHAPTER TWENTY FOUR

George and Mike agreed on a two prong tactic in the hunt for the escaped prisoners.

Both men headed up teams combined of Armed Response and plain clothed officers. George and his team headed north which included the abandoned trading estate where the warehouse that Tilley and co was held and Mike took his team south. Both teams had trained sniffer dogs which were given articles of the two men's clothing to give them their scent.

Mike's and George worked out that Brice would want to either get to the train station or take the back roads to town, his strategy was for the two teams to fan out and gradually close in on each other meaning they could very likely push Brice and Simon into a corner.

George had worked out that Brice would want to leave the area but would need papers and ID and that is why he sprung Simon from jail. With this in mind he sent two officers to the Junction telling them to have another look around and see if there was anything that pointed to where he may go. He was convinced that he would want to contact his people in the states and he could force Simon to take him to the pub to call them.

As the two teams were slowly converging on each other George received a call from one of the officers at the Junction to confirm that his hunch was right and they had found something. He told George that he had checked the last number dialled and it was indeed to America and he gave George the number. George immediately called the FBI agent who visited him giving him the number so that the Bureau could apprehend the yanks contacts.

Meanwhile the search was proceeding well and the two teams gradually closed in on each other. Mikes dogs were the first to pick up a scent they started barking pulling their handlers towards the wooded area Brice and Simon had hid over night in the van. Biscuit wrappers and water bottles were found but because the men left in the van the scent was lost. However the ground was damp and there was mud at the edge of the area and the van had left tracks which Mike decided were fresh. Mike told his team to spread out and they moved off in the direction the tracks went. The tracks led to the road and Mike radioed the find to George, he told Mike that he had just been informed that a man had reported his white van as stolen the afternoon of the escape after being hijacked by two men, one was American and he had gun. He was also told that another man had his wallet pick pocketed only a few hours ago, this occurred just yards away from a Post Office on the outskirts of Parkview where a man answering Simon's description used the man's ID to collect a package. He told Mike: 'It looks as if they are going to the railway station you and your men get there ASAP.' Mike acknowledged George and ordered his team to speed off to the station.

They entered the station from the goods yard and luckily the station was quiet. Brice told Simon that HE would have to buy the tickets as he may be recognised but he warned Simon not to try anything Simon said he didn't have any money but Brice reminded him that he gave him fifty pounds from the wallet. Simon said that was for him to use and wouldn't be enough to pay for the tickets to Heathrow anyway. Brice sighed loudly and gave Simon a wad of notes demanding he gave back what he didn't spend.

Simon went to the ticket office and asked for two single tickets to Heathrow. The woman asked if he was sure he wanted single tickets because it worked out cheaper to get returns if they wanted to come back at a later date. Simon saw a chance to maybe get some help, he told the woman: No! 'My "AMERICAN" friend and I are not coming back.' He pronounced the word American loudly hoping the woman would catch on who the American was but unfortunately the woman made no connection.

She handed Simon the tickets and Simon rejoined Brice handing him his change. Brice looked at the tickets and noted that the train left at six twenty eight pm meaning they had ten minutes to wait so he handed Simon a ten pound note telling him to go and get some food and coffee, Simon said it wasn't enough money as station cafes were expensive, Brice reluctantly gave Simon another ten pounds and grumbled: 'That's another reason to get out of this dump it's too expensive, now go and get a move on.'

Simon returned five minutes later with sandwiches and two take away coffees, Brice moaned in his characteristic way: 'Sandwiches, haven't you heard of hamburgers over here, I can't wait to get home and eat some real food.' Simon not caring any more replied: 'It's clear now how you got that fat belly, eating trash like that.' Brice moved to swipe Simon's face but as he did so the train arrived. They walked out onto the platform and Brice kept his head down. The train stopped and they boarded, Brice whispered to Simon to walk through the carriages and find an empty one but, all were occupied.

Much to Brice's disgust they had to settle for one with two passengers in—a man and a woman—and Brice had to accept the situation.

The train moved off and Simon was sat facing Brice, he handed Brice his sandwiches and coffee but he looked disinterested so Simon took them back, the look on Brice's face however soon convinced him to hand them back.

They consumed their sandwiches and coffee, Brice looked out of the window for as long as he could so as not to let the other two occupants see his face. Simon used this situation to taunt Brice by continuously talking to him or asking questions such as where he lived in America, pronouncing America as he had done when he had bought the tickets.

Brice just grunted short sharp answer's such as Baltimore etcetera. This though only made the two other passengers look at him, making him even more nervous.

It was a long journey and it was rush hour causing the train and their carriage to fill completely with many passengers having go stand up. Brice couldn't take anymore so he went out and stood in the space linking the adjoining carriage. Time went on and as they were approaching the station which was only two away from Heathrow Brice decided he wanted to get off. He caught Simon's attention and beckoned him with his finger to go to him. Simon reluctantly edged his way through the standing passengers to join Brice, he told Simon: 'We are getting off at the next station.' Simon knew by the tone of his voice that he had no choice but to agree. The train pulled into the station and the two men got off and made their way out into the street. Simon suggested getting a taxi to the airport and for once Brice agreed.

There was a taxi rank outside of the station with a line of taxi's waiting. They climbed into the first in the line and Brice instantly sat in the back. Simon sat in the front and the driver asked where they wanted to go and Simon told him Heathrow.

They had been travelling for about ten minutes and Simon noticed the driver kept looking in the rear view mirror. He spotted Simon looking at him and quickly looked back to the front. It was obvious that the driver was interested in Brice and assumed that he had recognised him so Simon knew he had to act fast, he called out to Brice: 'Not much further no Mr Forbes and you will be on your way home.' Brice didn't respond to the name so Simon began to say it again but Brice interrupted him . . . . I'm sorry I was miles away.'

Simon was relieved and said: 'No problem, I was just saying that there wasn't much further to go and you will be on your plane.' Brice answered: 'Yes won't I just?'

Simon looked at the driver and said: 'He's exhausted from too many business meetings but he is going home now for good.' The driver nodded but gave a look as if to say "I hear you but I'm not convinced".

They continued on in silence for a while then the driver discreetly tapped Simon's right knee, Simon looked up and the driver moved his eyes towards the rear view mirror.

Simon caught on and looked behind to see that Brice had dropped off. He looked back at the driver who once again used his eyes to indicate to Simon to open the glove compartment. He opened it and found a newspaper and took it out looking at the headlines, they read: "Armed murderer still at large" and showing Brice's picture.

Simon froze because he knew what Brice would do if he was recognised. He looked behind again then back at the paper pointing to the words "armed" and put his finger to his lips. The driver nodded shuffling around in his seat indicating he was uncomfortable with the situation but continued driving not knowing what to do.

Brice awoke as they pulled off the motorway and took the slipway to the airport. They pulled up outside of the departure's entrance and the driver got out and opened Brice's door and Brice kept his head pointed to the ground. The driver remarked inquisitively that they had no luggage but Simon was quick to say that they had been held up and someone else was bringing their luggage.

Brice got out and went straight into the airport and Simon acted quickly saying: 'yes you are right he is the wanted man as I am but he is the one you have to worry about. Leave now and call the Police, he is travelling under the name of "Jack Forbes" and his flight is leaving at eight forty five tonight.' He paid the driver and told him to get away fast. He didn't need telling twice, he got in his taxi and sped off. Brice was just coming back out to see what was keeping Simon and asked why the driver drove off so fast. Simon thought quickly again and told him: 'He had an urgent booking and he's late.' Brice grunted and said: 'Yes well come on let's go.'

When they entered the airport Brice wanted to get checked in early. The documents they had included express check in so they could avoid meeting as many people as possible. Simon on the other hand hoped that he could delay Brice to give the taxi driver time to notify the Police.

Brice headed for the check in desk so Simon had to think quickly, he grabbed Brice's arm blurting out: 'I think those two men over there are plain clothes cops.' He was pointing to two cleaners who were mopping the floor. He shoved Brice into the gent's toilets and told him to lock himself in one of the cubicles. Brice protested but nevertheless he did what Simon suggested.

Simon took the opportunity to look for Police or security but there were none to be seen so, he went over to the two cleaners and told them who he was and that Brice was in the toilets and asked them to alert someone.

Simon waited as long as he dare then went back into the toilets and was relieved that no one else was in there, he and banged on Brice's cubicle and told Brice that it was all clear so he gingerly came out and followed Simon back out, Simon looked around and he was amazed that the Police were nowhere to be seen.

"Unbeknown to him the cleaners had alerted security and they and the Police were actively placing armed men in a position to close in on the two men.

Meanwhile George and Mike received the news that the taxi driver had reported taking the two fugitives to the airport. He reported that Simon had kept calm and helped the driver through the traumatic journey. Not long after that they heard that the two men had been spotted in the airport and they were under surveillance and armed officers were in attendance.

George immediately recalled the officers from the manhunt and redeployed them to the airport, he then put out a call for a helicopter to whisk him and Mike off to the airport hoping to be in on the arrests. Back

At the Heathrow the word came through that the Detectives were on their way and the senior officer in charge ordered that no move was to be made without his express orders.

As soon as George and Mike arrived at the airport they exited the helicopter, the senior security officer met them and guided them to the security office where the two men were being observed on CCTV monitors.

The officer asked George if he wished to make the arrest but he said that he would be happy just observing but would be taking them back to Parkview for processing.

The two men were kept under close observation, they were watched going through the check in process and then they went to the VIP departure lounge awaiting the boarding announcement. Simon had no choice but to follow Brice not wishing to alert him to the fact he had spoken to the cleaners. The public announcer had also been advised of the operation and all other passengers on that flight had been taken to a secure area, they were informed that the flight would be delayed as Police and Security were dealing with serious situation.

When it was time the announcer was asked to make the departure announcement. Simon and Brice made their way to the door that led out to the waiting plane not aware that the door was manned by Police wearing airport staff uniforms.

The men produced their papers and they were checked, they were handed back to them and was wished a safe flight then ushered out onto the tarmac.

Brice emitted a huge sigh of relief but then suddenly they were pounced on from three directions by armed Officers who were screaming: "ARMED POLICE GET DOWN ON YOUR KNEES NOW". Brice turned to run back into the airport building but ran straight into the disguised officers, they were also armed and they wrestled him to the ground disarming him then he was roughly turned onto his stomach and handcuffed behind his back whilst surrounded by armed officers all pointing their guns at him.

Simon meanwhile gave himself up tamely and was also cuffed. Brice began a string of verbal abuse at everyone including Simon whom he warned that if he got his hands on him he was dead. The senior officer told Brice to shut up then formally arrested both men.

George and Mike arrived after observing the arrests on CCTV and told Brice and Simon that they were being taken back to Parkview and will be locked under armed guard. George then praised all the Police and security staff who aided in the men's apprehension. Six armed officers took the men to a secure prison truck and observed as they were locked in and driven away. George and Mike were then taken to their helicopter and flown back to Parkview.

On his arrival back at the station George went straight to his office and called Tilley's parents house, Tilley had returned from the hospital and answered the phone. George asked: 'Hello is that Tilley?'

'Yes it is, that's DCI Carter isn't it?'

'Yes Tilley, good news we have apprehended the two escaped men.'

Brilliant! 'Is Simon alright? Did that pig hurt him?'

'No both men are unharmed and they are on their way back here at this moment.'

'When will I be able to see Simon, he must be in a dreadful state.'

'No I can assure you he is alright, in actual fact it was due to him that we caught them, he hindered Brice as much as possible to allow us to find them. All this will help him get a lighter sentence and I will definitely be speaking on his behalf, I'll will call you when you are able to see him but it will probably not be until tomorrow or maybe even the next day.'

'Thank you detective, give him my love and tell him I will see him soon.'

'Of course Tilley now go and tell your parents the good news.'

'I will goodbye.'

Tilley didn't want to tell him that her parents were angry at her, she hung up and went into the kitchen and made a pot of tea, she placed it on a tray with cups, saucers, milk and sugar and took it up stairs. She knocked on her parent's bedroom door and gingerly opened it and went in. Her parents were sitting on the edge of the bed, her mum still sobbing and her dad had his arm around her shoulders.

Tilley placed the tray on the dressing table, she went over and knelt down in front of them and said softly: 'I am so, so, sorry for endangering and distressing you both, I love you with all my heart and would never willingly put you in that situation, please, please forgive me. DCI Carter has just called they have recaptured Brice and Simon so the danger is over.'

Systematically they both put their arms around Tilley and her mum told her: 'We know you weren't directly responsible, it was just that we have both had enough and want to forget it all and get on with our lives.'

'Me too but I must tell you that I intend seeing Simon as soon as they let me, the DCI said that he was instrumental in the recapture and he should get a light sentence.' Her mum then said: 'Ok ok you do what you have to but just keep your promise not to get involved in anything like this again. Do you hear me Tilley?'

'Loud and clear mum now let's have a nice cup of tea and then we can go downstairs and I am treating us all to a Chinese takeaway tonight.' Thank goodness for that, I am starving.' Her dad chipped in.

Later while they were eating their Chinese her dad asked: 'What's all this interest in this Simon character, you haven't fallen for him have you? Because if you have you must think very seriously about it, he is almost definitely going to have a criminal record.'

'No dad, I just feel so sorry for him, he is one hundred percent sorry for the hit and run in America AND the fact that they used it to force him into helping them. He didn't know they were going to commit murder, he just thought they were going to do a robbery or something.'

'That's as it may be but all I am saying is, just be careful.' Tilley kissed her father on his forehead and told him she would heed his advice.

CHAPTER TWENTY FIVE

The two prisoners were transported back to Parkview and put in separate cells, Brice at one end of the block and Simon the other, this was to prevent the two men conversing—not that Simon wanted to, he'd had enough of Brice and the less he saw or heard from him the more he liked it.

George called Brice's solicitor informing him of the recapture and enquiring whether he wished to continue representing Brice. The solicitor said he did but only under armed guard all the time he was with him. George confirmed that would be normal policy under the circumstances so the solicitor confirmed he would be there in about an hour or so.

As Brice would have to face extra charges George called Mike into his office to discuss this and go over the events of the last few dramatic hours. George told Mike that he intended interviewing Simon first as his role in the matter seemed very clear and all they wanted from him was the names of the contacts in the states. He said: 'I'm sure he wasn't given any names but his evidence would have to go on record. He asked Mike to call Simon's solicitor to come in straight away.

When the solicitor arrived he was shown into an interview room and Simon was brought in and sat down next to his solicitor and George gave them fifteen minutes to update Simon's situation.

When George was informed that Simon was ready he called Mike and arranged to meet in the room. Once George and Mike were seated Mike went through the pre-interview process for the tape and the interview commenced.

George reminded Simon of the original charges and informed him of the new charges of escaping Police custody, aiding and abetting the escape of and armed prisoner, actual bodily harm of a Police officer and unlawful imprisonment of a civilian. He asked Simon how he pleaded and Simon replied: Not guilty! 'I had no choice but to go along with Brice in the escape because he had a gun and threatened not only to hurt me but to harm Tilley. I did everything I could to get us recognised but was unable to attract anybody's attention until the taxi driver. As for everything else I was not aware what those yanks were getting me involved in, Brice blackmailed me into helping him when he witnessed the hit and run in the states but said he just needed help with a "little job". He said he wanted a go between to send and receive coded messages back and forth, it wasn't until the murders were reported in the papers and on TV that I started to wonder, it was soon obvious though what was going on of course but I was in too deep by then so, I just kept my head down and hoped they would go home soon and then I was going to contact you people. Obviously I really regret Tilley getting involved and kidnapped, I dearly wanted to tell her but didn't dare for fear of getting her involved, I may just as well of done as it turned out. I was really getting to like Tilley and it was painful having to lie to her, in the end I just wanted it all to end.'

'And that is why you let her escape from your pub and gave Franks up?'

'That's right, when he turned up there I nearly died, she was in such a state and hated me because she felt I had betrayed her, luckily I was able to talk to her and explain my predicament and she forgave me, that's when I thought up the plan of letting her go as I was not going to put her in any more danger, I knew everything was over however it turned out. By the way how is Tilley? I have been thinking about her although she probably won't want anything else to do with me.'

'Just the opposite actually Simon, she wants to see you. I will arrange it as soon as we are finished here but for now can you give me the names of the yanks contacts in America?'

'No, They never used names just code words, I can give you those but they knew the "business" here was compromised so I would think they are long gone from wherever they were operating from.'

'Ok Simon give them to your solicitor, you will be going to court for your bail hearing in the morning but we will not be opposing bail. You will be expected give an address where you can be contacted and you will have to surrender your passport. Tilley has put in a good word for you and I will be speaking on your behalf also the authorities in America have been in contact regarding your outstanding charges over the hit and run but we have told them that you are helping us in a double murder and kidnapping, and we are holding you until the case is settled. In the meantime your solicitor will draw up papers to get you absolved of that as your help here has secured the arrest of two of their citizens, we will also tell them that we are willing to talk to them regarding the junior Minister helping with their case of the shooting of the son of the gang Lord. Now stay in here and give your solicitor all the code words you used and the names you and the contacts were known as. I will call Tilley when I leave here and arrange for her to come in and see you, I will let you know when she is here and I will arrange for you to be brought up to see her.'

'Thank you Detective I don't deserve it. Simon put his hand out and shook George's hand, George reciprocated and the men said their goodbyes.

Mike and George left the room and Mike said to George: 'I thought he was going go burst into tears in there, you are just a little softie deep down aren't you.' George looked sideways at Mike and replied: 'Shut up "Detective Chief Inspector" or it will be the shortest promotion in history, now go and arrange for Brice to be interviewed.'

Brice was informed of the new charges and insisted he wanted a new solicitor as he was convinced that he would not be defended probably considering recent events. This was arranged and he remained in his cell awaiting his new solicitor.

Later that evening Tilley and her parents were in the process of going to bed when the phone rang, her dad answered and it was George Carter he asked to speak to Tilley, when she answered George said: 'Tilley; you can come in and See Simon whenever you wish, just let us know and we will make the arrangements.'

'Oh lovely, can I come now please?'

'Well yes of course we will send a car to collect you, we don't want you going missing again do we?'

'No we don't.' Tilley replied Laughing. She thanked George and went to tell her parents.

When she arrived at the station she was escorted to a meeting room by George, minutes later Simon was brought in handcuffed to a PC. The PC sat Simon down then released the handcuffs from his wrist and attached them to the arm of the chair then the PC moved and stood by the door. Tilley couldn't resist rushing around the table and hugged Simon, kissing him on the cheek. George said to the Constable: 'I think we can leave these two lovebirds alone for a while.' They left the room and locked the door. Tilley was quick to say: 'Oh Simon I am so glad you're alright, I have been so worried.' Simon replied: Ditto! 'I am so sorry Tilley I wouldn't have gotten you mixed up in this mess if I'd know what they wanted please forgive me, I will make it up to you I promise. The DCI said you had put a good word in for me and he is going to have a word with the judge, so hopefully I will get a light sentence, will you wait for me Tilley?'

'Of course I will silly and you have nothing to be sorry for, I'm just glad Brice didn't hurt you.'

Simon and Tilley chatted for over an hour until she looked at her watch and said she had better get back, her parents would be worried, they said their goodbyes and Tilley was taken home. She let herself in and her parents had gone to bed, then Tilley saw a light coming from under their door so she knocked and her mum told her to go in.

She told them that Simon would more than likely to get a very light sentence and that she would be waiting for him. They told her they were very happy for her but she should think very carefully before making any final decisions. She kissed them both and told them that she loved them and that she would be going back to her apartment the next day. Her dad said: 'If you are getting married you will have to move to a larger property, so can we have your new sofa?' Tilley looked at her dad and said: 'Dream on dad, dream on.' She said goodnight again and went to bed.

That evening Tilley tidied up her apartment before going to bed. The next morning she was suddenly awoken by a continuous buzzing of her intercom. She forced herself out of bed and went to the hall, she pushed the button but before she could speak she heard her mother's voice saying: 'Tilley were you still in bed? Surely you haven't forgotten we are going shopping today to find you an outfit for your thirtieth birthday . . . .!!!

Lightning Source UK Ltd.
Milton Keynes UK
UKOW040315041212

203134UK00001B/14/P